ADVENTURES

OF A

SPACE BUM

BOOK 2

IN SEARCH OF A LEGACY

by

JON BATSON

First Edition

ISBN-13: 9780989372626

ISBN-10: 0989372626

Midnight Whistler
http://www.midnightwhistler.com
info@midnightwhistler.com

Cover Art by

BREAKIRON
Animation&Design
www.breakiron.com

ADVENTURES OF A SPACE BUM
BOOK 2
IN SEARCH OF A LEGACY

Glossary

Abigail — Starwort's friend from school, named Father's joy.

Achilles' daughters! — Exclamation bordering on profanity

Adonis — A planet, named for the beautiful youth beloved by the goddesses Aphrodite and Persephone.

Androgenos — A place famous for its medical facilities and healing spas.

Anubis — In Egyptian mythology, god of the dead. It is the name of a planet in the middle ring.

Aristaeus — Doctor Genus, named for the Greek god, son of Apollo.

Baal — Hindu deity. When used with "son of" or "in the name of" it is profanity.

Bacchus — Starwort's family name, in Greek and Roman mythology, god of wine. Also, home planet named for the family Bacchus.

Be-demoned! — Exclamation of having erred in judgment.

Bishop — Brand of speeder

Borth — A large and angry dog used to guard locations.

Camel — Wheeled vehicle for use in desert areas on Ceres.

Carte bancaire — A card for a reader holding Universal credits.

Ceres — A dry and desolate place where work was scarce and supplies were dear.

Ceres Segundo — A secondary town on Ceres.

CG — Central Government of Earth, an oppressive body.

Chandler — A purveyor of ship's goods and supplies.

Copernicus	A town named for Copernicus, the founder of modern astronomy.
Daedalus	A planet named for a respected Athenian artisan descendent from the royal family in Greek mythology.
Dagon	Name of a crewman, for the Philistine fish-god
Daphne	School friend of Starwort's, still living on Khons, the home planet.
Daughter of Ra!	Exclamation bordering on profanity.
DCR	Digital Control Ring for operating all aspects of the ship remotely.
Dodd	Grantham Dodd, who also wants Star's fortune
Fangdu	Short for Fangdu Kouzhao & Fangdu Shoutao, matching surgical mask and glove sets.
Flax	Name of the entity of the vessel, after a flower meaning benefactor "I will call you Flax, for you are my benefactor."
Galium	A friend from Sterope, named for a flower signifying rudeness.
Gold-backs	Slang for Universals.
Grecian Flu	Illness created by the Central Government to control the population.
Hades	The ancient Greek god of the underworld, in this usage, Hell.
Helia	A waitress who betrayed Star, now deceased.
Hermes	In Greek mythology, messenger of the gods, in this story, a GPS unit, a tracking device.
Inner Ring	Planets close to Earth and under control of the Central Government.
Juno	in Roman mythology, queen of the gods, the wife and sister of the god Jupiter. The largest city on the planet Jove.
Khons	A planet named for the god of the chase. Egyptian.

Levitator   An elevator.

Liber   A moon near Earth supporting life.

Malameris   Shapeless aquatics, a delicacy with a sting.

Manchineel   The name of Starwort's aunt, a flower meaning "betrayal."

Mithra Tavern   a tavern on Sterope, named after a goddess worshiped as the mediator

New Babylon   a planet with both low-life bars and healing pools.

Osiris V   Brand and designation for a speeder, popular at the time.

Pallas   A planet named for Pallas Athena, Greek goddess of war.

Phorcys and Ceto!   Exclamation bordering on profanity.

Red Stroke Drive   Propulsion system for interplanetary vessels.

RRD   Remote Repair Drone.

Semiramis   A residential community on New Babylon.

Shakti   Brand of speeder.

Souci   French for Marigold, a flower that could mean foresight, but could also mean trouble.

Starwort   The name of a low-growing north temperate herb having small white star-shaped flowers; has an alleged ability to ease sharp pains in the side. Meaning: afterthought.

Sterope   An island on New Babylon, named after one of the Pleiades.

Trebium latch   A tool for opening a trebium scuttle, a part no longer used on vessels.

Universals   Denomination of money common to all worlds, using the symbol Ц, as in Ц20.

Victoriana   The planet where Dr. Genus lives.

Willamette Police officer who once helped Star, but is now after her inheritance.

Wind Pools Expensive resort at New Babylon, famous for its healing vapors.

ADVENTURES
OF A
SPACE BUM

BOOK 2

IN SEARCH OF A LEGACY

Starwort (stärwôrt) n. Any of various water plants having star-shaped flowers. Also, low-growing north temperate herb having small white star-shaped flowers; named for its ability to ease sharp pains in the side. Significance: Afterthought

"I got a tattoo: a tiny, white, star-shaped flower on my left shoulder blade. It was to remind me that I am a weed growing in still waters. So I kept moving, avoiding the still waters; vowing to be a weed no more."

Starwort Bacchus

Starlost Child

The time before we landed in Adonis was carefree. I awoke with a peaceful feeling and a curiosity about our journey. I set a bare foot on the cold, metal floor, stood up and walked to the refresh room. I splashed water my face and stood before the mist-covered mirror. A chill in the air told me it was early and still dark. Ridiculous, of course, because in the far reaches of space there is no early or late, no natural light or dark; there is only space and it's dark and cold. Space was where we were. I didn't know exactly where, only in space. If I had to point the way out, I would be at a total loss. I was a starlost child.

I looked into the mirror and ran my hand over its face. My own face appeared, that of a girl barely two summers out of school, surrounded by brown hair, not quite shoulder length. My eyes appeared tired, my face held a bland expression. I turned my left shoulder, to the small tattoo on the blade: a starwort, a tiny flower growing in still waters. I wore the tattoo to remind me to keep moving, to stay out of stagnant waters.

A sound caused me to turn my head, a growl? No, a snore. It was Chineel, my friend, my ship-mate, my aunt, but not by blood. Being married to my uncle only meant she had bad judgment when she was young. I knew what that felt like.

I turned back to the mirror, focusing on my neck, on the

left near the collarbone, the scar my uncle gave me on the night we parted. He wanted to give me more, but he couldn't muster the strength, not with a broken whiskey bottle in his eye and an iron rod through his head.

Another sound caused me to turn. Beyond Chineel, in the next bunk in crew berthing was Dagon, the boy we rescued from Pallis, a planet always at war. We brought peace to Pallis by removing the last soldier moments before the planet died from lack of water and air. Dagon, whether he knew it or not, was named for the Philistine fish-god. It didn't matter; it meant nothing in the scheme of things. I was sorry we could only rescue him and not the other children. It was too late for the others.

Dagon would correct me if he could hear me call them children. He would say, "You mean soldiers." Yes, Dagon, of course: Soldiers.

The chill distracted me again. If the boy-soldier were to wake and look up, he would see me completely nude, without even a hand-towel to cover me. I smiled, thinking it wouldn't matter. Dagon was a boy becoming a man, but he was a soldier first and I was his captain. He would see my nakedness and would wonder why I stood in the cold without covering. Nothing else would occur to him.

Why did I stand in the cold? Flax must have wondered as well, though she didn't say anything. She was ubiquitous and could see me and hear me in any part of the vessel, inside or out. Out would not be possible in our current location, far from any planet.

"Can't sleep, Star?" asked Flax, in a whisper so as not to wake Chineel or Dagon.

"I'll come forward," I said, turning from the mirror. I

picked up a blanket from my bunk and wrapped it around me, only for warmth. Flax didn't care if I was nude. I pulled my hair over the scar on my neck, an automatic movement since my schooldays. Only Abigail knew how I got it. She was my best friend in school and we shared every secret. I was heartbroken when she died.

In the galley, the chill of the cold deck suggested I should have also donned slippers, but I didn't stop or go back. I kept on toward the bridge.

I remembered a planet we visited where everyone had a scar and showed it off with pride. A scar was a sign to announce your digital implant was removed; you were no longer tethered to the Central Government. Often these people tattooed something around the scar, a fashion statement as much as a freedom statement. The CG responded by making the implants smaller, infecting tattoo ink with them. I had no implants in my tattoo: I had been scanned by my one-time lover, Galium.

For a moment I remembered Galium. I missed him.

No, I missed the idea of him.

At the entrance to the bridge, I considered calling Galium on the interlink, but we were too close to home system and the trans might be picked up. We were headed for the space between Mars and Jupiter, The Main Belt. Being only two planets away from Earth, and knowing the colonies on Mars were under close CG supervision, calling radical activists on the interlink was not a good idea.

"Are you cold?" asked Flax as I settled into the pilot's seat.

"Yes, it's chilly." I pulled my feet up and tucked the blanket around me.

"You wear a skirt and blouse most of the time, as a way to

regulate your temperature and to give protection to your structural covering."

"Yes, my skin; a tender covering for certain. I suppose I didn't feel like clothes. Hope you don't mind."

"As you wish." Flax had become more accommodating of late.

We sat in silence, moving though the darkness at speeds I had read about in school, the blackness speckled with a trillion dots of light, some of which had burnt out a thousand years or more earlier, their light getting to us only now. I sighed at the beauty.

"Yes," said Flax. "It is beautiful."

"How do you know, Flax? Can you see beauty?"

"Beauty is a thought, a consideration one way or the other. I sense you are pleased with the sight and are of the opinion it is beautiful. I believe you are wise and would evaluate the level of beauty. You believe it to be beautiful and I have faith in your judgment."

"Thank you, Flax. I appreciate it."

"It's quite all right, Star."

I smiled. Flax had taken to calling me Star when we were alone and our conversations were private. In public, she called me Captain. Back when I was the only rider aboard, I had taken on the position and responsibilities. Now I had a crew and a passenger.

"How is our passenger?" I inquired.

"Aristaeus sleeps soundly. We talked until well after you and the others had turned in."

The man named for the Greek god, son of Apollo, was a technical genius. He tagged along for a free ride to Adonis.

4

We were on our way to fulfill a repair request from a fully automated functionary on the planet.

The repair contract in Adonis was not an emergency, more preventative than anything. The advanced systems of Adonis predicted breakdowns and requested maintenance automatically when they did. Our response occurred according to the proper time line. All was right with the universe.

Aristaeus had saved my bacon before. He was a good friend. Still, it was good he slept and couldn't come in to find me nude, which might be awkward. We weren't friends in such a way. He enjoyed speaking with me, but enjoyed so more with Flax.

"You two speak a common language," I told Flax.

"We do communicate on a different level. I am glad you understand."

A small rush of warmer air came in from the side and from beneath the console. I smiled. Flax had noticed my shivering and raised the temperature.

"Where will we land?"

"The main platform on Adonis. It will give us a chance to take on provisions."

"How long until we get there?"

"Time enough to nap and dress before you must meet people."

"Good. Tired and naked is no way to greet your public." I pulled the blanket tighter around me, looking at the lights on the console and those in the blackness surrounding us.

Adonis

Flax set us down gently and we prepared for our different directions. Chineel was off to the chandlers and I was headed to the market in search of what I could find. Dagon came with me, as I was his captain. He was eager to serve.

Aristaeus left to catch a transport back to his home on Victoriana. He hugged Chineel and me, waved goodbye to Dagon and Flax and stepped off in the direction of the giant transport vessel at the end of the free port.

"I'm going to miss him," said Flax, confining her voice to the common area. She didn't want to be heard throughout the ship, it was for me alone.

"So am I, but we have an open invitation. I should buy something to give him at our next meeting, a present." He had, after all, given me a present, a pin with a star shooting out of a circle. I wore it on my blouse.

"What invitation?" asked Chineel, coming in and dropping her bag on the table.

"Aristaeus, he said to come and visit anytime."

"Oh, well, he had to say so. What does one say? Stay away, I'm busy?" Chineel was still a cynic.

"He meant it. You'll see," hoping to settle the matter. Apparently, I did.

"I know. Are you ready?"

"Ready! It's a short walk into town. We shouldn't be long, Flax."

Flax bleeped, which was what she did when she didn't know what to say. She was not much for long goodbyes.

"What did you see in him?" I asked Chineel as we walked toward the marketplace. Dagon walked a respectful distance behind, taking it all in.

"Who?" Chineel cast a casual eye around at the growing number of stalls. We had not been in Adonis before so everything was new, though little different from other places we had been.

"Uncle Lazar. How could you have ever married him?"

"Oh! When he was younger, he was handsome and a charmer. Of course, liquor would touch his lips and he would turn into something else, a monster. I discovered it late and tried to keep spirits out of the house, but to no avail. After a while, the man I married failed to show up at all. I was alone in the house with the monster. So I left."

"I understand why you left."

"Still, sorry."

"Not your fault. You didn't know."

It was true. She didn't know my parents had died leaving me to my uncle, so didn't know she would be abandoning her coming-of-age niece to the monster. We didn't discuss whether it would have changed her mind.

"I paid for it in my way," said Chineel, continuing her cynical, hard edged introspective. "Ending up in a harbor town charming rich widowers, pondering, 'How long can he last, anyway?' Turns out some of them were heartier than they looked."

"You're out of the life now."

"Thank you," said Chineel, touching my arm.

We walked in silence for a while, turning whatever private thoughts were still in our heads over for their relative value. Should these thoughts be shared, kept to ourselves or forgotten? It was a constant conversation within us. In the end, *forgotten* won out as the market drew near.

Dagon paused by the speeder-caddy, a place where two, three and four-wheeled vehicles were parked while their owners walked through the market. The universe was new to Dagon, as he had never been off of his home world of Pallas, which had been at war for centuries. He was familiar with speeders, but had never seen so many and so sparkling new. His eyes took in every nuance.

"See you when done," said Chineel as she sauntered off down the lane following the sign to the Chandler's.

The Marketplace

It was mid-day and the market was at full capacity. Businessmen came from the center of town for lunch, kids took time from classes to run in the heat of the day and anyone with a need for company came to the market.

While looking through a stack of skirts, I noticed a man at the next table sorting through the ladies' undergarments. He wasn't looking at them, though; his eyes were on me. If he were a young rogue, with a jaunty smile and a twinkle in his eye, or a middle-aged executive in a costly suit, I would have understood. This man, however, was dressed in traveling clothes with the dust of a dozen planets on him. He was unkempt, which made the sight of him holding ladies' underclothes even less appealing. He didn't look at me with desire or admiration, but recognition. I didn't care for it. As if on cue, Dagon appeared at my elbow.

"Let's move along," said Dagon, taking my arm in his hand. He pulled me down the lane, past a covered drink stand. He motioned for me to stop and peered around the corner. He returned to me with a hardened look on his face. It had until recently been his only look. We moved to the back of the stand and behind two scrubby trees. I followed Dagon around the other side of the stand and out onto the street as the man turned the corner walking away from us.

"You have the same bad feeling, eh?" I said, trying to

shake off the chill I felt.

"There's something not right with him. Let's go back."

"I don't get it," I commented as we moved toward the crowded square. "I've never been here. I don't recognize him. If he has some dispute with me, I don't know about it."

Dagon didn't respond, he took my sleeve and pulled me after him. He stopped and peered inside a small cafe. There was a back door next to the kitchen. He pulled me in and sat me at a table near the rear door.

"Any reason why he should be following you?" asked Dagon.

I tried to think and catch my breath at the same time. At the counter, a girl looked up, sighed and looked back down again. She would be over to take our order, but not right away.

"I doubt he's any kind of lawman. I've never been in this sector before, so it can't be an old warrant. I've left a few people with a bad taste between their teeth here and there, so he could be someone with an old grudge, or could work for someone with an old grudge." I raised my head, stretching my neck, as if to get a look above the crowd outside.

Another face in the middle of the crowd was familiar, a man looking to the side. He scanned the crowd for someone or something. I wasn't sure where I had seen him. Then he looked in the other direction and I remembered. I pulled my head down and averted my eyes, as if looking away would keep him from seeing me.

"What?" asked Dagon, his eyes wide.

"Willamette!" I said, as if one word would explain everything.

Dagon stood up, looking out at the passing throng.

"No!" I pulled him down into his seat. "We need to go."

The look in my eyes said it all. Dagon looked around at the rear door, used for deliveries, and went through it staying low. I was on his tail feathers. The face I had seen in the crowd was the man I knew only as Willamette. The dark, ugly scar on the right side of his face was put there on our last encounter.

"You know him?" asked Dagon.

"You remember the last port? Copernicus?"

"Yes," he said, looking at me with worried eyes. We passed an enclosed stand with art on the walls. An old woman sat in the corner eating a colorless mush from a ceramic bowl.

"He was upstairs in the landlord's apartment. The wife of the landlord hit him with a red-hot skillet straight from the fire to the side of his face. He'll carry the scar for the rest of his life. It's not only my father's map he wants; he wants revenge. He blames me for everything."

"We had better head back to the ship, and grab Chineel on the way." Dagon looked out and started off to the left, waving me on as he went. Two steps from the corner, a large hand reached out for me, stopping me in my flight. I felt his grip around my arm above the elbow, biting into my flesh.

"Hold it right there, Miss Bacchus. I would like a word with you."

It was Willamette. The dark, gravelly voice offered no kindness; his hand hurt my arm. I whirled and sank my ceramic blade into his shoulder.

"Do you think your little sliver will hurt me?" he grinned. He cried out, letting my arm go. He staggered as if drunk.

When he turned I saw Dagon standing behind him. My larger blade stuck out of the back of his leg. Dagon had taken the blade from the galley. I was glad he did.

I grabbed hold of the large blade and pulled it from Willamette's leg, twisting as I pulled. He screamed again, whirling in place at an odd angle. The smaller blade was still in his shoulder, but as he reached for me, I could see it hurt him. I reached up and pulled it out, letting a spout of blood from his shoulder and another anguished cry from his mouth. Willamette went down, holding his shoulder with one hand and the back of his leg with the other, unable to stop the showers of blood from either.

The sight of his hideous face screaming and distorted was truly ghastly. The scar made him the ugliest man at the market, one to make women faint and little children scream. The landlord's wife must have been trying to kill him with that frying pan. I wished she had succeeded.

"Time to go," said Dagon.

"Here," I said, handing the big blade back to him. "You're smarter than me, I only brought a toothpick."

Dagon replaced the blade in the sheath, took hold of my sleeve and pulled me along through the marketplace. I sheathed my own blade, lest anyone see us with drawn weapons.

A cry went up behind us. A crowd gathered by the art stand. One of the men running to see was the other man who had been with Willamette. We ducked behind a group of onlookers, craning their necks to see what the yelling was all about, and ran back toward the main intersection. At the road where we left Chineel, we found her again.

"Done shopping already?" she asked, smiling.

"Willamette! And others with him! We've got to go now."

Chineel changed from cheerful to panic in an instant, pulling her parcels closer to her breast and turning toward the free port.

Dagon ran on ahead, no doubt to get Flax to have the door open but also to avoid being seen with me. If anyone had seen us, a description of a woman with a boy would identify us. I fell in step with Chineel and urged her to quicken her pace.

"How did he know you were here?"

"I'd like to know, so we could avoid meeting him at our next port of call."

"There!" cried out a rough voice behind us. It was the first man we saw, the one I couldn't place. He ran toward us, anger written across his face. Behind him, I could see other men break into a run, eager to join in a chase, any chase, for the excitement of it.

With Chineel and me both in full skirts, I doubted we would out-sprint them. A roar from the other direction caught my ear. It was Dagon on a four-wheeled speeder, coming at us full-tilt.

Fast Getaway

It was a signature move for Dagon. He pulled up at full-speed, jammed on the brakes and skidded sideways into the target zone. There was lots of dust, but he landed where he intended.

"Get on!" he yelled, his voice lost beneath the roar of the four-wheeler and the screaming men. I threw a leg over the speeder, pulling as close to Dagon as possible. Chineel did the same, pulling close to me.

A hand reached out and pulled at Chineel's skirt. It was the first man we had seen, the one who looked suspicious. She kicked high and caught him in the jaw. We didn't have time for the niceties, like getting situated and hanging on. I felt Chineel tilt as Dagon hit the accelerator and we were off.

A glance back told me his friends weren't wasting time picking up Willamette, he was on his own. The man was at full-speed behind us. He pulled a pistol from his coat, but caught his foot on a loose paving stone sending him sprawling before he could use it. Another fell in behind us as Dagon pushed the limits of the speeder.

Though on wheels it felt like we flew past the speeder-platform, the place where someone would miss his four-wheeler later today. Dagon sent a plume of dust up behind us as we short-cut the turn to the sky dock.

A glance to the rear confirmed we were no longer chased

by the men, but I knew not to underestimate the length and depth of Willamette's resolve.

Flax must have heard us coming. She opened the port bay door. A flurry of dust blew out to the sides as the take-off thrusters warmed up.

Dagon cranked the handle and the speeder jolted forward. We were traveling far too fast for the turn and Dagon had to lean out to prevent the speeder from tumbling as we slid into the port bay door. I leaned with him, happy to see the bay door closing behind us.

"I'll shift the cargo later, let's get out of here," said Dagon. Flax complied. We were all thrown to the floor of the bay, skidding back against the aft wall. The speeder slid toward us, still running but out of gear. Dagon threw himself on the speeder and stilled the engine.

The light from the bridge grew darker and the landing thrusters cut off. There was a tremble throughout the ship and another surge as the Red Stroke Drive kicked in.

I exchanged looks with Dagon. Chineel was pale, as if she had seen a ghost. There was a moment when we shared our frightened faces, followed by a feeling of relief. We all laughed at once.

"What is funny?" asked Flax, as if we were sitting around a tea party.

"Happy to be alive is all," I said.

"Want to tell me what's happening now?" asked Dagon.

"Phorcys and Ceto! Why not?" I stood up and held a hand to Chineel, who took it and pulled herself up, smoothing herself out as she did. We picked up her strewn packages and walked to the galley.

"On Copernicus," I began, dropping myself into the Captain's seat at the end of the table. "I went to return 40 Universals to the landlord. It was not the most well-thought-out plan, but it was a step in a plan, none-the-less. Willamette and his lady, Helia, had followed me there, their purpose being to steal my father's map."

"Why?" asked Dagon. Chineel secured the parcels and sat down as well. Stores could be stowed later.

"Some people decided my father's map was valuable, valuable enough to fly from planet to planet and risk everything looking for it. Helia gave her all for it. When she lunged for me, I pushed her against Willamette and his gun went off, which no doubt fuels his hatred some."

"The man called Vesta was at the front door," said Dagon, who had himself plunged a dagger into Vesta's eye up to his brain. The headmaster of my old school had been chasing me all these years for a map I couldn't figure out. Perhaps he knew something I did not, but if he did the knowledge died with him.

"Carthanian in the market," added Chineel, recalling how close he was and who killed him, her old lover from the Wind Pools, the name she wouldn't speak. But I would.

"Osiris," I said. Chineel and I exchanged looks. They had been lovers. If events had gone differently, it might have been me in his bed. Still, I thought we were friends until he showed up to kill Carthanian, revealing in the process he and Carthanian both were after the map.

For a moment I remembered Flax tilting as the inner doors closed. I remembered the sound Osiris had made as he fell to the market below to be impaled on a flagpole in the center array, his long arms outstretched as if asking for forgiveness.

I looked up to see Dagon still fixed on me, waiting. I continued.

"Willamette and Helia tracked me to the landlord's place. He had a gun. He came after me, but she was in the way and the shot killed her. He became a madman, filled with rage. The landlord's wife hit him with a hot frying pan and left him with a mark."

"Easy to spot," said Dagon.

"Easy to see why he's so angry!" said Chineel with furrowed eyebrows at me.

"It wasn't my fault!" I protested. "Willamette tried to kill me. Helia had a knife; she wanted to cut my face off. If I ever see the landlord's wife again, I'm going to kiss her."

"So," said Dagon, bring it back to the subject at hand. "This guy is after you for the map and your father's treasure. Also I assume he holds you responsible for him killing his woman and getting scarred across the face."

"You've summed it all up in a bundle."

"We have another problem," said Flax, who had been listening but had been silent until now. Dagon jumped, still not comfortable with having an entity be so ubiquitous yet invisible.

"What, Flax?" I turned, though it wasn't necessary, as Flax was everywhere on the ship.

"The repair was interrupted. There wasn't enough time to complete it and get you off the sky dock as well."

"Thanks for making the right choice."

"Happy to do so. The repair still needs to be done and there is a query logged as to why it has been left incomplete."

"What would you suggest?" I asked.

"We return, noting a short in the circuitry as an excuse, make the repair and leave. Those men will not be at the repair site but they might be still looking for you in the market. You would have to stay aboard for the duration of the repair."

"That's not a problem. We could all use some downtime."

"What's that?" asked Dagon, his face scrunched up as if a bad taste were coming.

"Downtime: when you're not trying to kill someone or trying to avoid being killed by someone. When it's too rainy to play outside, we play inside. It usually turns into a pajama party or an excuse to spend the day with a reader. Either way, it's rest and recuperation."

Down Time

After a fast sweep around the town below the horizon, Flax approached from the south, making a report saying she had to get out of the way of a power surge threatening to damage her system. She returned to the repair and settled in. There were no humans involved at her end, so no questions were asked. She left the life support on and turned her attention to the repairs. I had no doubt she listened in, enjoying whatever would occur during our downtime activities.

Chineel and Dagon settled in the galley reading from the library while I took the opportunity to play at my clarinet. In the bridge cockpit, I assembled the parts and turned the ring on the bell to a soft blue, reflecting my mood. I searched for the opening notes of "Homesick," the piece I had composed while at school. It always reminded me of Abigail.

After a few false starts, I found the note, the one I lingered on until I felt the vibration between my temples. The somber notes of "Homesick" wafted through the bridge and out into the bay, all the way to the galley. I hoped it was not a distraction for my crew.

"It's not," a voice said. I looked up, but didn't expect to see anyone. I knew her voice: it was Abigail, though she had no voice. A small opening at the side of the console, covered in thin tissue, vibrated as if a breeze had touched it. But I knew there was no breeze.

"Star?" said Flax. She had been listening.

"Yes, Flax," I whispered, wondering what to say to explain the disembodied voice.

"Someone is here."

"Yes, Flax, a friend from school, Abigail. She visited once before, when you were having a maintenance check."

"Do you mind if I listen?" Flax asked.

"No," Abigail said.

"No, not at all," I said at the same time. Two giggles were heard, one from me and one from the small, covered opening at the side console.

"I've missed you, sister," said Abigail.

"And I've missed you." I started to tear up. I longed to see her face, to hug like we used to.

"You remember to create vibration you must have a harmonious rate of motion. Have you been arriving where you mean to go?"

Abigail always had a familiar lilt to her speech and I heard it, though it seemed strange to have it come from a console speaker. She had a better grasp of the concepts involved, as she paid better attention in Life Class than I did. My attention wandered.

"It always did," she giggled, reading my thoughts. "And it is again. You are out of sync, Star, out of harmony."

"I know," I said, pulling in my lips like a schoolgirl. "I welcomed the free time so I could play." I held up the clarinet, as if she could see it.

"You have more voices in your life now," said Abigail. "The woman and the boy are both in disharmony with themselves. They have much to scatter their attention."

"Yes. It's been a rugged road since we last spoke. But I have a clarinet now. I'll find my note. I'm getting closer. Would you like to hear 'Homesick?'"

I placed the reed between my lips and sucked in a breath.

"Rather would I hear your own vibration, the one from your heart, the song behind your eyes. What would bring you back into harmony, Star? What would make your heart sing?"

The map came into my mind's eye as I recalled pouring over it with Chineel and Aristaeus. Sailing across the galaxies to find the planet *Bacchus* and making it my home; Flax being free, autonomous; to see Chineel and Dagon happy.

Without being summoned, Galium came to my mind's eye, my old lover from my first days out of school. He was always difficult, always rude, but never cruel. In fact, I missed him. We had last spoken over the interlink. These days he hid from the Central Government, out to shut him down. He had a lover, so no chance for me. But it was not him I wanted.

No, I wanted the idea of him. I wanted someone to care for and who cared for me, to love, to hold, someone special.

"They are all special," said Abigail.

"No, not like friend-special. Like a lover-special."

"Ohhh!" said Abigail, as the idea came into focus. "Then the same rules apply. When you have a pure vibration, harmonious motion occurs. When you send a flow out, a flow will come in. Look around. Do you see him here, your man?"

"No," I said, looking around, though I knew no one was there. Abigail giggled.

"And you will not unless you bring him. To do so you have

to go out and find him."

"There's an ex-policeman in the way, Willamette. His vibration is quite different."

"Yes, it is. It is confused and distorted, discordant and inharmonious. His vibration will never win. Yours will. You have greatness in you. Let it flow, precious Star. Let it flow."

I felt Abigail leave. There was a flicker of energy against my left cheek and a soft 'whoosh' more known than felt. And so, I was alone. Well, not quite alone.

"She's nice," said Flax.

"Yes, she is. She is a strange and special friend."

"She is welcome anytime. Shall I set up a vibration chamber?"

"She tends to find her own. She prefers it. Would you like to hear a pretty note?"

"Yes, I would," said Flax.

I pictured her putting two hands behind her head and leaning back to hear. I put the reed between my lips and blew a crooked note killing the whole mood.

"Hold it, wait a minute. Here it comes."

I blew again and the note held true this time. It vibrated between my temples and set the small console speaker moving. A harmony note was heard, higher and lighter. I let the note ring in my head while I searched for the source of the harmony note. It was Flax, she sang with me.

As I relaxed into the opening notes of "Homesick," Flax sighed, which I believe she picked up from Chineel, and sang harmony notes as they occurred to her. It was how we spent most of the afternoon.

Galium

Galium had been my lover on Sterope, in the low islands of New Babylon. We spent our time at the Mithra Tavern, where I later found Chineel. She had not known Galium; handsome, rude, thoughtless Galium, who I loved in spite of myself. When I left him, I cried for days, but would not go back. Since then, we have spoken by interlink. He told me about implanted trackers of nano-technology, so small they were hidden in tattoo ink, unknown even to the artists. Innocent people had been implanted with info-chips and trackers without knowing. It was insidious.

We were friends, not close, but I had need of him, to hear his voice and to get his advice. I logged onto the interlink, hoping I could find him. Much of Flax's resources were in use, but perhaps I could find enough to push out a signal.

The screen flickered. The sound was intermittent. The lights in the cockpit dimmed as Flax cut the power drain to boost the signal. A familiar voice filled the bridge.

"Hello, Little Wort! To what do I owe the honor," said the pirate rogue of Sterope, trying to be his old, crude self. He couldn't be as rude as he once was; he had mellowed.

"I outgrew that name not long before I outgrew you, old man. Are you still a thorn in the Central Government's derriere?"

"I do what I can. The flu does the rest." He sounded tired.

23

The fight had gotten to him. One man against the Central Government was a hard battle.

"Flu? What flu? Are you OK?"

"Grecian Flu, Little Wort. Have you been living on the outer rim? The latest control mechanism of the Central Gov. Haven't you seen Kouzhao and Shoutao all over the place?"

"No. I have a set, but they're not in fashion out here."

Fangdu Kouzhao and Fangdu Shoutao, matching surgical mask and glove sets, known simply as Fangdu on planets I had recently visited, were becoming more popular. Not being a slave to fad and fashion, I didn't notice.

"They're all over the place here and on the Inner Ring. Grecian Flu first showed up on Earth where ten to twelve percent fatalities are common and more are predicted. It's moving out now, to where the few who travel from Earth go."

"But no one leaves Earth," I said, parroting what I had heard so often.

"They're leaving now. Any destination will suffice; any excuse will do. Pick a secondary location and people make a dash for it. Where the Central Government goes, implants are required. Once the CG is in place, Grecian Flu follows."

"Copernicus was our last port. I didn't see it there," I said, remembering the tourist vessels two and three deep at the free port.

"You wait! People travel farther out into the cosmos to avoid it these days. Where are you now?"

"Adonis, but I don't expect to be here for long." The planet, named for the beautiful youth beloved by the goddesses Aphrodite and Persephone, was not beautiful or lovely for us. On Adonis, we ran and we hid.

"Check where you're going. Don't go out without your mask. You might find some cities empty and others full as people scurry around looking for a safe place to live."

"What's it like?" I asked, hoping to get a handle on this new piece of terrible news.

"After a near-death experience lasting about fifteen circuits you either die or get the vaccine."

"There's a vaccine?"

"Yes, Wort. You're still slow getting off the launching pad, aren't you? The vaccine is the whole idea. Once you are on the vaccine, you need to take it daily. You can only get a day's supply at a time, so you have to check in to the CG Grecian Flu Vaccine Station every day or else you convulse, spasm and die. If the Central Government doesn't like your politics, you don't get the GFV - the Grecian Flu Vaccine."

"Catchy name."

"Great way to keep the population in check. All the preventative measures in the world won't stop the boys back at Central Gov from giving the flu to everyone eventually."

"Why?" I couldn't believe it. The Central Government wanting people to be sick?

"Wort, have you not been listening? If you don't get the vaccine, you die. If you don't sing the central theme song loud enough and with enough enthusiasm, you don't get the vaccine. It's a control mechanism, nothing more."

"Insidious," I muttered.

"I thought I said that."

"You did. I repeated for emphasis."

"If I were you, I'd stay away from anywhere you see a scanning station. If you need a chip, you'll need your mask.

Kiss the wrong guy and you're under the thumb of the CG for the rest of your life, long or short."

"You're always full of cheery news, aren't you, Galium?"

"Happy to be of service, Little Wort."

A flicker on the screen caught his attention.

"They're close to getting the signal; we have to break off now. Good to hear from you. Keep in touch. Wear your Fangdu."

"Fangdu, will do."

Before I could chuckle at my own rhyme, he clicked off. A fuzzy, blank screen greeted me. Flax turned the screen off before anyone could see us sending. Talking to a dissident like Galium could get you jailed forever.

"Sounds serious," said Flax.

"Where the Central Government is concerned, the conversation is always serious. Now they're making people sick so they can give them medicine."

"It is a good plan, if you have no conscience or soul."

"Such as the CG. Let's check where we will be going before we accept any contracts."

"If possible," whispered Flax.

"Yes, if it's possible." I raised the clarinet to my lips and played. It wasn't anything impressive, I needed to zone out, to think. Galium always made me think.

I missed him.

No, I reminded myself, I missed the idea of him.

Pageant

"Star," said Flax, interjecting herself into my dream.

"Yes, Flax," I said, rising to a sitting position. Napping in the crew quarters, I had been hanging on the edge of sleep, still aware of everything, the hardness of the cot, the chill in the room, the buzz made by a button on a jacket hanging on the wall, vibrating with the ship as we tore through space at Red Stroke speed.

"Sorry to disturb you, but you have a call."

"You aren't disturbing me. I wasn't sleeping. Wait! A call?" All at once, I was awake.

"Yes. Why don't you come up to the bridge and take it?"

"OK. Be right there."

On the way through the galley to the bridge, Chineel and Dagon looked up from their reading.

"What?" asked Chineel.

"A call."

"A call? Who?" Chineel stood up. Dagon looked from her to me and also stood up, leaving his reader on the table.

"Don't know. Going to find out now."

I slipped into the pilot's seat and saw Chineel follow me in, settling in the co-pilot's seat. Dagon took the navigator's chair behind. The whole crew assembled to find out who would be calling at this hour, or any hour. In space, the clock has no orientation.

"Hello, Star," said a familiar voice.

"Daphne!" I winked at Chineel with a grin across my face I couldn't help. "What brings you to our corner of the universe?"

"A request, if you have the time."

"We will find a way to make the time." I could feel Dagon and Chineel rolling their eyes. Somewhere deep in the console, I couldn't help feeling Flax rolled her eyes as well, or the Artificial Intelligence equivalent.

"It's so silly, but I couldn't get you out of my head ever since I heard."

"Heard what, Daphne? You're driving me mad!"

"It's a beauty pageant! It was set up and organized before the news of the Grecian Flu arrived, but the promoters decided to proceed with it anyway. It's been decided everyone will wear Fangdu. I've signed up! I simply can't go into it alone. Mother has permitted you to come and stay with me and she will buy your dress. You must come and help me through it. I'll die if you don't."

"Steady on, Daphne. You won't die. I'll see what I can do. Send us the where and when. It'll take some coordination."

"Make extra time front and back for inspection and quarantine. We live in paranoid times," she warned.

"Yes, we do. I'll get back to you."

"Good roads, fair weather, sister." Daphne clicked off.

I had not heard the parting phrase of our school days, not since the money ran out, and me following close behind. The money ran out a few weeks before graduation, but without a Universal in my account, I wouldn't be among the graduates of the Vesta Academy for Young Ladies. Penniless young ladies did not graduate.

"It might be pleasant for a change, to go somewhere where they're not trying to kill us. What do you say, Flax? Are you up for a beauty pageant?" I asked.

"I am sure I would win," said Flax. "But I will sit this one out at the sky dock. You can go in my place. I will make arrangements."

Flax practiced humor of late. Her delivery was still a bit stiff, but she nevertheless raised the corner of my mouth at least once a day.

"Beauty pageant? Are you serious? Aren't we looking for a planet at the far end of the universe? Remember your father's map? Bacchus? Treasure?" Chineel pleaded, waving her hands in the air.

"Yes, but we are on this end of the universe and there is an awful lot of space to fly though to get there. It wouldn't kill us to take some time in Daphne's world. Come on! You always wanted to rub elbows with high-society."

"I didn't," said Dagon.

"Yes, but you're a boy, and a young one!" I shot back. "Let the girls have some fun. It's dress-up and girl-talk. You wouldn't like it on your best day."

Dagon turned toward the window, as if finding interest in the darkness outside, in the millions of stars floating in it.

Chineel grinned and blushed. She wanted to do some girl stuff and didn't know how to say it and not sound dumb. She now had permission and was pleased.

Quarantine

The approach to Khons was the same as it always was, but before the doors opened, the similarity ended. Orders came to not open the doors or disembark until the local authority had checked us through quarantine.

"Quarantine doesn't sound good," Chineel said.

"Full masks and gloves will be required ashore." Flax read the directives relayed to the vessel once we had landed. "You'll need full protective gear. There is a twenty-eight hour quarantine in effect. Do you have Fangdu?"

"I do," Chineel said.

"Me too," I added.

"Not me," said Dagon with a frown.

"You will keep me company," offered Flax.

Dagon stood by the bridge hatch with a stoic look. He would not acknowledge keeping Flax company as a good idea or a bad idea, but he wasn't jumping for joy either. I could see he wanted to be part of the fun, though twenty-eight hour quarantine didn't sound exciting to any of us.

"Quarantine, Dagon. You wouldn't like it," said Chineel, looking out for his feelings. Dagon took in a gust of air and held it, his face like carved granite.

We stood apart as a scanner beam went through the ship. The readout was three life forms. Although I always counted

Flax, they did not. Flax logged on the names of two life forms who would be exiting the vessel, one would remain aboard.

This was our first encounter with what Galium had foretold, the Grecian Flu. In full skirts, long-sleeve blouses and press-front jackets, Chineel and I stood by the port bay door, waiting for the signal to disembark. The dark red gloves and mask I had purchased as a fashion statement proved to be prophetic as they were now required. Chineel sported Fangdu of green, predictably, to set off her red hair, barely showing beneath what we called a French Sea Cap. We both wore them, hats of soft material but with stiff rims and bills. Whether they were ever from France or worn by anyone who sailed a sea was beside the point.

When the doors opened, uniformed guards stood on either side waiting for us. We stepped out and were handed goggles to wear in public. The broad, clear eye-coverings had no strap but secured to the face as if by magic. I heard a short sucking sound and felt a minor irritation, but it was dispelled by a few blinks of my eyes.

Three guards on our left and three on our right seemed like overkill. There were only two of us and we weren't wanted for anything, not on Khons, at any rate.

"Please forgive these precautions," said a metallic voice. "So little is known about the Grecian Flu. We left nothing to chance. This way please."

The first guard extended a hand, indicating he was the source of the filtered voice and we were to come with them. I nodded and fell in step between him and another guard on the left. Chineel was behind me. The final two waited until the bay door was secured and fell in line behind us.

We were taken to a preliminary room where female

attendants in face-masks and clear face-shields asked us to disrobe. They gave us loose-fitting pajamas to wear with matching slippers and Fangdu, all of soft gray. They stayed to watch the disrobing process. I supposed they were also to check for contraband items we might be smuggling. They didn't even wince at the blade I had strapped to my leg under the skirt, or the smaller one Chineel had in the back of her belt. They saw such precautions on a regular basis.

They went through our clothing and then packaged it up, each in a bundle in a separate container. Before it had even been fully sealed, we were shown out to a holding area, a cell where others who had come in recently were waiting. Waiting for what, I didn't know.

The cell was three windowless walls with benches in the middle. The wall on the fourth side was glass with small vent holes in it and a door of gray metal.

We sat on a bench and nodded to the others in the room. There were two families: one a mother, father and two small girls; the other a mother, father, a girl and a boy. One mother was clearly pregnant. All had worried looks. Behind us was a young couple who would not let go of each other. With them were two women and a man, all older. The two lovebirds, we guessed, were newlyweds and this was the family. If they were here for their honeymoon, it was off to a rocky start.

It was an hour before a woman in full protective gear walked up and looked through the glass. She checked a reader and made a note, then spoke into a wrist communicator and looked up at us. She opened the door and directed us to continue down the hall to the door at the end.

What we had been waiting for was the quarantine rooms

in the next section, which had been sterilized and changed, providing new bedding and furniture. We were shown to a largish room with bunk beds and a number of perfunctory reading chairs. There were several readers on the tables, each secured by a metal cord. A screen in the corner had a moving picture of nature scenes but no sound. The control panel was built into the side table. Chineel and I were shown in, as well as the two older women and the newly-married girl. The door shut and we were in for the duration.

"I'm sure they try to be as accommodating as possible," said one of the older women. "They have so many to process."

"Yes, I'm sure. Do you know how long?" I asked, though I remembered what Flax had said.

"Twenty-eight hours appears to be standard," said the other older woman.

"We've been traveling for so long already," said the young woman. She was barely a girl, but wore a ring, so our guess about her being married was correct.

"Where are you from?" asked Chineel. It seemed like a natural question, from the girl's statement. It was the girl who spoke again.

"Liber, a moon of Vulcan. It's about the size of Mars and in the next solar system. They say Liber is so like Earth it could be a double. I don't know, but we miss it."

"Yes," I said, seeing she was emotional about it. "So many people miss Earth, it's only natural. Earth is where we're all from originally. But tell us about Liber."

"Too much like Earth," said the older woman sharply. "Earthers come and go like it's theirs to contaminate. We were doing fine until a vessel arrived bringing refugees from the Grecian Flu. In no time, it was all over Liber as well. We barely escaped with our lives."

We sat looking at each other for an uneasy moment, when the woman spoke again.

"I'm sorry, please forgive me. I'm Juniper Blossom, my sister Jasmine and our daughter-in-law, Fuchsia. She and my son, Acer, were recently married. It was announced we could stay and undergo treatment, whether or not we had the Flu, or leave. Given the complete shutdown of Earth, we decided to leave while we could."

"I'm Starwort, this is Chineel. I am originally from Khons, though we are travelers now. What brings you to Khons?"

"We have family here. Our cousins live here: Mari and Marvel, and their daughter, Daphne."

"Blossom!" I said, without realizing it. "Of course, Daphne Blossom. I should have recognized the name immediately. Daphne is my dear friend and the reason for our visit. We're here to assist her in a beauty pageant. We were in school together."

So delighted was I to find someone with whom we had a connection, I completely forgot about being in quarantine. Juniper and Jasmine were on Khons looking for shelter, a place to live, as they could no longer live on Liber.

"I'm afraid I have not heard of you. Our family branches have not been in touch. Now, however, it is necessary. We have to reach out to someone."

Juniper's disgruntled look told it all. She was forced to seek help from cousins they never spoke of, those in the middle circle of planets: Khons, of all places. In better times, they turned their noses up at the Blossoms of Khons. Now, things being what they are, they were hoping they could become bosom buddies in short order. I had a feeling they would be asking for deluxe accommodations, regardless of who was put out.

"I'm sure Daphne and her family will welcome you," I said. My attempt at positive reinforcement met with pursed lips and disapproving glances from Jasmine and Juniper. Fuchsia seemed above it all, happy to be married and counting the minutes until they were reunited with their men, meaning with her husband, Acer.

The door opened and five more women and a young girl entered. They didn't speak to the rest of us and kept their fangdu on the entire time. The young girl sat looking forward, as if looking at another person would be enough to catch the Grecian Flu.

"Are you here for the pageant?" I asked the oldest woman, the closest to me.

"Yes." she showed a wrinkle in her brow which could indicate a smile beneath her fangdu. She then turned her head and looked straight forward again.

"So am I," I said, as if we were now in a conversation. "I'm here to help my friend through it and to walk with her. We hope it will be an exciting experience. I believe every young girl should experience a pageant. Don't you?" I stopped, blinking my eyes, smiling and waiting.

"Yes," said the woman, then returned to her stoic pose.

"Good, then." I waited, trying not to fidget. When I couldn't stand it any longer,I blurted out. "It would be wonderful if we could meet the young lady who is to be in the pageant – for if we don't have a conversation of some sort, we will experience ..." I lowered my voice and furrowed my brow for emphasis. "... the longest twenty-eight hours of our entire lives."

I could see Jasmine and Juniper smiling. They exchanged

glances; I was someone who was all right to know, having said such to total strangers even snootier than they were.

The tense mood was broken as the door opened. A food tray was wheeled in by a uniformed matron. She counted heads, counted covered plates on trays and decided it was an even count. The food was predictable and perfunctory, being meant to neither nourish nor entertain. If asked, no one could say we didn't get a meal.

After the meal, a heaviness came over us and we slept. I suspected the food had been laced with a mild narcotic, something to make us rest. When I awoke, it was hour twenty-six of the twenty-eight hour ordeal. Others were also getting up.

"Is there is a sedative in the air?" asked Chineel, yawning.

"In the food, I think. Or possibly both."

Another meal was wheeled in, complete with a stimulant drink to wake us.

When the door opened, we were guided out to a locker area where we could shower and put our own clothes on once more. At each juncture, our identification was checked and double-checked to make sure no one slipped by with the flu. It was a great relief when I saw Daphne's face on the other side of a glass door I knew would open soon. Before we could leave, an hour's worth of administrative details remained. The health officials of Khons were taking no chances.

When the final door opened and we were allowed to enter the city of Khons, I rushed into the waiting arms of Daphne and her smiling family. Her parents, who once paid me to leave, now welcomed me as a returning daughter; someone who could show their child what growing up looked like.

Perhaps then she would find a man, get married and move out.

The Jumper

On board Exterra 4136A, Automated Repair Vessel, crewman Dagon watched his Captain and First Mate step out of the port bay doors onto the landing deck at Khons. He watched as Flax closed the doors. He stood looking at the doors, wondering what to do, since he had some time to himself.

"Dagon?" said Flax.

"Yes," said Dagon. He had no experience talking to a vessel.

"The bay doors are closed, and yet you stand before them."

"Yes, I know." Dagon couldn't think of a good reason to do so, but continued to stand there anyway.

"The doors will not open to admit the Captain and First Mate until they are done with their business and have returned. It will be twenty-eight hours before they are out of quarantine. It will be longer before they have completed their business."

Dagon thought for a moment, turned around and looked at the four-wheel sport speeder in the far corner. The speeder was strapped into the corner for transit. A loose speeder flying across the bay could cause damage.

"Why is it twenty-eight hours, Flax?"

"The time is arbitrary. The use of a Standard Earth Hour

provides uniformity from city to city. What on Earth is twenty-four hours, the complete planetary rotation, takes four more on Khons."

"So one day is twenty-eight hours here?"

"Yes."

"But doesn't it make the day longer?"

"Yes, by four Standard Earth Hours."

"So, at the end of the day on Khons, it's the next day on Earth."

"Yes." Flax was happy to be patient with Dagon. Both of them would remain aboard until the mission was complete.

"What happens when the end of the year comes?"

"Time is relative, as the planets are all different in regard to rotation and revolution around their central star. A year on Khons is shorter than a year on Earth. There are twelve months, but only twenty-three days each. Every January first, Earth and Khons are in synch."

Dagon furrowed his eyebrows. He had never been to school and didn't know how to behave when learning something not related to killing an enemy.

"Why don't they have their own system of keeping time?" he asked.

"In the beginning, the first residents were used to hours, days and so on. They also had a great deal of traffic and communication with Earth. As settlements grew and the planets became more separate, they discussed independent methods of keeping time, but by then everyone was used to the system in place."

"Oh," said Dagon. He looked across the bay to the speeder. "It looks too tall and slender."

"You are correct. This four-up model has acquired the unofficial name of 'Jumper' among those who ride them."

"But it doesn't jump, it rolls on four wheels."

"Correct. It is not designed to jump, but often does so, sending many riders to the infirmary. A wider wheel-base and a lower center of gravity should remedy the problem."

"Do we have tools?"

"Yes, we have tools. I can direct you to the tool locker. Please indicate the need so I may point you to the correct section."

"It's a large tool locker, then?"

"Yes. It is a large tool locker."

Dagon looked at the sport speeder strapped to the bulkhead, 'The Jumper.'

"It's also sluggish and rough on the turns. I can fix it so it's quick and stable. It will take some time and parts."

"The tools you will need are in the second section."

A row of dots lit up on the floor where Dagon stood leading to a line of lockers across the center divider between port and starboard bays. He followed this trail to the second locker and opened it. There were five stacked tool kits, each heavy and secured.

"Thank you," said Dagon.

"You're welcome," replied Flax.

Dagon took the first of the tool boxes to the speeder, unstrapping it from its tie-downs. He looked over the speeder, getting an idea of where to begin. The main engine housing seemed like a good start. Dagon opened the tool kit and took out a hand tool to use. He held it gingerly and was surprised when it slipped from his hands and fell to the bay deck. He reached down and touched the tool, but found it magnetized to the deck.

"I'm be-demoned!" cried Dagon. "What is this?"

"The tools in the smaller kits are magnetized. The estimated effort required to lift the tool will be sufficient to overcome gravity plus the magnetic pull of the tool to the deck. All life is a matter of estimated effort, one way or the other. For example: If you used more effort than needed to stand up from a chair, you would fly across the room. Too little and you would remain in the chair."

"Thanks, I think I understand."

Dagon picked up the tool and removed the first fastener to the main engine housing.

"It's going to be a long few days, is all," said Dagon, under his breath.

"If you say so," replied Flax.

The Khons Plaza

The new central shopping district in the redesigned downtown area took up sixteen city sectors. It went up nine stories and held hundreds of shops. As we drew close, riding in Daphne's family speeder, all I could do was gawk. I had never seen anything so grand in all my life. Inside it was even more spectacular, with seven sprawling hubs, each with a central food court. Carts and kiosks crowded the broad lanes, doubling the number of shopping outlets available. Every type and class of bauble and trinket was available in the Khons Plaza.

"Traffic has been down since the Grecian Flu scare," said Daphne, as if to apologize for the reduced number of people. It was, in fact, more people in one place than I had ever experienced.

The Grecian Flu might have been only a scare on Khons; there had not been a single reported case. Even so, the health authorities were taking no chances. The consequences of the flu getting loose amongst the population were too gruesome to consider. I turned my thoughts to more pleasing things.

"So many stores, all enclosed, all under a single roof! It's amazing!" I said, not sure if I thought it or had spoken the words out loud. I guessed I had spoken them, for Daphne laughed. I must have sounded like a rube from the outer ring.

"The dress shop I want is this way," said Daphne, taking my hand like a child.

We had come to find a dress for her to wear to the upcoming event, the beauty pageant. Daphne was entered, in spite of the nose dominating her face and the wideness of her cheeks. Fangdu would be worn at all times as the Grecian Flu scare was widespread. The pageant had to be either canceled or masked. Masks won out. As registration day approached, three times the number of young ladies stood in line to sign up. Daphne was among them. Now all she needed was a dress.

"Come, you have to see this!" she said, pulling my sleeve. We skipped to the central food court, passing so many shops, each more interesting than the last. I hoped they would still be there when I returned to see everything. Daphne continued pulling me along.

When we arrived at the central food court, I was amazed. It went up the full nine stories to a domed glass ceiling and spread out farther than I could see. The first three levels were quick-stop restaurants with tables in front from the doors to the central opening. From there up were finer dining places, set back further from the edge to give a grander view. A levitator with a glass cage went to the third level. I imagined another, more set back, ascended to the higher levels.

Daphne stood me in the exact center, under the glass dome.

"Wait here!" she said and skittered off to the levitator. She entered the glass cage and touched the pad. The levitator lifted from the floor up to the third level. I saw Daphne get off. She disappeared from view, leaving me standing there, in total childish wonder at the sights in view.

"Do you hear me, Star?" said a voice at my elbow. I spun in place, but saw no one; there was only a faint giggle. I spun around twice in a circle, but could see no one speaking to me. It was only a whisper, but one I heard for certain.

"You won't see me. I'm up here," said the disembodied voice.

I looked up to the third level to see Daphne waving to me. I smiled to her and waved back. She beckoned. Her voice whispered in my ear, "Come up and see."

The levitator had returned, so I boarded it and touched the pad on the third square. It flew up so quickly, I was frightened I might take off through the dome and launch into space, but it halted at the third level and the glass side opened.

"It was discovered after construction was complete. If you stand at the edge and speak, they can hear you down there. Right now, people walking by hear us. See the woman looking around?"

Far below, where I had stood, a woman carrying bundles stopped, turning her head as if someone spoke to her. When she heard "See the woman looking around?" she spun in all directions, and then hurried off as if possessed. Daphne giggled and in no time we were both laughing like schoolgirls.

"Come," said Daphne, pulling my sleeve. "We'll go check my plaza account. Fathers put money aside for their daughters for pageants and wedding days."

"One at a time, Daphne. Pageant now, wedding day much later."

"If I had a boyfriend, I'd be making plans already. My parents want me wed and settled. Don't you want to be wed and settled?"

I looked at Daphne, prepared to plead my case, but instead I said, "You'll be a grown woman for a long time, during which you will often wish you were a girl again. Don't rush into being grown. Stay a girl for a while longer."

Her parents would have disapproved.

Where Credit is Due

"Bacchus?" said the clerk. I looked up at him, trying to judge whether or not he was a threat. He didn't appear to be reaching for an alarm or a weapon.

"Yes?" I replied, still ready to fight or run at need.

We had stopped to see if Daphne's father had deposited money into her plaza account. He had, she had enough for two dresses, one for her and, as promised, one for me. I was far removed from grand dresses, and had never attended a pageant, especially in Fangdu, but the thought excited me.

After Daphne asked for her bundle, she asked if they held something for Star Bacchus. She giggled at the prospect, but to my surprise, the clerk recognized the name.

"Any relation to Doctor Bacchus and his wife, who I suppose is also Doctor Bacchus? Are you the daughter?" He looked at me with a twinkle rather than a suspicious eye. He might have been a holiday elf about to give me a sugar-coated treat, he so glowed with amusement.

"Yes, I am Starwort Bacchus. Doctor Bacchus was my father. He passed away some time ago."

"We were sorry to hear of it, but we all wondered when you would come around. We have been keeping your credits safe all this time. Would you like to collect your account?"

"Credits?" I stammered. Daphne and I exchanged glances.

It was the first I knew of credits.

"Oh, yes. A carte bancaire holding Universals for the time when expenditures would be heaviest. Are you to be married?" The old man twinkled all the more with the possibility of a wedding in the offing. He expected me to blush and glow at the same time.

"A pageant," I offered. "We're here for a dress for the upcoming beauty pageant."

The clerk darkened for the first time. His bald head wrinkled and his thick brows furrowed. "It's not going to be much of a beauty pageant if all the contestants have their faces covered."

"It will be better," interjected Daphne. "All the girls will be able to participate, not only the same old beautiful ones." Daphne appeared a full two inches taller, having stood her ground. Her neck was straight and her head high. She was not to be trifled with on this point.

"But it's a ... Oh, I suppose so," said the clerk, more to be agreeable than anything else. "Would you like to receive your credits? I'll need to see identity, of course."

"Of course." I produced my identity card, grateful I traveled under my own name. Khons was my home.

The clerk vanished into the back, to return a minute later carrying a card with a holographic image of a shimmering landscape across the front.

"I have it. You are in time; we were going to close for lunch in a few minutes." The clerk put the card in a reader on the counter. The reader whirred for a moment and popped the card out. The clerk placed the card into a red velvet sleeve, tied around with a scarlet ribbon and handed me the full package with a broad smile. "Here is your carte bancaire.

You can verify the balance in any terminal reader."

"Thank you. How much do I owe you?"

"No need, it's all covered," said the clerk, though his finger tapped expectantly on a tip jar located on the counter. I took the hint and placed two Universals in the jar hoping it was enough.

Daphne received a similar card chock full of Universals. She gushed, holding the card with both hands. It seemed the card was so small, and yet the spending power it contained was so large. Daphne looked over at the red velvet bag holding my own card, also still in my hand.

"What's on it?" asked Daphne as we joined the stream of people in the avenue.

"I'm not sure, but from his statement earlier, it might be enough to buy a wedding."

"Do you have a wedding planned?"

"Not even remotely. You need another person, it turns out." We both giggled.

"Here is my next stop." Daphne pointed to the refresh room marked for women.

"Always a good idea," I added as we stepped inside.

The booths were enclosed and discreet, made large enough for clothing to be changed comfortably. Privacy must have been a concern as they were being designed, as was security. I wondered if the carte bancaire was the legacy my father promised me. If so, it was a lot of fuss over what would fit on a card.

On the other hand, a thought which stilled my excitement, it could be credit of a mere handful of Unies and recorded advice for my coming nuptials. As I had no nuptials upcoming, such advice would be for a later time.

I was also glad for the privacy of the booths when I heard the door open and several people enter. It seemed odd to me to hear no further sound once the door had closed. The expected chattering of ladies out on a shopping spree, faucets activated, booth doors opening and closing, and dress fasteners being unfastened did not occur. There was an uneasy quiet in the refresh room.

When I stepped out of the booth, Daphne stood by the wash basins. She was stilled and wide-eyed. There was a slight tremble in her stance. I saw the reason for her fear. Three large men stood in the woman's refresh room, one by the door, one next to Daphne and one, the largest, close to me. The one by the door spoke.

"Just like Mister Dodd said." He grinned and opened his coat. He had a gun stuck in his belt.

"Relax, sweetie, and behave now," said the man next to Daphne. "Make no trouble and you won't get hurt too badly." His smile told me all I needed to know: we weren't merely being robbed; there was more in store for two young ladies cornered by three armed men.

I glanced at the big man closest to me. He also had a gun in his belt, on the left side so he could reach it with his right hand across his expanse of a belly. I remembered something Galium had said about most people not acting in the midst of a conversation. I stammered, quivering as best I could.

"Please, sir, whatever you do, don't..."

I spun around mid-sentence and grabbed the big man by the waistcoat with my left hand. We twirled together as the other two men pulled their weapons and fired. The big man reached for his weapon, trying to keep his balance with his other hand. He couldn't get to his gun; I was in the way. I pulled his gun and fired it from beneath his coat at the other two men.

As the shots intended for me flew into the back of the big man, I fired by instinct, nothing more, through the coat. I hit the man next to Daphne twice in the chest and shot the one by the door in the shoulder. He crashed back against the door, his eyes unfocused with surprise and pain. The man next to Daphne appeared to lunge at me, so I fired at his head. A small hole appeared on his forehead and a larger one in the back of his head as it rocked back with the blast. He fell into the line of basins and crumpled to the floor.

The man at the door pulled at the handle and disappeared out into the mall, leaving a deep red blotch on the door and a trail of blood across the tiles.

I glanced up at the big man. He had a look of wonder in his eyes, surprised to be spun around and then shot several times in the back, and by his friends.

"Sorry," I whispered. I pushed him away from me and he fell to the floor, dead before he hit.

One glance at Daphne told me she had reached her breaking point. Her eyes glazed over and she began to lean forward. Her fear showed itself as a dark spot appeared on her trousers. I dropped the gun on top of the man and reached out to catch my friend before she fell to the floor.

"Come on, Daphne. This is no time." I splashed water onto her face and she began to perk up. She looked with shock at the scene before her. The big man was dead on the floor, his eyes staring straight up at nothing. The second man had collapsed against the basins, leaving splatters of blood on the mirror behind him. He then fell to the floor where he lay in a heap. On the exit door, a large blotch of blood showed the exit wound. A trail of red led out to the mall. Somewhere out there, the third gunman was either dying or waiting.

Deception

Not far from the refresh rooms, a resting place with massage chairs beckoned us. For a Universal, aching muscles would receive a vibrating rejuvenation. I deposited Daphne in one of these and set it to work, massaging her from head to toe. I wanted to take the other, to feel the loving, though mechanical hands caring for my body. I wanted to sit beside Daphne and tell her it would be all right, but someone still stalked me and I had to find him first.

"You stay here, Daphne. I'm going to find out what's happening. I'll be right back for you."

My friend from school looked up at me with trusting eyes. She didn't nod but I had to assume she understood. I didn't have time to go into details or explain why armed men were after me. I squeezed her hand and rushed out into the lane filled with carts and shoppers.

The sound of shots from the refresh room had attracted the security people, uniformed men and women were headed down the lanes toward the refresh rooms. I looked left and right in an attempt to see the man who might also be looking for me. Of course, he might be looking for a medical facility, or he might be looking for a quiet place to die. All were possibilities.

A face turned toward me in the crowd. I recognized it as the man from the refresh room, the one I had wounded.

Apparently, I had not wounded him enough.

He smiled the evil smile I so hated. He opened his shirt to show me the pistol in his belt. He worked his way through the crowd toward me. At his shoulder was a smear of blood. He was wounded, but driven by hatred and anger. He must have been running on pure adrenaline. I turned away from him and ran as fast as I could through the crowd, my heart beating and my head racing.

I stretched my brain trying to come up with a plan. My thoughts came in bursts. He would shoot me no matter who was in the way. Innocents would die. It was near lunch, so there would be an increase in the traffic, more yet at the food courts.

The food court! An idea blasted into my head like an angry bat. But I was headed in the wrong direction, away from the central food court.

At the massive seven-levitator array I turned left and ducked around the structure. As he paused to locate me, I darted past him. In my peripheral vision I saw him look up and smile. It was as if I had failed to elude him.

I ran down the lane, pausing occasionally to make sure he still followed. He was right behind me, confident in his success at stalking me. I passed a center-lane cart overloaded with ribbon-festooned hats on sale and snatched one as I went by. At the next turn, I put it on, making sure he saw me do so. Once again, I had not fooled him; he saw me put on the hat. I could not disguise myself from him, his smile said. He must have felt like a king with the knowledge of his prowess.

At the central food court, the lunch trade traffic picked up and so did security. Uniformed guards emerged from the side doors and stood around to make sure everyone behaved themselves. The recent report of shots fired had heightened their presence.

Running with this many in the court was difficult, but my life depended on it. If he caught up with me, he wouldn't care how many were in the way, he would end me.

At the center of the court, I dropped the bonnet and turned sharply to the right, heading for the levitator. It was about to rise so I slipped in between two ladies, trying to blend in. I smiled at them so they wouldn't think me too rude. I alighted at the third level and ran to the rim. The man stood in the center, holding my bonnet and looking in every direction.

"I'm behind you," I whispered.

The man whirled around, still clutching the bonnet, but with his right hand perched over his open shirt, ready to draw his pistol and strike me down on sight.

"You're mine now!" I said, trying to sound as evil as him if he had said it.

He spun in a circle again, attracting the attention of two security guards. One tapped the other and indicated the man in the middle of the court with a bonnet in his hand.

"You don't have long to live," I whispered.

The man pulled his gun, looking one way then the other. The guards spoke into small pods on their shoulders and stepped forward, pulling people around behind them.

"No! Over here!" I whispered.

He twirled, eyes crazed, gun pointing left and right. Women screamed and ran, pulling children along with them. Men dropped to the floor and covered their heads. More security guards and several troopers arrived. They drew guns and spoke into radios relaying information and instructions.

"Prepare to die now!" I said.

The man whirled around and fired into the crowd of security guards and troopers. The bullets flew past them, fired so wildly all they struck were stone and marble behind the guards.

Five troopers returned the fire and the man in the middle shook as if hit by lightning. He went down, his gun clattering along the tiles, the bonnet falling from his hand.

A trooper went up to him and kicked the gun further away. He bent down and felt the man's neck. When he looked up at his partner, he shook his head.

People stood up, coming out from behind counters and columns to see what had happened. They would all have a story to tell tonight. I sat down at the nearest table and allowed myself to breathe.

Grantham Dodd

Watching the scene from the shadows were two men, Grantham Dodd and Adox Willamette.

"I told you he was an idiot," said Dodd. Grantham Dodd was tall, quiet and well-groomed.

"He was the best I could do on short notice." Adox Willamette, on the other hand, had fallen far from his days as a thin and dapper police officer. Now, he was rough and unkempt.

"At least he can't tell them anything." Dodd darkened as the security detail lifted the stretcher bearing the body of the unknown man who had been shot by plaza guards on the food court floor.

"They'll be sorting that one out for decades," snickered Willamette. "They'll never figure out what happened."

Dodd turned to him with the same look of disdain, wondering how he could have selected this moron in the first place.

"You miss the point. The point is we're no closer to our goal, we're farther away. She knows we're looking for her. She'll take to her heels. We have to put a tracker on her."

Grantham Dodd loomed over Willamette. He was taller than most men. Much of his height was due to the family trait of natural tallness, but the rest was his stick-straight posture and his air of superiority. He held his head high, the better to look down on the rest of humanity.

On this day, however, the regal brow was furrowed as he held the frayed lapel of his expensive waistcoat between his fingers. Time had not been good to him of late.

Having inherited young, Grantham Dodd had spent most of the family fortune before he left school. By the time he emerged from the halls of learning, little was left of his fortune. But Grantham Dodd knew of a way to earn barrels of riches: he could lie convincingly, though no one would believe him capable of it, not his teachers, not his friends, not his friends' trusting parents and not the many business partners he made easily and cheated profusely.

His downfall came at a time when he rode the highest, when he enjoyed his reward in the best of places, the Wind Pools of New Babylon. The day was burned into his memory like hot iron.

Grantham lay on the chaise in his cabana dressed in white silks sipping the citrus flavored waters for which Wind Pools are so famous. He had not a care in the world: his investments paid regularly, his accounts swelled with money and his acquisitions ran themselves, giving him the opportunity for an open-ended vacation high in the clouds, often called the Playground of the Gods.

Of course, the investments belonged to those he had cheated, the money in the accounts was embezzled and the acquisitions were the results of craftily worded contracts that somehow always seemed to come out in his favor. Those who brought charges against him found themselves hopelessly bound in iron-clad contractual clauses and inundated by endless legal motions, tying them up in trivial court details until the last of their money ran out.

Grantham Dodd was completely relaxed and confident in his position. He was ahead of the pack with a long trail of broken men behind him, completely helpless to do other than whimper at their own inability to gain any advantage.

So when armed members of the New Babylon Constabulary pulled aside the leading flap of the cabana, placed him in manacles and dragged him from the resort, he was surprised to say the least. The court-appointed attorney did nothing to brighten his day.

"Mr. Dodd, your accounts have been frozen, your credit suspended and your investments confiscated. You won't be able to sell any of the businesses or real estate you have acquired, they have also been frozen in anticipation of the charges brought against you. Without resources, I'm afraid other representation is impossible and you have not the wherewithal to secure your release. You'll be the guest of New Babylon until you can be transferred to the Central Government Command Center at Copernicus."

The blood drained from Dodd's face. A queasy feeling in the pit of his stomach made him throw up in the metal toilet next to the bed. The lawyer pulled his brief closer to avoid spatter.

"Be-demoned!" he cried, beating one fist against the stone wall.

"There's nothing more I can do. The court says you need representation. I have been assigned. If there is anything, anything at all you can mention in your defense, I will bring it to the court's attention. In the meantime, I will try to get you some sort of deal to make the blow easier. Given the extent of the damage, though, if I can get you a life sentence instead of the paddles, I will do so."

A shudder went through Dodd. Those convicted of the worst crimes, those who were considered beyond redemption, were placed on a gurney while electronic paddles were attached to either temple. The current running through them fried the brain. Death was not fast, but certain.

The lawyer returned the brief to his brushed metal case and stood at the cell door waiting for it to recognize him. It did and opened for his exit. He stopped in the doorway for a moment, hoping he could think of something to say to make it better, but nothing came to mind. He turned left and walked down the corridor as the door closed automatically behind him, locking Grantham Dodd in his cell.

Minutes later, a racket distracted him from his misery. Down the corridor two constables dragged a wretched man kicking and screaming toward the cells.

"Full," said the taller constable as he walked by cell 214. At 216 he stopped for an instant, looked in and shook his head. At 218, he smiled. "In here."

The door opened and a drunken and dirty man was thrown onto the floor. Grantham Dodd recoiled at the sight. The twisted, imploring face of Adox Willamette turned upward to him, as if begging to be beaten no more. Adox, named for the flower signifying *weakness*, was a large man but not larger than two constables with clubs. Besides, they were most likely sober, whereas Adox was certainly drunk.

The man at Grantham's feet stunk with old sweat and cheap booze. He moaned with pain from the blows he received at the hands of the constables and he spat blood. He spit as he spoke of the one who was to blame for it all. The image of a young girl came into his mind: a young girl gripping a parcel containing the route to a family fortune larger than one could spend in three lifetimes.

Grantham smiled. Here at last was someone he could exploit, to win over and use to his own ends. Where the constables and the worm attorney were a loss, Adox was someone who could be fashioned into a weapon to use against them. First the attorney, then the constables, then his old business partners, now organized and joined against him, would take their deserved falls. Sooner or later, he would find the young girl who filled the eye of this unfortunate drunkard, and when he did, he would then become the new owner of this same fortune, for there would be no one left alive to lay claim to it. He would see to it.

The next time the lawyer came to the cell, he was met with the twisted face of the drunkard. Adox held the lawyer in front of the door. When the door opened, it was the prisoners who exited, not the attorney. He lay on the floor, his neck broken.

"Where in Hades' realm will this lead?" asked Dodd, as they hid in a gully on the edge of the free port awaiting some unsuspecting tourist wearing fine, new clothes to wander by.

"The lowlands, a tavern I know, the Mithra. We'll pick up her scent there. We'll need some money." The scarred man looked at his cellmate.

"Working capital. Yes, money's what's needed. Not a problem. I will lift a credit ticket at need. I'll get us something to run on. There's only one point to mention."

Adox looked up at the man who somehow seemed taller and more self-assured than before. Dodd continued:

"I'll be making the plans; you'll be carrying them out. If you understand, we'll proceed."

60

Adox Willamette's options were non-existent, so he nodded. He didn't need to be in charge, he needed to be rich and free. It's what he deserved and it's what he would get, even if it killed the girl. In fact, her death would be a bonus.

Grantham Dodd allowed himself a quiet smile as his new ally nodded his agreement. This was, Dodd assured himself, the beginning of a new chapter, one which would leave his former life in shadow.

Adox Willamette

At the Khons Plaza bar, after the excitement at the food court subsided, Adox Willamette drummed his fingers as he waited for his drink to arrive. He had been looking to his right when the hostess took his order from a few feet away. She saw his less-ugly side, the side without the disfiguring scar which made his right eye and right ear useless and deformed his mouth into a constant sneer. The hostess smiled as she looked up, as she did with all her customers. A smile is as good as a wink when it came to her tip jar.

The smile faded as Adox turned toward her. The gnarled right side of his face, the drooping eye, the twisted mouth made her recoil.

"Some of that," he said, pointing to the bottle already in her hand.

The hostess poured and found other duties to attend to rather than linger by the frightening man with the scarred face.

The girl! Willamette thought. That rotten little girl! She's the one who made his life turn to guano.

As a young man, he had gone to the military with his friends. Being younger, he had been held back from actual battle, until all battle was done. Peace is a death sentence to a soldier out to prove himself. Being named Adox didn't help, the flower signifying *weakness*. His name alone gave him

62

something to overcome.

When peace arrived, all of his friends were dead or crippled. Those still alive resented him for accepting a hero's welcome, having never seen action. The boys in the PR department needed a hero in one piece to show off; presenting a broken, embittered wreck simply wouldn't do.

After the service, he took a position with the police. There he met Helia, a married woman needing saving. After her husband beat her senseless, Adox found the man and returned the favor, causing him to be unable to speak up in protest at the divorce hearing.

A year later, Helia's ex-husband was found dead of a drug-induced overdose. His fellow police officers questioned Adox, but he had an alibi: Adox had been with his girlfriend, Helia.

After the inquiry died down, they tried to make plans, but plans take money. Then a girl walked into the cafe where Helia worked, a girl who needed a friend.

"She has an inheritance," said Helia. "If we are smart, we'll befriend her. We could use some kindness from the little rich girl."

The girl left school before their plan could get started. And there were others with the same idea, the school administrator and his scheming partner. They had scared her off and she developed allies. By the time Adox found her, he was two steps behind the competition and one step ahead of the law.

"I had the drop on her," Adox said to his empty glass.

He remembered the swinging kitchen door, the landlord at the window crying out: the constables had been alerted. Helia reached for the girl but was pushed back into him. The gun went off of its own accord. Helia fell to the floor, dead.

The landlord fell out of the window, screaming all the way to the ground below.

Blinded by anger, Adox leveled his gun to the offending girl. It was all her fault! She should have stayed where she was, been protected. He would have cared for her. Helia would have been like a mother to her. But no, she had to take her fortune and run. Now he might never get it, but neither would she. She would die for Helia.

Faint memories of the kitchen door swinging open, the landlord's wife screaming, the landlord falling from the window ran in a jumble through his brain. The door struck him in the head, knocking him sideways. The woman screamed, returning to the kitchen. The schoolgirl waited for him to charge. He was about to kill her. She looked as if she expected it. Adox raised his pistol to finish her. This would be ended for all time!

The kitchen door swung open again, striking him in the same place, on the left side of his head, knocking him to the floor. He remembered the sight of the wife, screaming like a crazy woman, wielding a black, steaming fry-pan, dripping hot grease. She swung it at his face and he remembered nothing more.

He awoke in police custody, charged with the murders of the landlord and his own girlfriend, Helia. There were other charges, but he didn't hear them. Instead, he took stock of what he'd lost, all he needed to regain and who was to blame.

No sight came from his right eye, no sound from his right ear and the mouth didn't quite work on one side. His woman was dead, his plans destroyed and he was destined for death row, all because of the dumb luck of one stupid little schoolgirl. He nearly had her fortune in his hands, but in an instant everything was taken from him. No! He would not let it go! He would find her and he would take her family fortune, her father's inheritance, all she had. And he would take her life as well.

Sometimes, in his imagination, he would kill her quickly, snapping her neck. Or maybe putting a pistol to her head, smiling as he pulled the trigger while looking into her eyes. He would make sure his face was the last she would see. Then she would be sorry. Then she would know. He would smile as he watched her brains fly out of the other side of her temple. He would sit there and enjoy watching the blood seep from her body.

Other times he would imagine killing her slowly, taking carnal pleasures denied him since Helia's death. She was gone and no woman would have him, for any price. He would take it all: her fortune, her body, her life, and do it with a smile. He would get all he had coming to him.

The escape from incarceration was supposed to be quiet and bloodless, but Adox made sure the guards knew who escaped. He paid them back for everything. They would not laugh or sneer at him again, not any of them. He killed seven as he left. The rest were beyond his reach, but they knew.

"I told you, no killing," said Grantham Dodd, his cellmate, the mastermind of the breakout. Adox held a guard by the neck when he said it.

Adox snapped the guard's neck for spite. "There. Now I'm done."

"If you're going to get the prize you seek, we're going to have to put some rules in place. You can't kill everyone you meet. You got it?"

"Yeah, I got it." Adox looked forward to the day he could

snap the neck of Grantham Dodd, who was far too cocky and far too handsome.

The bulletin for his capture was out across the Central Planetary Circle, but the girl wasn't likely to travel those lanes. Adox would find her on the middle ring, hiding from the authorities herself. Little did she know she would also have to hide from him. Once he found her, he would be rich and free and closer to even, though it was difficult to think the score would ever be even.

If he could, he would take her face and leave her with no sight, no sound, and no face. He would wear her face over his, as spoils of the personal war he waged. Any way he envisioned what was to come, it was not enough.

Adox tapped his glass. The hostess picked up the bottle and held it at arm's length, setting it down within his reach. She didn't want to get any closer to the man with half a face than necessary.

Adox Willamette's one good eye narrowed with hatred for her. He would make Starwort Bacchus pay for that, too.

Secrets and Dresses

Three floors below me in the whisper court, security guards were questioning witnesses and taking the names of those who saw the carnage, while troopers placed stanchions around the place the body had fallen.

It was time for me to slip away. I walked to the place three floors above where I left Daphne and rode a levitator to the ground level. She was still there, where I left her.

"There was some excitement at the food court, but you didn't miss much," I told her, as if of no interest.

I sat in the massage chair next to hers and ran my credit tag over the pay-dot. The chair vibrated, beginning at my feet and working its way up my body at a mechanical pace.

"I have had all the excitement I can stand for the moment, thank you." She paused, turned her head and showed me her worried face. "Star, I'm afraid I made a poor account of myself. Please forgive me. I'm not naturally brave, I'm rather quite timid."

"Please don't, Daphne. It was an unexpected situation, overwhelming. It's understandable."

"I'm going to need another pair of pants."

"Luckily, they sell them here." I looked over at her and smiled. "We'll get you some pants, we'll love each other as usual and we'll never speak of this day again."

"Promise me? It'll be our secret?" Daphne's face implored me. I couldn't refuse her. I didn't want to. She looked so pitiful.

"I promise. Best friends should have secrets, things they never speak of. This is ours."

Daphne sat back, feeling the vibration reach her head. She closed her eyes and the events of the day were forgotten, as forgotten as secrets between best friends could be.

It took another hour of vibration, a new pair of pants and fresh dainties before Daphne felt like going to the dress shop. When she finally ran out of distractions, she turned to me and gave in.

"All right, Star. Let's go and buy dresses. Only please tell me we've seen the last of such men. I can't take much more."

We readied ourselves, fortified our courage and strode off to shop for dresses. It was an effort for me, as much as for Daphne, though it was different with me.

How was I supposed to keep my mind on dresses when I had killed a man and caused the deaths of two others? How could I choose a theme and formulate a presentation? Daphne had a short attention span. One minute in the dress shop and she was as giddy as a schoolgirl. In fact, she still was a schoolgirl in many ways. I looked over my shoulder at every opportunity, searching for those who sought to kill me.

Whoever sent those men, Dodd he said, wouldn't stop simply because he lost three employees. It could be they weren't after my father's map at all. There was little left of his legacy in the parcel I toted. No, they saw me pick up a line of credit at the plaza and guessed it was money they could steal. But why send three armed men to overcome one little girl for a card of unknown contents? Daphne didn't count;

she could be overcome by a juvenile boy with a bad attitude.

"Don't you think the violet is a lovely dress?" Daphne said.

It was a rhetorical question. She wasn't looking for an answer. By the time I had one, she was already on the next table.

"Look, there's fangdu to match! Gloves all the way up and a decorated mask to catch the judge's eye." Daphne danced around the dress shop like a sugarplum fairy.

"Oh! Shoes!" She pirouetted off to another department.

It would be a pageant of dresses and hair arrangements. Even the favorite event, the height of the pageant, had been canceled due to the ridiculousness of young girls walking across a stage in two-piece bathing costumes and fangdu with long gloves. With three times the number of entrants, the opening introductions would take up the allotted time.

At the end of the day, we walked out with two dresses with matching shoes and fangdu. Daphne didn't stop chattering the entire time.

We spent the evening and into the early morning talking about school and how beautiful the pageant would be. When we finally fell asleep, it was from sheer exhaustion.

In the morning, we sat at the breakfast table and listened to the news: the pageant was canceled.

Three men had been killed in the plaza the previous day, two in a shootout in a refresh room and one killed by security guards in the main dining court. They were believed to be terrorists, part of an advance guard sent here to disrupt the pageant and perhaps to kidnap some of the young ladies who would be participating. In the light of this information, of course, all festivities were canceled until further notice.

There were heartfelt apologies by the pageant originators and promoters. There was footage of pitiful girls in tears as their young dreams were dashed to pieces on the plaza's marble floor. The usual collection of talking heads retold the same information over and over "for those who have recently tuned in."

All three of the dead men had police files, all three were wanted in many systems and all three were cold-blooded killers. Whoever put this pack of thugs together wasn't messing around, he was out for blood.

"Well, I suppose the store will take the dresses back," said Daphne's mother. Daphne looked up at her with a sour face. Her mother felt the need to justify her statement. "I mean, they haven't been worn."

"Yes, of course," I said, trying to be obliging. "It's only right if the pageant is off."

What I wanted to do was to scurry back as fast as I could to the dress shop, drop off the parcels, kiss my childhood friend goodbye and beat a hasty retreat to my ship. What frightened the pageant committee into canceling the entire event also frightened me, and I had more information than they did.

"Perhaps I can take the dresses back this morning, Star, darling. You can stay and comfort little Daphne." Daphne's mother was afraid we would change our minds and decide to keep the dresses anyway.

"Good idea," I joined in. "However, if the pageant is canceled, I should return to my vessel. It is a repair vessel after all, there may be contracts."

Having business to do around the galaxy beats simply not

wanting to hang around and talk about how we missed our childhood school days, the same way we did every time we saw each other. I liked Daphne well enough, but we had grown apart. She was a debutant with a broken heart because the pageant was canceled, and I was a pirate who had caused the deaths of three feared terrorists.

"Oh, just go!" cried Daphne. "You didn't want to be in a pageant anyway!"

"It's not that, Daphne. I have obligations. One day you'll have obligations. Then you'll understand."

In the end we hugged and waved, but while she turned sullenly back to her life, I strode boldly onward to mine.

Options

"Anubis in four hours. There is an open market there if you want fresh food."

I jerked awake. I had drifted off into a middle world of neither being awake or asleep, sitting at the console in the pilot's chair. A million stars played out before me.

"Thank you, Flax. What would I do without you?" I said, grateful for the nudge.

"You would explode! There is no atmosphere here."

"You have a point." I laughed. My friend who was once voiceless, then stiff and all business, now made jokes.

Sitting there, watching the black constant of deep space, surrounded by the light of stars, which might have burnt out a hundred years earlier, I had drifted off into a netherworld, a drama unfolding as it had once, not a flashback of the past, but a replay of events cut in stone. It was always thus.

Other people had no grasp of how it was in the early days on Khons. Even the police thought my uncle was a comfort to me in my grief after my parents died, and a loss to me at his passing not long after. The truth could not be further away if it were in another universe.

My Uncle Lazar's desk came into my memory, unbidden. It was an ugly desk in an ugly den. Most of the drawers were locked and I had to use the fireplace poker to break the locks. In the large drawer was my father's packet, his legacy to me. It felt light, as if something was missing. I should have taken the desk apart, the entire den, the whole house, brick by brick, until...

"That way lies madness, Star," I said to myself aloud. "Should-have-beens and might-have-beens will make you crazy. Don't travel in those regions."

But there was a carte bancaire in my possession yet to be inspected. My father left it for me at the market plaza, hoping sooner or later I would come there to shop, perhaps for a wedding dress, as many did. Now the carte bancaire called to me, its secrets begging to be revealed.

Chineel brought out a reader and we gathered at the galley table. The carte bancaire looked ordinary, despite its exotic name. The ornate hologram aside, it was simply a reader card used in most of the known worlds.

"Go ahead," Chineel said. "Open it."

She saw this as a frustratingly slow ballet. All I had to do was to slip the card into the slot and follow instructions from the screen.

"I'm afraid."

"For Achelous' sake, why?"

"I don't know. Suppose it's something I don't want to see?"

"Why would your father leave you something you wouldn't want to see?" Chineel asked, unfolding her arms.

"Oh, I don't know," I said, like a spoiled child.

With a flourish, I picked up the card and pushed it into the reader slot. The screen came alive with a liquid display. It rose like a ghost and hovered over the reader, awaiting my fingers to select the right dots floating in the air. The readout rippled with the air currents, patiently awaiting my decision while I procrastinated.

"Yes...?" Chineel said, pushing me.

"OK, OK, I will!"

"Then do it," Chineel chided. "Don't stand around. Is this the fearless Captain Bacchus we all know and love?"

I threw her a look to back off and turned my attention to the reader again. It seemed to taunt me, but after what I had gone through to get it, I wasn't going to stop now.

With trembling hands, I poked the air, tapping several dots from my point of view, telling the reader I wanted to open the carte bancaire and investigate its contents. The reader complied and showed two items, one was a balance able to be activated at any system bank and the other was a personal message. I tapped the balance first. The number Ц 250,000 came up on the readout. I gulped.

"There's a fortune in Universals here."

"Are they accessible?" asked Chineel. "The CG Reserve sometimes makes them inaccessible, you go in to claim them and find them taxed down to zero or less."

"The entries appear to be six years old, about the time my parents died. He must have put this in for me right before my mother passed on. He followed her within a week."

"It must have been a hard time for you." Chineel put a hand on my shoulder.

"Yes. It was. But I've cried my tears. It was expected. Even in these times of medical advance, no one lives forever. Only, I was a kid and wasn't ready. I'm not a kid anymore."

Turning back to the reader, I tapped the message. It came up taking up the full space of the holographic image. In earlier times, my father would have written me a letter, on paper and in an envelope, no matter how antiquated the art form. This was a new wrinkle for him.

In the image, I saw my father's flourishing hand. As I read the message, tears formed unbidden in my eyes and an unexplained catch came into my throat.

"My dear, dear child. If this is not enough for your undertaking, try the main plaza on Adonis and the smaller bank on Copernicus. I love you dearly, as does your mother. Fondly, Father."

"Fondly, Father? Is it how he addressed you?" Dagon asked.

"You knew one life, I knew quite another. We were polite when I was a child. We could do with some politeness now. There is much I miss about the way we used to be. I'll ask you to show some respect, please."

It was true. Chineel knew it. She had wished and hoped for the kind of life I had, but couldn't find it. The world of my childhood, in the rarefied air of academia, where my parents made their lives, was one of extreme politeness. There was tea in the afternoon, people complimented each other and rarely, if ever, said anything hurtful; it simply was not done. If one could not be courteous, my mother used to say, it is best to remain in one's room. For my father to end his letter "Fondly," and to sign it "Father" was completely in keeping with the fashion of the time and place. The rest of the universe would descend to rudeness, but the Bacchus family did not. It was a source of pride.

"What does it mean?" Chineel asked.

"I believe it means something from my father waits for me in the plaza at Adonis and at Copernicus."

"We should go," Dagon said. He seemed to be starting out on a quest instead of making a statement. The prospect of visiting new places and getting treasure in one swoop was too attractive for mere words. He needed action.

"We recently came back from Adonis," Chineel added.

"Yes," I pointed out. "But we didn't go to the market plaza there. Nor did we ask if anyone had left anything for me. Besides, and more to the point, we were able to go to Adonis because Flax had a contract. We will have to either wait for another contract, fake one, which we have done before but cannot do often lest we arouse suspicion, or..."

A thought formed inside my head. It had come up before but not in a while. It was a radical thought and would take all the fortitude Captain Starwort Bacchus could muster.

"Or?" Dagon said, tapping a finger in the galley table.

"Or we buy Flax." My statement was met with blank stares. The thought had not occurred to Chineel or Dagon. To them it was a new concept and hard to get your head around.

"Is there to be a vote?" asked a disembodied voice from the wall console as Flax joined the conversation.

"I believe such a vote would be unanimous. Don't you?"

"I hope it would be, but then I am new at the concept of hope. My experience is things either are or they are not. To hold out a desire for one outcome over another is not in my nature."

"We all are changing our nature. Daphne went home with a whole new frame of reference for her outlook on life. It's time we did the same."

Two sets of eyes looked at me, but I knew there were three

76

entities listening as I continued.

"There will be no vote. We will make an offer on Flax's contract at the earliest opportunity and then set our course for Adonis, Copernicus and finally, Bacchus, where we hope we can make a home."

Anubis

Before we went dashing around the universe in search of treasure, there was another contract to fulfill; we were still under the orders of another.

"Anubis is in its fall season, with warm days but chilly nights. I suggest you return to the vessel at darkness. I will leave a light on for you," said Flax, always accommodating.

"Good idea, Flax. Anything you need?"

"What did you have in mind?"

"I don't know, a software upgrade, more memjars, a toy?"

Flax took an interesting pause, as if thinking. But then, she could do more thinking in an instant than I could in an hour. She emulated me, taking as long to think something over as I took. Of course she would reach a conclusion in an instant, but I took longer, so she did as well. It was polite.

"Thank you, Star, but no; I have no needs at this time. Nice of you to think of me though."

"My pleasure." We got on famously these days, Flax and I.

On Anubis I headed for the market. It was not far from the space-port to the center of town. It was a lovely walk, which was good, because there were no speeder-taxis to be had.

The food stalls were serving and everything looked delicious. While deciding what to get first, the peaceful scene erupted into chaos.

"There!" a voice cried. A large man with a scowl pointed at me. He ran toward me as several others as mean-looking, took chase.

Old habits kicked in and I ran too, away and fast.

I only just arrived! I thought as I ran through the market. What could I have done already? I haven't even mentioned my name! Could it be someone from another place, another time, another universe?

It had been some time since the incident on Copernicus. Besides it was a small matter, four dead, one wounded; too small to follow me to this sector. Yet, here I was, one step ahead of mean looking men, turning over barrels and pushing past stalls, chasing me down alleys and over culverts. I pulled a scarf over my head and ducked into a side street, running with unladylike strides to the next row of stalls.

I could not for the life of me place these men, but they were intent. Faces turned toward me, trying to discern what the fuss was, not knowing whether to protect me from the men in pursuit or hand me over to them.

At the end of the row I turned left and found a surprise: it was a dead end. I should have gone right. A hand reached out for me and pulled me over a table full of melons. I was lifted off of the ground, my hands held and my feet unable to find a ground to get a foothold. The scarf was ripped from my head. The man turned me over and looked into my face.

"It's not him!" he said.

He let me go and I dropped to the ground like a rag doll. The man strode back into the street looking left and then right. The three with him followed without comment.

"Oh, please! Don't apologize!" I called after them. "It was

clearly my fault! You cretins!"

The men moved on without noticing me. No one came to apologize for roughing up a lady. None of them extended a hand to lift me from the ground. They had less interest in me than in any of the cobblestones over which they had chased me.

"Are you all right, miss?" said the man whose cart I had disturbed. He did extend a hand and I took it gratefully. "Did they hurt you?" he asked.

"Yes, thank you. Only my pride. Are your melons intact?"

"Yes, thank you. Here. Have this one; you look like you could use refreshment."

He handed me a melon, clearly the pick of the stack, and smiled warmly. A friendly smile! How nice! How welcome! How rare!

"Thank you so much," I said, taking the melon. "What did he mean, 'it's not him?'"

"I don't know," said the melon man. "You don't look like a 'him' to me!"

I nodded thanks, tucked my melon under my arm and continued to walk down the lane. I needed to find a cup of something warm and soothing to settle my nerves.

"Are they gone?" came a voice from the potato bin. I turned to see a head poking out of an otherwise empty bin.

It was a boy dressed in a woman's clothes. Clearly, I was not the object of the chase. As he stood and extricated himself from the barrel, I saw the likeness. The boy wore makeup and earrings, a full skirt, plain, white blouse but with short hair. The makeup was done badly, so he was not a bonnie-boy; they knew how to do makeup.

"Yes, they're gone."

The boy adjusted his skirt, which was odd to me. He looked both ways and started walking, taking my arm as he went. "Let's walk together," he said.

"Oh, so if they see us, they'll arrest me as an accomplice? No thanks, miss. Good roads and fair weather to you." I walked off in the opposite direction.

"No, wait, you can't leave me like this!"

"Watch me," I shot back over my shoulder.

"But..."

"Good roads,"

"You don't understand..."

"Fair weather," I waved over my shoulder, leaving him behind me.

"No, No, I have to get my own clothes back, I need your help."

"Oh, but yon skirt is soooo attractive." I continued walking away.

"It's yours!" he yelled. "If you'll help me."

His cry stopped me. Before me stood a young man in dire need of aid. Somewhere a young lady stood wrapped in a sheet wondering where her clothes had gotten to. I had to know more.

"Where are your own clothes?" I asked, taking a step closer.

"In my rooms, not far." He pointed off across the square. He looked hopeful.

"And the owner of these garments, where is she?"

"One of the boys down the hall had his lady friend in.

When I ran from my room, I left in what I had on: nothing. I had to put something on, though I'm not sure this is better."

"Better than naked? Yes, it's better."

Around us, business continued as usual. The chase being over, the vendors wanted to get back to selling their produce.

"Will you help me?" the hapless boy pleaded.

"It will necessitate a return to your rooms, if for no other reason, than to return these clothes. The young lady must be in a state."

"I'll take you there, but we must be careful."

"Guarded?" I asked.

The boy tilted his head and looked away.

"Guarded," I answered my own question.

I walked in the direction he had indicated, across the square with the boy following close behind, skipping to catch up to my stride. He had difficulty walking in skirts, which was a good sign. I always say, show me a boy who can walk in skirts and I'll show you a boy who couldn't meet a girl in a lady's academy while holding a pie.

Taxus

"Althea," whimpered the boy, as we walked back to his room, "is my heart, my life. But her father disagrees. He has taken her away and to make it stick, he has leveled false charges against me."

"Is Althea derived from a flower?" I asked, always interested.

"Althæa in the Latin is a flower meaning *beneficence*."

I didn't want to tell him the English name for his love: *marshmallow*.

"Ah, yes. And the father, rich and powerful?"

"Do you know him?"

"You have no idea!" The boy continued to look at me. "I mean no, only the type."

"He won't let me see her. He has taken her to one of his homes. He has many homes; I don't know where they have gone. It could be anywhere."

"What's his position?" Men who can muster an army of thugs usually have a position, rather than a job.

"He is the richest man on Anubis. He owns everything worth owning, including the local elected officials. He is a good man to befriend but a bad one to offend. When I developed a love for Althea, he took offense."

"What do they have against you?" I asked.

"Nothing of substance, but any reason would do to get me into a small cell. From there, those men will do the rest. In short order, no one would see a way to love me."

The lad looked so dejected it touched me to my heart.

"We'll make it all better," I said, trying to comfort him.

"He decided I was not good enough for his daughter," said the boy, his eyes on the ground.

"That is often the case. When my father was alive he told me, one day I would meet a young fellow who would want to win me away, and he would put fear of the gods into said young fellow. He was a good man, my father."

"Sounds like it. But I do love Althea and my prospects, while not impressive, are not too bad. I am educated and am quick to learn."

"Yes, aren't we all," I said, more to make space in the conversation than for any other reason. "What's your name?"

"Taxus."

"For the taxus baccata, the yew, strong and supple, it thrives no matter where it is. It's a good name."

"You know names and histories? Tell me your name?"

"Starwort, signifying *afterthought*, but also good for soothing a pain in the side."

The boy called Taxus said nothing, showing some intelligence. We walked in silence until something else occurred to him to ask.

"Tell me about your vessel," said the boy dressed as a girl. We walked quickly through the market with one eye sharp for the constables. Taxus walked with the added distraction of having to watch his feet while holding up the hem of his skirt.

"I'm the captain, but not the real brains of the operation."

"Who's the brains?"

"Flax."

"Who's ax?"

"Flax, the ship's computer."

"Oh! So there's you."

"No, there's Flax." I stopped, turned and looked him straight in the eye. How dare he prejudge? How dare he correct me? "The Flax flower signifies *benefactor*. She is so to me, I call her Flax. And there's Chineel."

"Who's Chineel?"

I continued down the line of stalls. "She was married to my uncle, so I guess she's my aunt. Of course, he's dead, so she might not be my aunt anymore, technically, but she's still my friend."

"So, the two of you."

"No, Taxus, three of us, Dagon, Chineel and me, plus Flax, making four."

"Dagon?"

"He's harder to explain. He's a protector and deserving of respect."

"And you count the computer as a crew member."

I took Taxus by the blouse and pulled him to me. I spoke calmly and quietly, but my eyes said to tread lightly. "You have to stop thinking of Flax as an 'it' and start thinking of her as a 'she.' She is, as I said, the brains."

"OK, OK. Can she take us off this rock?"

"Yes, she can," I said, before I could think. Would Flax welcome this new obligation, this additional responsibility?

Would Dagon appreciate another man on board? Would Chineel think I'm collecting suitors as I ramble through space? Did I commit to an impossible task? Was I an idiot?

After all, I thought as we passed by a stall vending closed circuitry systems, the boy could be called attractive, or might be in his own clothing. Or out of them, came a thought unbidden.

I halted mid-step. Wait! What had I seen? Or rather, what had I not seen? I spun around and pulled Taxus back to the stall featuring a camera and full screen, such as one might put up in a shop. As we walked by, there was a distortion on the screen, but no image, not from me and not from Taxus. The camera didn't pick us up.

On my blouse was the pin Dr. Genus had given me, the one with the power to distort such systems and make me invisible to surveillance. Could it be it hid both of us? We walked close beside each other, but not holding hands.

"Stand there," I instructed Taxus, as I stepped aside, away from him. There was no change in the screen.

"What is it?" asked my companion, in a voice too deep for the skirt and blouse combination.

"Come on! We have to get out of sight. Where are your rooms?"

"Up ahead, not far."

We ran to a student riser, inexpensive temporary housing for those still at school. Above the door hung a security camera, hastily placed there from the look of it. The location was within easy reach and it didn't look like a permanent installation. We walked by the camera, expecting armed thugs to leap out at us at any moment. None did.

At an unmarked door along a hallway lined with unmarked doors, Taxus looked both ways and slid a slender card into a slot. The door opened and we slipped inside.

"What are you wearing?" I asked, turning him around and looking him up and down.

"You see what I'm wearing."

"No, I mean, what else? Do you have something like this?" I pointed to the pin on my blouse, the star within a circle with one arm of the star reaching out to the universe beyond the circle. Dr. Genus said it symbolized both my travels and my attitude.

Taxus looked at my blouse, at the pin Dr. Genus had so boldly placed there. While he was at it, Taxus stole a look at what else filled my blouse. He was not impressed, but I was on another quest and had no time for trivialities. His eyes grew wide with recognition.

"Yes, Althea gave it to me as a token of her love." He reached into his blouse and pulled out a thin chain from around his neck. On the chain was a pin similar to mine. Two birds perched within the enclosure of an oval. Charming and precious as it was, I had no time to admire the cuteness of new love. I pulled the pin to me for a closer look. There was a mark on the back, a flourishing, stylized "AG" inscribed on the metal. I pull the pin from my blouse and saw the same "AG" across the back of my own pin.

"Take off your clothes."

"Here? Now?" The boy's eyes grew wide for a moment. He looked around to the left, then to the right. He turned red from his neck to his hairline.

"We have to get to my vessel. Change to your regular clothing, you stand out like a borth in a dancing dress. We have to get back to Flax and contact Dr. Genus."

"Who?"

"I don't have time. Strip!" I said between my teeth. Would I have to say everything twice for this boy? How could I possibly think him attractive when he was such a dullard?

"I'm keeping my token, you can't have it."

"Yes, yes. You keep it. Wear it around your neck as you have been. What does Althea's father do?"

"He does nothing, he's rich. You said you knew the type."

"More than is comfortable. Take only what you can carry. We have to move fast and unseen."

The pins would protect us from technical eyes but there were still human eyes to see us. They mistook me for him when he was a "her" so they didn't have much of a description. Perhaps a boy and a girl traveling together would throw them off their game.

"Hurry! We must return your friend's girlfriend her clothes."

"He's two doors down the hall."

"Good! We'll drop them on the way out. Do you have any hats?" I remembered a trick from earlier flights of my own.

"Hats?" said my new dullard friend.

"Hats. You wear them on your head."

"I know what hats are," he said as he tucked his shirt into his trousers. A light jacket lay to one side, but I saw no head coverings.

"Good. Do you have any?"

"Yes, I have one, it's around here somewhere. My roommate is the one with the hats."

Taxus opened a closet and pulled a soft cap with a stiff bill from the collection of headgear hanging there.

"Aha! That's more like it!" I chose several: a fedora with a brim and a French sea cap like the one I had back on the vessel; two more like it for Taxus and we bundled up a few belongings. I put the fedora on him and a similar hat with a wider brim on my own head. Thus disguised, we turned to go. It was time for Flax to meet Taxus.

Wrinkle on the Screen

As we went through the town, keeping a close eye for those who sought Taxus on his girlfriend's father's warrant, we had no effect on the cameras we passed. The security looming from every store and doorway of business buildings often turned as people passed, watching them until another caught its robotic eye. Such held their searching mode, unchanged by our passing. We were barely a wrinkle on the screen. It would take a human to come out and look at us for our presence to be known.

We passed a vendor selling Fangdu who smiled as we went by. He only saw a young couple hurrying through the town, no doubt heading home for lunch. A store clerk sweeping in front of his shop with an air broom stopped his labors until we passed. He didn't want to stir dust as we went by. Behind us, the sound of the air broom resumed.

We felt as though we were in the clear, but the feeling didn't last long. We attracted the attention of two men with hand-screens. They looked at us and looked at the screens. They then looked at each other and followed us. We had been spotted.

We quickened the pace and scooted around a corner onto a crowded avenue lined with tented shops, shedding the fedoras along the way for the French sea caps. As we went, we walked by a man who jerked at irregular intervals and seemed to be looking around at everyone. He wore a long coat over a tuxedo. It looked as if it had been on him for a year or more: the tie was crooked and worn and the cuffs were ragged. He was unshaven and had slept on his hair.

He saw us and made a face, like a child chiding us. I made the face back to him.

"You're invisible!" he said. So sudden and insistent, it stopped me.

"You see us?" I asked, more to play along than believing us to be invisible to anything but security cameras. The strange man reached a finger to me.

"No, mother, and you cannot see me. I am invisible as well. Did I not say so before? I'm sure I said so before."

"How do you know you are invisible?" I asked, pulling him along with us, mindful of the men who tracked us, who knew we made no image on their screens.

"I travel the shadows, the back roads and the underground. I am of the cobwebs. I live in the netherworld. I am not here. How did you find me, Winifred?"

"He's crazy," said Taxus, a fact made clear to me when the man didn't know if I was his mother or Winifred.

"Shh! Yes, but crazy might be what we need." I turned to the man and joined him in his madness. "Well, brother, show us these back roads. Does one of them connect with the free port?"

The man stepped to a table in a sidewalk cafe, picked up a cup and drank from it. The woman who had been discussing the events of the day with her friend looked at him with disbelief. She exchanged disapproving looks with her friend, but said nothing. The madman returned to us with a smile.

"You see, Old Tom? I am not here. I am somewhere else altogether."

"Free port?" I repeated.

"Certainly, but first: a demonstration." He took us to an alcove off to one side and pulled us back around him. He turned to me and held a finger to his lips. He spoke as if commanding the universe, "Time will now stop!"

For us, time did indeed stand still. Taxus and I held our breaths, anxious to see what came next. The two men who had been following us with screens in their hands came next, loud and agitated.

"I was sure they came this way," said one man. His voice was deep and rough.

"That's what I thought, but I don't see the wave, nor do I see them in real space." The second voice was higher, shriller, like nails on a slate.

"He won't be happy if we let it slip away," said the first.

"You look further down, I'll retrace and see if they have ducked the other way," said the second man.

One of the men walked past us, intent on the crowd before him. I turned to Taxus. He had a guilty look about him. I tilted my head, like I knew something.

"What are they talking about?"

"I don't know. Do you think they're after the token Althea gave to me?"

"Could be. It scrambles the signal so we can't be seen on the screens. It's how they tracked us. They weren't looking for what they saw on the security cameras but for what they didn't see. They didn't see us in the screens, yet we were there."

"Come, sergeant," said the crazy man, snapping out of his trance. "We are no longer here, we are elsewhere."

We followed our unusual guide along a darkened alley, across a wide boulevard with no people in sight and into a large building closed to business long before. It was an amphitheater, dark and empty. The seats were worn and many of them had been taken out. The only light came through open places in the ceiling where the sky shown through. We went on tip-toe, down the side aisle to a door next to the stage.

"Right, doctor," said our guide. "Step lively, no time to waste. Time!" he said, as if it had only now occurred to him. I had the feeling it had. He pulled close to me and whispered. "Time is not our friend. Beware thereof and thereunto."

"Will do," I replied with a wink.

The man pushed us through the door and closed it behind us with a slam. We were in a darkened space with no hint of where we stood and no sound.

Searching for some clue to our location I sniffed for a smell of identification. There was only the mustiness of old and neglected spaces. I felt a hand on my arm. It was Taxus, shaking with fear.

"Wait," I said to him. "I think I see something."

As my eyes became accustomed to the dark, a sliver of light appeared, dim at first. I moved toward it until I was within arm's length. I reached out and felt a bar at hand level. I pressed on the bar and the door opened outward. On the other side of the door was a back alley, all brick, with brickwork on either side. At the far end I saw the free port. The crazy man had led us to exactly where we needed to be.

Wanted

"Starwort Bacchus." The voice was unfamiliar.

"What?" I said, automatically.

We were a block short of the free port and hand-made stands of souvenirs and drinks were scattered along the old road. Over the counter of the bakery cart hovered a news screen for the entertainment of those waiting for their order. The man stood in line waiting for a biscuit and breakfast brew, watching the screen as it ran the local news, weather and shuttle departure times. Slipped into the mix was a segment on wanted criminals at large in the town. The man was short with a bald head and wire-framed glasses. He had the same readout in the corner of his lens.

"She's wanted, supposed to be dangerous, part of a gang. Gotta be on the lookout." The man winked at me, turned around and stepped up to the bakery cart. I moved to the side so as not to be in the way and therefore obvious.

An image of the free port came onscreen with vessels arriving and departing, followed by a talking head, simulated, giving the local weather. It was a lovely day, if breezy.

A face appeared on the screen, a young woman with dark hair and a crooked left eyebrow. "Starwort Bacchus" it said underneath her picture. I could barely hear the announcer as she told of a bulletin sent out to be watchful for this fugitive, said to have crossed several checkpoints with forged ID tags rather than implants.

I pulled my hair over my neck, a nervous tick, to cover my scar. We wouldn't want anyone to think I had removed my chip, not in this port.

The face on the screen was not mine; it was someone else. There was a likeness of Taxus with his name underneath. It was not a good likeness, younger and not in focus.

"It's from my school days, when I played ruckus-ball," Taxus noted.

Chineel's round face appeared next, younger and framed with the colorful feathers of a dance hall girl. "Manchineel Delancy" was displayed beneath her photo, her maiden name. Next came a poor attempt at a drawing of a child, only in military gear. "Unknown Child" was beneath the picture I could only guess was supposed to be Dagon.

Chineel waved at me from across the square on the edge of the free port. She motioned for me to come across. It seemed urgent. I looked around to see if I was under surveillance and trotted across the square as calmly as I could. Taxus followed me as if on a tether.

"Where's Dagon?" Chineel asked.

"I don't know. I thought he was with you. Have you seen the screens?"

"Yes. I don't know where they obtained an old picture of me, it's ancient. I haven't looked so young since before I was married to Lazar. They have my maiden name as well. I'm going to have to get a new identity."

"Luckily, they don't have Dagon yet, not even a photo. Did you see the photo over my name?"

"Yes. I did. Who is that?"

"I don't know, but if they catch her it won't take long for them to find out they have the wrong person. We have to get out of this sector."

"No, I mean who is that?" she pointed at Taxus.

"Oh, a friend. We're going to help him."

The Hermes in my skirt pocket vibrated. Flax was sending a message. I slipped around Chineel to the corner of the building in the shade of a doorway. The readout on the Hermes said, "Dagon here. Leaving early. Come now."

"Flax is lifting off, we have to move," I said to Chineel.

Without a further word the three of us crossed the lane and stepped onto the free port toward Flax and passage to another world.

The Trinket

"Hold it closer," said Dr. Genus, his face taking up the entire screen on Flax's center console.

Taxus leaned in, holding the trinket given to him by his sweetheart, Althea.

"Yes, it's one of mine, the piece I loaned to Mr. Cronus to show to investors." Aristaeus frowned, something I had never seen him do before.

"The family name of my beloved Althea. She is Althea Cronus," said Taxus.

"Cronus is a business partner of sorts. He sought funding for the project. I had enough in-house to fund a small operation, but if this project was to go further, it needed more. I wonder if he showed it to anyone other than a reverse-engineer. If he gave this to his daughter as a plaything, he didn't consider security. I should have a talk with him."

"We don't know where he is," I pointed out.

"Oh, I know exactly where he is," said Aristaeus. "He's at his summer home on Juno. I put a tracker on him at our last meeting. We may have been partners, but I didn't trust him for borth-spit."

"So, we all go to Juno; we get the girl back and you confront Mister Cronus."

"Only if there's a contract," Flax piped in. "We haven't bought me yet. I go where I'm told."

Chineel leaned in between Taxus and me, "Aristaeus, don't you know people on Juno? Couldn't someone put in a repair request?"

Aristaeus smiled. "I'll have one drawn up immediately. You can swing by and pick me up on the way. It will be good to see you again and to meet the young man who came to inherit the sister piece to yours. Starwort, how do you keep finding the things in the universe you were meant to find?"

I couldn't help rolling my eyes. "It's a mystery to me."

"There's one item more," said Aristaeus. "If we go to Juno, it will be masks and gloves. They have recently had a Grecian Flu scare. If you ask me, it's being engineered. Outbreaks occurred at the exact right time for the Central Government to step in and save the day. Too convenient for my taste."

"If my friend Galium is to be believed, it's not a coincidence. Where the CG goes the flu follows, so it figures they might send the flu first and have the CG step in to be heroes with a vaccine."

"That makes sense, in a twisted, sadistic way. All right, come and get me, but take care along the way. Whoever engineered this flu did a wonderful and terrible job of it."

Victoriana

Flax settled in on the allotted spot, a large "X" painted onto the free port tarmac. She read the temperature and predicted fair weather, then closed down for a welcome recharge of her batteries. As I stood up from the console, I heard the gentle clicking of her internal sensors as they checked accuracy and realigned accordingly. Dagon was already at the port bay door.

"Why exactly are we here again?" asked Chineel, still putting herself together before meeting the world outside.

"Doctor Genus wants to look at the trinket and will take us to find Althea's father. He also wants to have a chat with Flax. I think he is infatuated." I listened for a tart response from Flax, but there was none; she was indeed closed down for recharge.

"And where are we?"

"Grandville is Dr. Genus's home base, the central city on the planet known as Victoriana. For once, I don't think anyone will be chasing us. The security here is superb."

"Good, a breather for all of us. I'm ready now." Chineel had on her Town Hall dress, green to set off her hair and proper for a lady.

Dagon was in a brown suit Chineel had chosen for him and Taxus was in his cleanest shirt with a light coat over it. It would have to do. I wore my deep red skirt with the white blouse. We were suitable but hardly the fashion plates we would like to be for a visit with a man of Dr. Genus's standing.

Dagon activated the bay door, letting in a rush of fresh air, which carried with it the refreshing scent of flowers in bloom.

The lane in front of the landing zone was red brick and flawlessly cared for. Trees lined the roadway and grass grew on the other side in a lawn stretching on for a mile or more until we couldn't see beyond it. Flowers lined the roadway at the grass and a split-rail fence of simulated wood ran along the road as far as the eye could see in either direction.

There in the center of this picture-perfect scene stood Aristaeus Genus, our host, in an elaborate coat and waistcoat, a silk cravat with a green, cut-stone pin, wire-frame glasses and an outlandish top hat. He grinned and held out his arms.

"Welcome friends! How wonderful to see you."

"Aristaeus, it's been too long," I said, though it hadn't been long at all.

"Welcome, welcome, Chineel, lovely as ever. Dagon, don't you look smart! And someone new. You must be Taxus, of whom I have heard so much. Well, not a great deal, as you just arrived. There's more to tell, I am sure." Dr. G. was over-the-top, even for us.

"Uh, Yes, sir. I'm Taxus," though he didn't look sure of his name as he said it.

"I can hardly wait to show you Grandville. All of Victoriana is quite something, of course, but Grandville is the cherry on top, as it were. We'll see it after we change."

"Change?" I said, my eyebrows jumping up in surprise.

"Certainly," said Dr. G. "You can't go out into polite society looking like that." He emphasized "that" with a raise of his own bushy eyebrows. He turned around and motioned to a driver.

The transport was new to us all. I had seen pictures of the first automobiles, but had never been in the presence of one. Aristaeus beamed as the vehicle approached, driven by a uniformed man in a full coat, cap and goggles. The car was a metal box with an elongated front and curved back, open with no roof, painted bright yellow and polished to a shine. It had four wheels with spokes like an old wagon or coach. It spewed white smoke and made a clattering sound as it approached. Next to the flat wind-screen sat a large horn with a black, flexible bulb on the driver's end. The strange vehicle screeched to a halt and Dr. Genus opened the second door, the one to the back seat. He turned to see four child-like faces with jaws dropped. He chuckled.

"You've never been in a steam-jitney before, have you? Well, then, this will be an experience. Come on, get in. This is the yellow roadster I might have mentioned."

"No, you never did." I shook my head, still in wonder. Aristaeus smiled broader.

Chineel and I settled into two form-fitting, stuffed-leather seats in the back while Dagon and Taxus pulled up two jump-seats and balanced themselves for the unexpected ride. Dr. Genus stepped into the front seat next to the driver and with a spine-tingling jerk, we started off.

Dr. Genus turned in his seat, explaining.

"It's the same basic operating system as the Red Stroke Drive, but instead of propelling us forward, it creates compressed steam, which drives the pistons which turn the wheels. It's new but it's old, which is what we like here. Most everyone walks or they ride bicycles, but there are still many uses for vehicles such as this. For transport to and from the landing dock it's ideal. Don't you think?" He turned around again without getting agreement, as he already knew it was ideal.

"This is my man, Runyon. He drives the roadster and sees to a great many details for me." Dr. G. turned to Runyon, "This young man is in love with little Althea. You remember Althea Cronus?" The driver nodded.

Taxus turned to me with a face on the edge of panic. These people knew the family. I patted him on the shoulder and he turned around, calmed enough to continue the tour in silence.

The town itself kept the same antiquated feel, with a town square boasting a large gazebo in the center, quaint shops on the streets around the square, a town hall on one end of the street and a library on the other. Men in full suits with hats walked to and fro, some carrying satchels from a by-gone age and some sporting outlandish mustaches. Ladies moved about in twos and threes with parasols and large hats held on with silk scarves. Their dresses had bustles behind them, making each woman look as if a full lunch sat in a trunk strapped to her rear part. The men tipped their hats at the ladies' approach while the ladies took no notice at all. Once the encounter was behind them, the ladies giggled to each other.

On one street, two children in short pants and suspenders played with a dog, much smaller than a borth, with brown and white spots. They appeared to be younger than Dagon, but he took note of them with some surprise. They didn't appear to be training, they appeared to be playing. Playing was new and foreign to Dagon, the boy soldier.

The houses we passed were mansions with large front porches and columns. Each had a short road leading up to the front door and then around to the back. The driver stuck his hand out as if motioning for someone to stop, but there was no one in front of us. He then turned into one of these small roads and up to the house, pulling in front of the steps to the main door. The vehicle shuddered to a stop and we all sat for a moment, unsure as to what to do next. Dr. Genus leaped out and opened the rear door with a flourish.

"Here we are, home sweet home. Out you go, there's lunch being made as we speak."

Runyon took the vehicle around to the back of the house as we climbed the steps to the broad front porch. The doors opened as we drew near. Inside was a woman in a long dress with a white apron. Her hair was fixed in a loose bun on the top of her head. She smiled as if we were long lost family.

"Myrtle has been waiting lunch for us and has laid out some clothing. I think you'll be pleasantly surprised. Hello, Myrtle. These are our guests."

While Dr. Genus recounted our names, even getting Taxus right, I looked at a staircase even larger and grander than the one in my father's house. The walls were covered in patterned silk and the accents were simulated wood. The whole effect was one of opulence and elegance.

Lunch consisted of small sandwiches, lacking the crust, with a salad of cut greens and a soda type of drink the color of tea but with bubbles tickling my nose. The conversation addressed our curiosity at his home, the town and the whole planet.

"Victoriana is only a quarter inhabitable, with much of it covered by water. Grandville is the capital, though by no means the largest city. There are others larger, but none nicer in my opinion. We have harkened back to an age when people were civil to one another and technology had not yet taken away their humanity. The reason my roadster runs on Red Stroke technology is we can't burn wood or coal, there is no liquid fuel to be had, there simply are no resources such as were abundant back when this era was the height of fashion. It has taken us some time to get the details right, and I had no small part in creating the technology behind the lack of technology."

"You run your vehicle on steam?" said Chineel, still a sentence or two behind the conversation.

"Oh, yes, the drive heats the water, the steam created gets forced through the ... well, you saw it. It's an interesting reverse engineering feat."

"Why?" I asked.

"Yes, that is the question, isn't it. Why? Runaway technology was blamed for all the evils of the universe. Implanted identity chips, over-controlling government influence, even the Grecian Flu. In many of the systems, on many colonized planets, there is rampant crime. It's not safe in the streets, people are suspicious of one another. You've seen it," he said, looking at me.

Yes, I had seen it. I saw it on Deoius where I bought my clarinet. We also stopped for memory ewers. There we met men fixed on stealing the doctor's most recent prototype, a memory ewer containing liquid memory of ten times the strength of those in use at the time. The encounter did not end well for them. I was still breathless at the thought of it.

Dr. G. continued.

"It was decided: rather than have police on every corner, we could create a society slow of pace, polite in its daily encounters and proper in its behavior. Creating the trappings of such a society also gave us something exciting and fun to do. Whole industries have grown up making hats and clothing, barber shops, called 'tonsorial parlors' have become the rage. Demand for roadsters, all utilizing my steam technology, grows as people realize the need for transportation. As are other innovations, which while making life easier, also lend to this slower lifestyle."

"How wonderful! Everyone seems happy with the way it turned out," I said.

Aristaeus beamed with pride, and the best was yet to come. "What it was designed to do was to keep the ills of the world out. You will not find the Grecian Flu here, security is strict and well maintained. You will not find implanted identity chips. Anyone new would stand out. If you were to walk out in what you are wearing, you would be suspect. Because you are with me and were expected, you are welcome. All is well and in order in our little town. Later we will go to the town square for a concert and you'll see."

The Gazebo

Within a short time, we changed into clothing appropriate to make our foray into the Victoriana world of polite society. Chineel wore a full-length dress of dark green with long sleeves, closed up to the throat and with a large bustle behind. It was topped off with a giant hat of green felt held on with a silk scarf of light green.

"Some ladies have rather large behinds. This makes all equal. Quite thoughtful, don't you think?" said Dr. Genus, putting our uneasy feelings to rest.

"I should say so," said Chineel, admiring herself in the mirror.

My own dress was similar in a deep red color. Aristaeus handed me a hat with a large brim and a silk scarf attached. The scarf kept the hat on in the open roadster. A small, beaded bag, just large enough to carry a handkerchief, was the finishing touch.

Taxus looked like an early century explorer in a pith helmet and jodhpurs. Dagon blushed deep red in a suit Aristaeus called "Lord Fauntleroy," consisting of shorts and a jacket of blue, knee socks with shoes buttoned up the sides and finished with a hat bearing a tassel off to one side. He didn't look soldier-ish; more like a child of school age.

Both Chineel and I had our hair done up in a loose bun to fit under our hats. Myrtle, the maid, named for a flower meaning *love*, helped us with our hairstyles. She giggled most of the time, she had so much fun preparing new visitors to meet her town.

"There will be a band playing," announced Aristaeus, letting us know no expense had been spared for our visit. "No data chips spouting replicated music, these are actual instruments, played by real people." He looked at me. "There's even a clarinet."

We all filed out to the yellow roadster with Runyon behind the wheel.

"It chugs as if it's missing a sprocket," said Chineel, unsure of climbing into the seat in a full dress.

"Shh! It's all for effect," said Aristaeus, to keep her composed. "It's supposed to sound like an old steam roadster, so we made it to sound like one. You'll see many a strange sight before the day is up, I'm sure."

Out of the corner of my eye, I caught Aristaeus smiling. He was glad to have us to show off his town and his yellow roadster. And it was true, he had more in store.

On the green at the town square, people of all ages lined benches and sat upon the grass, some on blankets, others spreading their jackets to protect their ladies from the ground. Several young men in white pushing wheeled carts sold ices in many flavors. Aristaeus, while always a happy attendee of these concerts, was particularly proud to be able to show off in front of guests.

As the orchestra assembled, putting the finishing touches on their great display of tuning up, Mayor Attis stepped up to the podium to address the crowd. He wore a coat with tails, a top hat and red sash of office. He sported a large, gray mustache growing out to the side beyond his ears.

Without amplification technology, the mayor waited for the crowd to still so he could be heard. As the crowd grew quiet, I became aware of children running in the distance, a baby crying, a dog barking at something, but nothing else. No ever-present hum of technology, no lights buzzing, no personal alarms or reminders sounding, no rings or tones nagging people to interrupt current tasks to respond to a summons from their communicator. There were no sales calls, no surveys needing response, no requests for donations or political support and no government intrusion. Whether these people had their identity chips removed earlier or had never been implanted, they were free of such devices now.

There were also no slippery-men, no pick-pockets, hold-up men or thieves. The only visible signs of authority were a few uniformed constables in hard helmets, night-sticks and oversized mustaches who kept the style of the whole affair. We sat at peace beneath the shade of a simulated oak tree and watched the children play as the mayor welcomed one and all to the concert.

The band started off with a jubilant number setting every head tilting back and forth with the tuba and drums. Dagon, however, wandered off to find some other form of excitement. In no time he was surrounded by several boys his same age, all wanting to be his friend. He seemed to be lost amid the demands for his friendship. I knew he wouldn't embarrass me by starting a fight, so I didn't worry about him.

"Maybe I should dress more like her," said Chineel, pointing to a young woman teasing several equally young men at the edge of the square. She had on a short skirt, an open blouse and no sleeves at all. Her hair was loose and she wore a hint of makeup. "I'd be much more comfortable..."

Aristaeus stopped her: "Not without a permit, I'm afraid. She is a licensed familiar, paid to flirt with the boys to keep them from tearing someone's clothing off. There's a strict protocol in place here, and it keeps everything in line and running without mishaps."

"And a few police," I said pointing to the uniformed constables.

"Peace keepers of the first water. Better to have a social order and amiable constables than strict laws and stern police to enforce them. We have opted for a social behavior and agreed upon structure which we enjoy to the mutual benefit of all. In other words, it works; we're happy."

I smiled at Aristaeus and looked around. Yes, here was a peaceful community with its style and polite behavior, a proper way of doing things. Deep within me, I felt a stomach muscle relax, one I might have been holding taut for many years.

"I could be happy here," I said, more to myself than to Aristaeus. He heard me, though, and smiled.

"You know Althea's father," said Taxus. Aristaeus darkened at being brought back to one of the reasons for our visit. No doubt he enjoyed the concert in the town square and wished we would as well.

"Mr. Cronus was commissioned to locate investors. He was given the bauble you carry to impress potential money-men with the viability of my technology. He was to show it off and get those with money to invest to part with as much of it as possible. Clearly, he had another agenda, but I don't yet know what it is."

"Do you know where to find him?"

"Oh, yes, I believe I do. But you don't go running in to a

place; it takes planning."

"Shouldn't we..."

"Listen to the concert," said Aristaeus. "Everything will fall into place."

Misfit

"Aristaeus," I said, tugging at his coat. He turned his head to me and then to where I pointed. A man lingered at the edge of the square with his gaze straight at me who otherwise stood out as one who did not fit in.

It was in the middle of the fourth piece in the program. The breeze had stopped and ladies used hand fans brought for the purpose. Chineel was enraptured by the music, Taxus had calmed down and even Dagon was subdued, having been exhausted by his new friends. I questioned whether this man at the edge of the square had caused undue alarm in me or if the threat was real.

Aristaeus was not hampered by such doubt. He waved to a constable, who came over at a lope. He whispered in the constables ear and returned to his spot on the grass. The constable did not turn around to look at the man, but walked back to his little circle of similarly uniformed patrolmen. Aristaeus whispered to me as he sat down.

"The man doesn't fit. His suit doesn't fit. It's too short at the cuffs and sleeves, it hangs loose in front and the hat is too small. He is wrong tip to toe. Whether for your map or for the trinket Taxus brought to me, he came for other than good band music."

The scene changed instantly as three constables, wielding their clubs, ran from different directions to converge on the stranger. Before he could decide which way to run, the officers tackled and manacled the intruder. The band saw the activity and instead of ceasing their concert, changed to a fast piece of music which became a proper background to the action in the street.

The crowd marveled with gasps, cries and occasional applause, as constables descended upon the perpetrator and subdued him to a background track with full orchestra, triangle and cymbal.

A black roadster with outboard fenders and lights, a red light on top and a black box as its back, drove up and collected the man. As it roared off into the distance with its bell clanging, the constables bowed to the crowd. The band played a fanfare to accompany the applause of the people in the square. The constables returned to their former positions as the band resumed the program already in progress.

"They don't get much chance to show off," said Aristaeus, resuming his place on the grass.

At the end of the final number, the crowd stood up, applauded with enthusiasm, stretched and turned toward home. Some traveled on foot, others on bicycles and still others in jitneys and autos of many strange styles. Aristaeus's yellow roadster waited for us, as did the Sergeant of Constables.

"He was working alone for all we can tell. We found Mister Larkspur in the back alley with a bump on his head. The man had taken his suit and left him in his winter-longs. He hasn't said how he arrived here or what he was after, but we'll break him. One fact is inescapable, he doesn't belong here."

"Thank you, Sergeant. We'll be discussing possible motives

the man might have over dinner this evening. If I have anything for you, I'll let you know."

"Appreciated, Doctor Genus." The sergeant saluted, nodded at me and walked off at a brisk gait.

"Let's get home before this entire delicate balance is upset," said Aristaeus, hurrying us into the roadster. The crowd parted to allow us to drive through as Runyon guided us back to the house Aristaeus called home.

Once inside, bustles, hats and handbags were shed for plain shifts reminiscent of old time night shirts. Aristaeus donned a house coat with his initials monogrammed onto the pocket. He was the epitome of style. Dagon and Taxus joined us in similar night shirts, glad to be out of stiff collars and hot suit jackets.

"Let's begin with your trinket, Taxus," said Aristaeus.

Taxus brought out the gift Althea had given him and laid it on the dining table: two lovebirds perched in an oval, truly endearing. No wonder Althea gave it to her beau, it was the perfect symbol of love.

"Egad! Her father must have been furious," said Aristaeus.

"He set the police on me, said I stole it. Swore out a warrant and the complete disaster. The man is ..."

A ringing bell interrupted Taxus in his tirade. Aristaeus picked up a black device with a separate ear-piece swinging from a hook. He held the piece to his ear and spoke into the base.

"Genus." He paused. "Yes? Uh-huh." Dr. Genus turned his head and looked at the wide hat I had worn. Sitting next to my had was a small beaded bag with a leather strap. "Black and gold beads? Yes. Well, good. I'm glad no one was hurt.

Thank you." He hung the ear-piece on the hook.

"What?" I asked, bursting with curiosity.

"A woman was found, hysterical. Her purse had been stolen by another man. It was found, emptied onto the ground but nothing taken. She is shaken but uninjured. The entire force and several volunteers have taken up a search for the culprit."

"It will take us minutes to dress," said Dagon. "Can Runyon take us to where they are? We can help."

"You're needed here, Dagon, to figure this out. You also have to keep the house safe in case they followed us. Runyon, take this man and see to the perimeter, make sure all is closed and shuttered. We're in for the night and want no intrusion."

"Yes, sir," snapped Runyon. His hand reached up into a salute, but he caught himself and refrained. I guessed he was military at one time. Aristaeus wouldn't want to be saluted. He wasn't into such displays.

Runyon rushed to secure the windows and doors followed close by the boy soldier.

"Look, Captain," said Aristaeus, addressing me by title to indicate the official tone the conversation took. "This trinket is not a locket you pick up for five universals to give your sweetheart, it's a one of a kind prototype designed to evade the best surveillance the Central Government has to throw at us. With this you can walk through the center of town and never be seen on a screen. This shows no heat signature, no gamma sign, no alpha wave, nothing to a hint of you standing in the town square. Someone would have to be looking at you with human eyes to see you."

"Why would he give it to his daughter?" asked Chineel.

Aristaeus thought for a moment. "If someone looked for it and if you didn't want it found if you were searched, you could give it to someone and then you wouldn't have it. Similarly, if his house was searched, they wouldn't find it there either. The girl, where was she?" he asked Taxus.

"She lived at boarding school. I was there to see her at her school," said Taxus.

"And now he's taken her off to his summer home on Juno. They have higher security there than we have here. Not better, but more of it. Remember, you're not paranoid if people are out to get you. In such case, you are careful."

Preparation

We sat in the bridge, Doctor Genus and I, working out the details of a trip to Juno. Chineel and Dagon remained back at the house while we made plans and determined what sort of time line we needed to create.

The first step would be to land on Juno. If we couldn't get on the planet, the rest is academic.

"It will be difficult, but not impossible." Flax took her time answering. I could tell she not only considered it difficult or possible, but worked out exactly how it would be accomplished. She formulated a dozen different plans, working out the hard parts and making lists of items needed.

The visit to Victoriana had been made possible because of a request from Dr. Genus. Flax was still a repair vessel, designed to go where she was told. Her comings and goings were as a result of work requests filed at the home office. Payment would be expected. Luckily, when we arrived, weaknesses in the power array outside of town justified the trip. However, to falsify another for Juno could call attention to us and our quest.

On the other hand, time was of the essence. One uninvited visitor already attacked local citizens while another sat in jail awaiting the magistrate. How many more would land illegally on the outskirts and slip security to look for us.

For once, however, I was not the object of the chase. These

men were not after me, they were after Taxus and the bauble he wore on a cord around his neck, given to him by his sweetheart. He was the subject of this quest, not me. It felt good to be a protector instead of the protected, a hunter rather than the hunted.

"We could call in a favor from the engineers on Juno. They are always overworked. Any help would be welcome. Would you like me to test the waters?" offered Aristaeus.

"Yes, Doctor. Most obliging of you."

While Dr. Genus made the call to Juno, I reflected upon Flax, who took a while to respond verbally in the early days of our relationship. When she did, it was perfunctory, stiff and mechanical. Her transition from "it" to "she" was now complete.

Doctor Genus offered to leave her behind while we went to Juno in another vessel to retrieve the girl and hold Mr. Cronus accountable, but she wouldn't hear of it. Flax was not one to miss the action these days; she had become quite the pirate.

In fact, it occurred to me our crew shaped up better than I could have expected. Chineel had come a long way from the port tavern tease with too much makeup. She was the master of the galley and quartermaster of the vessel and in charge of stores and supplies. She was the first one off the ship and the last one on, her arms full of parcels. Often she would return with a tote-rover filled with goods. She was no longer the aunt who deserted me before she knew I existed, she was now the first mate who trusted my every decision and would do as asked without question or second thought.

Dagon was my soldier. I was his captain. He would fight for me and if needed would die for me. To instill such loyalty

117

in another was a big responsibility; it took my breath away and at times made me uncomfortable. Yet, many were the times when I was glad Dagon was there to lean on.

While I knew Aristaeus would not be coming with us on our adventure to Bacchus, he was with us now, which made me happy. He was a welcome crew member.

"There," he said, triumphantly. "All done. You will be receiving a request for Juno within minutes. As for us, we have to prepare to leave. Once the order is received, there will be no time for dawdling."

"I'll make ready the engines," said Flax. A gentle hum accompanied the statement, indicating she already started.

Aristaeus double-checked my dress to ensure I was properly attired for a foray into polite society. He hurried me out to the roadster where Runyon sat behind the wheel, ready to speed into town to retrieve Chineel and Dagon. We took off immediately, so quick it threw me back into the seat.

"Where's the 'chug-chugga' we usually hear?" I asked.

"It's an added sound, put in place for atmosphere, color. We don't need it to run. Whenever I can, I do without it. While this mode of living has its good points, some things are a pain in the side."

"Starwort flower soothes pains in the side, they say."

"Sometimes, dear Starwort, sometimes. Sometimes not. You keep me on my toes. There's always someone after you. Your father's treasure holds a predictable allure for some insistent and nasty people."

"Not this time. They're after Taxus, not me," I pointed out. "But remember, I was an ally when such men were after you." I remembered the encounter at the shop on Deoius, where his latest prototype was the object of considerable attention. We left the shop ablaze with a high body count.

"Yes, you were, and I appreciate it no end. But we're not keeping score, or even counting, we're doing what we have to do to get by in this universe we've created. It's going to take all we have to pull this off. This boy, Taxus: is he up for it?"

"I don't know. He's motivated, driven, and I've seen him run and hide, even adopt camouflage, but in a fight, I'm not sure how he'd respond."

"Let's hope it won't come to a fight."

"Yes, hope is good. Preparation is better."

Droids Don't Lie

The marketplace on Juno was made up of stalls twenty feet high, complete with holographic banners and music streaming from the microdot speakers on either side of tall posts. From the posts hung silken canopies, billowing in the breeze, causing the sunlight to change color on the street tiles. It was a beautiful but dangerous place. Juno had recently succumbed to the rule of the Central Government and heightened security regarding implants.

Juno was, in Roman mythology, queen of the gods, the wife and sister of the god Jupiter. She was the protector of women and was worshiped under several names. As Juno Pronuba she presided over marriage; as Juno Lucina she aided women in childbirth; and as Juno Regina she was the special counselor and protector of the Roman state. On Earth, the month of June was named after her.

Juno, the largest city on Jove, the planet next door to Copernicus, may have begun as Lucina, but now emulated Regina, playing host to the Central Government and all the evils inherent with it.

Coughing was heard in the marketplace for the first time; masks and gloves were the order of the day. I had been warned, and so wore my Fangdu, surgical mask and glove sets. What was once the fashion had become the norm, mandatory in some parts. My mask filtered the air as I breathed. It was necessary in public. Where the Central Government went, the Grecian Flu followed, went the commonly heard phrase. Though sometimes the flu arrived first and the CG came later with the healing vaccine.

Galium had warned me that the CG offered the vaccine to those who contracted the Flu. Of course, the cost was high while the dose was small. Qualification for the vaccine included having your implant scanned and updated, your record double checked and your name and likeness cleared by the CGMA, the Marshall Authority. At every turn there was more paperwork, though the term had little meaning in a world without paper. I wouldn't be there at all, but we had a girl to find.

Dr. Genus created a work order where there was none, which was difficult in a city where the CG had a strong presence. Today, thanks to his engineer friend, Flax had work to do on the sensor array high above Juno.

While Taxus, Dagon and Chineel sat in the cafe along a street with a view of the Cronus summer home, Aristaeus sat aboard Flax chatting with her about subjects far over my head. It was my lot to give eyes to the marketplace, where a myriad of helpful things could be seen and where I was able to fit in with the locals or run if needed.

It was chilly in the market, which was not expected. I had worn my light skirt and blouse, simple shoes and little else. It was supposed to be a pleasant day, with no severe weather in the reports, but reports can be wrong. There was a chill in the air. I wished I had brought something to wrap around me.

It's strange how something small can catch your eye and say a volume. A face from behind a fluttering bit of silk hung on a pole by the Dodonas stand spoke baskets-full.

Dodonas, steaming wraps filled with hot, tasteless paste, lay in rows along the three-tiered table. The woman behind the table sat as if asleep, not caring to hawk her wares at this hour of the day, so late, so near closing. The face I saw was a man, neither sleepy nor uncaring, it was watchful and focused. One blink and he was gone, I could no longer see him. Who was he?

A flutter of color caught my attention, red and flowing. It was a scarf, a beautiful scarf. I need something beautiful, I said to myself. I was overdue. My nerves had been shredded; I saw things and people who were not there.

I picked the scarf up from the table, smiled at the girl and gave her a torn Ц-20. The girl looked at it, unsure if she could accept it as currency. I had forgotten the CG encroached on this sector. Torn Universals would not pass as currency for long. She took it, but only because it was money and one less scarf she had to pack up at the end of the day. I draped it over my head and walked in the other direction from the Dodanas stand.

Another face turned toward me, then looked away, again a male face. A hand reached up to the mouth of the face, as if speaking into a wrist unit, as the face deliberately turned away from me.

A sound came from behind. I needed no more! I darted between the stands, under a low-hanging banner and down an alleyway. Footfalls followed me, coming fast and hard. This scenario was all too familiar. Someone had recognized me, enough to suggest further investigation. I pulled my skirts up and ran like a boy, without style or grace, through the back alleys of Juno's marketplace.

A cry behind me confirmed my worst fears. "Here! She's here!"

I poured on the speed, dashing to the right, then to the left, down an alley and straight into a brick wall. I had reached a dead end. I stood panting, footfalls growing closer behind me and stared at the unbroken brickwork before me. I was trapped!

To my left, a door opened. Inside, the face of a young girl peeked out. She was younger than me, though not by much. She beckoned to me with a pale hand. Not one to question kindness when moments count, I darted inside the door and closed it behind me.

In the darkness, I could hear footfalls outside. They stopped, shuffled around and paced back and forth. The sounds of men grumbling and swearing could be heard. Someone tried the door. I jumped, but didn't cry out.

When I turned around, I came face to face with the girl who had opened the door. She lifted the pale hand to her face, extended the index finger and held it to her lips. Outside, heavy footsteps growing fainter told of the men moving on.

Orders were barked from the mouth of the alley. "You stay behind. Watch for her. She's here somewhere." Next to the closed and locked door, I heard grumbling. Someone was not happy to be left to watch a dead end alley.

The girl motioned for me to follow as she slipped through the vague shadows of a darkened house. It was a private residence, secured and closed for the season. Plasticine wrap covered all the furniture.

"This way. You'll be safe," whispered the girl, leading me on through the ghostly house, draped in translucent tents.

123

Past a large hallway with a winding staircase, to an inner room between the dining room and the kitchen, the girl motioned for me to follow. I went, not willing to turn down an offer of help in these uncertain times. We stopped and the girl turned around. She looked at me, then giggled.

"I keep forgetting about the light," she said. She stroked a finger across the faded strip by the door and the lamps along the walls glowed, enough to see the room and my savior.

It was a preparatory room, where servants made minor changes to platters of food before serving them in the great dining room. Many of the large houses on Juno had such extra rooms. Before the Central Government's arrival, great wealth was the order of the day on Jove. Now the CG bled off its share, causing those of great wealth to relocate to the outer planets while they could still do so.

The girl was petite with soft brown hair tied with a faded ribbon. She wore a blue dress in need of pressing. She had a distant look in her eye, as if looking through me.

"I'm Cory," she said. "It's short for Coriander."

"A flower meaning *hidden worth*. You're such to me, certainly. Your value wasn't known to me until I was inside the door. Thank you."

"You're welcome. We are, after all, friends. Though I have forgotten what you are called."

I looked at the girl, noticing the strange look in her eye. Something about this girl was new and yet familiar.

"Star," I said, trying to sound unruffled by my suspicions. "My... my name is Star. It's short for Starwort."

"The flower meaning *afterthought*," said the girl.

"Yes, afterthought. Is this your home?" I looked around the

room, rather than at her. My uneasiness showed.

"This is the home of Doctor Icarus and his family, his wife and two daughters. I am ..." She seemed to stop as if paused because of a lapse in memory. Then she tilted her head, thinking, and said, "I am... her, their, your ... companion." The girl smiled, as if she had at last gotten it right.

"Cory, for Coriander, the girl of hidden worth. Yes, you are a companion, are you not? I can see now. Did the Doctor and his family leave in a hurry?" I asked, walking toward the nearest table.

I lifted the cover to see the table was far from clean. Plates and napkins were left as they were at the end of a hurried meal. The cover had been hastily thrown over it in an attempt to provide some protection. I pictured the doctor's wife casting the covering over her precious household pieces while the doctor urged her to get into the speeder before it was too late. When the Central Government arrives, it is often with disastrous consequences.

"Yes. We were all alarmed. Many items the girls wanted to take were left behind in the rush."

"And you, you were left behind." I turned my head toward her to see her response. She looked at me with the face of someone lost, as if the one important question of the day would go without an answer, no matter what else befell her. She snapped out of the trance to take up a new subject, a new idea, one which she seemed happy to present, as it was on another subject.

"I would offer you something to eat, but there is little left." She turned toward the kitchen and for the first time, I noticed the dark place at her hairline. A piece of scalp was missing; the inside of her head unit shown through. Circuit plates and tubes of liquid memory glinted in the dim light as she turned her head. She smiled, not noticing the missing piece at all.

"Perhaps some packaged food remains. I am not the cook." Her gaze drifted again. Apparently the cook had been taken with the family, but not the companion.

"Are the girls older now?" I asked, venturing a reason to leave behind the precious companion.

"Yes. Older. Older than they used to be."

"So you're here alone," I said, stating the obvious.

"No, silly, I'm here with you," she giggled.

As we stood there together, I shivered. The day had been chilly before, but now night came on and the temperature dropped in minutes. Cory saw me shiver.

"Come. We have heavier clothing upstairs. I'll show you."

"Perhaps I could help you with your missing..." I stopped, thinking I might wander into an embarrassing subject.

"I'm not sure where they went. I've been asleep. I only woke up to let you in."

I followed her up to the second floor where we found skirts and blouses of full length. The girls were not only older, they were grown. I held up a full skirt, noticing it was larger than I needed.

"No," said the girl with the missing piece. "If you want to move quickly, find some pants. Skirts are too cumbersome."

Cory pulled a single piece jumper from a lower drawer, feminine but sturdy. She helped me into it and pulled a pair of tall boots to go over. A short jacket completed the outfit and in no time, I looked like an adventurer from the back country.

The jacket was dark purple and black with silver buckles. On the inside pocket was a place I could secure the blade usually strapped to my thigh. It is always good to have a clear path to a blade at need.

"Is there a way back to the space dock, the free port?" I asked as we dressed.

"I could show you. I need only to find my traveling pack and we can be off. It's a long trek to the free port." Cory changed into a single-piece trekking suit as she spoke.

"I assume there is another way out of here. The side door is guarded."

"I will distract the man. You can slip by him. I have done it before with my sisters."

"Jumping curfew, eh? I've done so a time or two."

Cory smiled and an impish twinkle filled her eye. I could see she would have made an excellent companion for two young sisters. Now they were grown and she was relegated to the old toy bin with the jump-ropes and the dolls.

"Come, I'll tell him you have made your escape through the rear door."

"Wait!" The word came out too loud, but I remembered something. "Isn't it a thing with companions? You don't lie. You are not designed to lie."

Cory held her head erect, arrogant and challenging. She put her hands on her hips. "You are a borth-tick and I am the queen of the May festival."

"Oh, a borth-tick, am I? Well, you, miss Cory, are a liar. Now, let's go and lie to the man outside in the alley."

The jumper and covering jacket were stouter than my summer clothes and would keep me warm. Running and jumping would be easier as well. It could be my new companion foresaw some running and jumping in our immediate future.

As I passed the full length mirror, I pulled the hair over the scar at my neck and surveyed the overall image. "Demure as all hell!" I murmured to the mirror.

"What?"

"Oh, something I used to say when I was a girl."

"But you're still a girl." Cory tilted her head, as if she didn't get the distinction.

"Yes, I am, I'm still a girl. And now this girl needs to get back to her ship or it will leave without her. We should go."

Curfew

Cory slipped on a blue faux-leather Fangdu mask and glove set so as to blend in with the people in the street. I had my red leatherette Fangdu; it would suffice.

Before she could step outside the door, I held her by the elbow.

"Wait, Cory, let me fix your hair." I wrapped my scarf around her head, covering her hair and hiding the part along one side where the switches and lights shown through. "After all, one cannot walk out in polite society not properly attired."

Or with one's circuitry hanging out for all to see, I added in my head.

"Thank you. You're a good friend," she said. There was a twinkle in her eyes. Cory looked at me as if for the first time. Then a change in her demeanor told me she was back on the job. She touched the latch and stepped out into the alleyway.

Outside the door, a mountain of a man stopped her. He was twice her size with hands as large as her head. In his belt was a complex black pistol, rippling with side tubes. The black was rubbed from its sides and the extended barrel. It had been in his possession a long time and was much used. In his hands he held a rifle with a long muzzle fortified with cooling ribs. Two magazines stuck out from the belly of the weapon. If he hunted for me alone, he carried too much firepower.

"Where's the girl?" he demanded.

"The one who ran through? She was rude and mean. I hope you catch her. She threatened me and ran out the rear door, where the servants come and go. I think you can still see her going toward the uptown stalls by the marketplace."

Cory lifted her hand, indicating the way back to the marketplace. The man looked in the direction of her hand and ran off without a word.

"He could have said thank you," Cory said as I stepped out of the side door.

"Yeah, we'll teach him a lesson if he catches us. Let's go."

Cory took the lead, as she knew the way. She guided me along the darkened alleyway pointing out puddles. A gentle mist fell, making our hair glisten. I hoped it would be all the rain we would see.

I had heard of child companions. They were not mere playmates, they served as bodyguards and tracking units. If the child was kidnapped and the droid as well, it served to guard the child, to disable the kidnappers and to be a tracking unit for the authorities. If the droid was left behind, it was so attuned to its host child it would know her whereabouts within meters. Cory wasn't a toy, but a protector, a killing machine. This one could also lie.

Lying is a complex skill, involving knowing what is real, inventing an alternate reality and telling it as if it was real, while keeping the two in mind and knowing which is which. Even in Flax, deception was a recent development, a new evolution.

Cory had been damaged and perhaps repairs were in

progress when the family had to leave. She might not even know where the missing piece to her scalp had gone. I watched the red scarf bob down the darkened streets, empty of people though it had been filled to bursting but an hour before. Curfew might have been in effect. It was common when the CG was in charge. I hadn't gotten the bulletin so I didn't know what time curfew was, but the streets were empty; well, nearly empty.

At the turn, the large man appeared again, his rifle at the ready. He seemed to have been waiting for us to come around the corner, as if he had guessed at our route. His smile told him he was right.

"There she is, not going to the Market at all. Well, now I have you both."

Cory reached out a hand and struck the man in the mid-section. Sparks flew as she sent a charge through his body. He flew back, dropping the rifle. Cory stood as if recharging. A faint, high whine came from under the scarf. The man shook his head, pulled himself from the ground and looked at us as if focusing on his target. His eyes fell on the dropped rifle in the middle of the alley. We both saw it at the same time, but I was closer. I reached for the rifle, impressing him I was not some weak little girl. He darkened and spoke low.

"I'm going to skin you slow. You'll feel every piece of flesh being peeled from your hide."

In response, I raised the rifle and pulled the trigger.

Nothing happened! There was not even a 'click.'

"Ha!" said the man. "You don't know how it works!" He lunged for me, his arm out to take the weapon from my grip.

I flipped the rifle around, taking the long muzzle in both hands and swung the weapon hard and wide, crashing the

131

heavy butt into his head with a loud crack. His head spun to the side and he fell to the ground like a sack of grain. Bits of debris flew from beneath him as he connected with the alley brickwork.

"That's how it works!" I threw the heavy weapon into the shadows.

"Well done! We should go," Cory said.

We moved along down the alley to the main boulevard going to the market. It was well lit, so our hunters could see us clearly, but we could see them as well. Better to travel in the light than the darkness, though as we drew near the empty market, we realized more than mere men searched for us.

Zilla

Up ahead, silhouetted by the lights of the boulevard, stood the large figure of a man looking our way. It was joined by an even larger figure, all shoulders and mechanical arms.

"Zilla!" said Cory, stopping in place, one hand reaching back to stop my forward movement.

"What is it?" I looked through the fog creeping along the abandoned marketplace.

"Droid, but not like me: big, mean. We should go another way." She pointed to the side and we slipped through a narrow passageway between booths to a walkway winding around the back buildings.

"If he saw us..." I ventured.

"He did. He'll be coming around this way to stop us."

"Then we should go back..." I pointed back the way we came, but she didn't look around to see it.

"No. He'll think we did so. He'll send a message and have backup troops coming to cut us off. This is the safest way. Follow me."

A subtle 'tick' caught my attention. It had come from Cory, from her head. Something wasn't right. I worried what task the missing piece performed. As I worried, I followed her without question or hesitation down narrow back lanes and over make-shift bridges. There was little to absorb the sound along these back ways; our passing made too much clatter as we went along.

"Someone will hear," I whispered.

"Shh. They'll hear."

"My point! Shouldn't we..."

My statement was cut short by a blast of blue light from the lane in front. The blast struck Cory in the middle and doubled her over. She lay motionless on the rough pavement.

A sound from the side caused me to turn too late, a giant arm reached out for me. I tried to spin free but couldn't, a large hand held me, waist and hip, pulling me to him. The other hand clapped to my mouth.

My left arm was pinned to my side, but my right was free. I slipped it inside of my jacket and felt the handle of my blade, but the arm pulled me to the side. He carried me like a sheep to market, unable to break free or reach my blade.

The breath was squeezed out of me as I was bounced along on the man's hip. He spoke as if into a communicator. No doubt he had one attached to his ear or perhaps implanted. Either way, he was in communication with someone else.

"I got her. No, no trouble. The droid? The droid's scrap."

As he carried me along, I could only see behind us, where we had been. Cory lay motionless, cut down by the blast from the mechanical killer.

I kicked out hard with my right leg, then my left, striking the man in the chest. He shifted me to my feet to get a better grip, leaving me enough room to remove my blade from inside the jacket. I swung back, not sure what I would hit.

I heard a cry and whirled around, pulling the blade out.

The man screamed again, gripping his thigh. A shower of blood spouted from between his fingers.

I doubled over, struggling for breath, but he picked me up again, squeezing me as if to crush me. A thin gasp echoed in my ear. His head was next to mine.

Guessing at his height and form, I threw my arm back and felt his face against my hand as the blade sunk into his eye socket. The man cried out in earnest, sending a chilling scream through the narrow alley. He dropped me on the pavement and drew his weapon, searching for me with his one good eye. In the distance, I heard the footsteps of the mechanical killer, his huge, headless companion. In a moment it would be two-to-one.

I sunk the blade into his shoulder and pulled it back out with a twist, sending another stream of blood into the air. The gun clattered to the pavement as he rushed to stop the blood with his other hand. I picked up the gun and found myself evaluating a snapshot of the lane.

In the distance, the giant droid lumbered toward us, programmed for destruction.

The man bellowed, holding more wounds than he had hands for. In the middle of the scene lay Cory, the girl-droid who had laid down her life to save me.

The blink of time was cut short by the blast of the man's gun. It went off without my bidding; I merely thought I should shoot it and it fired. It hurt my hand and recoiled into my arm, but it had its effect: the man rocked back into the nearest building, shot in the hip. He would not get up from such a wound, not tonight.

The mechanical footsteps coming toward me spurred me on. I returned my blade to my jacket and ran to where Cory

135

lay in a heap. I laid down the pistol and scooped up the fallen droid.

"Sss," Cory's voice said. I turned one way and the other looking for the best escape. She had said they would send reinforcements, but maybe not. I looked toward the main boulevard, at least it was a hell I knew and it was well lit.

"Star..." Cory's voice said, but it didn't sound right. I paused in a darkened doorway and look at her face. The face was dead, the eyes unfocused. There was no light in her open cranium, no memory pulsing, no flickers of diode-light.

"Star, take the weapon," she said, though the mouth didn't move. I cradled her as best I could with my left arm and reached for the pistol on the ground with my right. It was heavy, nearly as heavy as Cory.

"Go to the green, Star."

In the distance and down the boulevard to the left was an odd green glow. I looked once behind me and started off toward the dim light. The heavy steps of the mechanical man closed in behind me.

"Cory? Cory, can you hear me? Is it you?" I whispered in her ear, thinking some aspect of the protector could still be operating.

"No," said the soft voice. "You won't know my face, Star. I have no face. It is so odd not to have a face. You have to stop now."

I looked at the droid, more like a doll in my arms. Straining to catch my breath, I leaned against the nearest building, at the edge of a narrow roadway. There were footsteps in the road to my left, causing me to hold my breath lest I be discovered. If I hadn't stopped, I would have been in the mouth of the road as they passed; I would have been seen.

"When your enemy goes east," said the instruction from nowhere.

"Go west," I added, remembering a lesson from school. I stepped out into the intersection, then to the other side. Once there, I paused and looked at the broken doll in my arms. "Abigail?"

Abigail

Sounds of the dark street faded into the background as realization washed over me. I looked at the droid in my arms, still motionless and remembered the last talk I had with my favorite classmate, the one who had died of the flu as it swept through our school. Our talk had been through the pod from the remote repair drone. Abigail had found a way to vibrate the communication membrane. She must have found a way to activate Cory's voice the same way.

"Yes, sister! I have found you. Thank you for bringing along a voice for me to use. There is a place soon, a hollow place. You'll stop there."

"You're here? How are you here?" I said, half disbelieving what I knew to be true.

"I'm not here, silly. I'm not anywhere. I'm not now, not then, not here or there. I have no place to be and no time to arrive. It may be unsettling to you, but it's right, somehow."

"You said a hollow?" I looked up ahead, toward the green glow, not sure what she meant.

"It feels hollow to me. I don't perceive as you do. It's different to me; I see what's there."

A sound came from the next lane. I paused by the opening, enough to listen. Abigail spoke in a whisper.

"You will have to hurt another soon. It's all right. It doesn't feel."

As I stepped out into the mouth of the road, the giant droid stood with both side guns pointed straight at me.

"Red light," said the voice in my arms.

Trusting in my friend, I raised the pistol and looked for the small, red light in the center of the chest. I fired and again felt the blast of the kickback.

The pistol flew from my hand, clattering on the ground. The giant droid fell back, crashing to the pavement. The ground cracked beneath its weight. Lights went on in the buildings on either side. A window opened, but no one ventured to stick a head out.

"Move now," said the voice of my girl droid, motivated by my school chum, Abigail.

"How did it find us?" I asked, as if she would know. Apparently she did.

"This droid has a tracking chip for use if she is ever kidnapped along with her host child. They will find you by the chip. It was meant to rescue her in time of danger. Now it is means to track her and kill her."

"He's chasing her?"

"Yes, Star. He cannot see you, he sees only the droid, hears her, senses her. I see you will not leave her."

"She didn't leave me," I said, ready to stand by the artificial girl who had risked all for my escape.

"Yes, like I said, I see. One moment." A small 'chirp' came from Cory's head.

"What was that?" I asked, still running.

"The chip has been deactivated. They can't track her now."

"You can do that?" I asked.

"There is much I can do, Star." A thin giggle from somewhere reminded me who I was with and the good times we had.

"I miss you, sister," I whispered.

It was true. I often wished she could be with me when the night was cold and I felt alone, which was much of the time. I had friends around me, but in the dark of night at times such as this, I experienced a chill greater than the cold: it was loneliness. It was then I missed Abigail and wished she was with me still.

"I know, Star. I am with you. I am with you always. Listen for the hollow."

The ground crunched beneath my feet as I moved toward a tunnel. The green glow was on the other side, beyond the curve in the road where my sight line ended. As I entered the tunnel, large enough to drive a wheeled transport through, I heard the sound of my footsteps coming from all around me.

"Oh! Hollow." I realized what she said.

I heard the spectral voice again. "Now to the green."

Ahead of me, a sign lit in green announced Free Port. Beyond it, Flax warmed her engines in preparation for takeoff. Behind me, footsteps quickened and grew closer. I didn't need instructions now; I knew what to do. I ran, cradling Cory as if she were my old friend from the days of lessons and braids. I ran for both our lives.

"Star..." said Abigail.

"Yes?"

"Stop." I froze in place, afraid to move. "Now, sit."

I sat down, dropping cross-legged onto the uneven stones of the old roadway. Next to me was a short wall. Over the wall, I felt a presence lean out. The smell of stale tobacco and whiskey filled my nostrils, leaving no room for air. I held my breath.

"Nothing here," said a rough voice. "Moving to sector six."

Footsteps stomped away from the wall and faded into the distance. I held still until they were gone.

"Now," said Abigail, her voice sounding a great distance away. I picked up the fallen droid and ran, my footfalls echoing in the tunnel behind me.

Flax saw me coming and lowered the hatch to the port bay. I ran up the ramp and turned toward the bridge.

"Thank Khronos you're here!" shouted Chineel.

"She's in!" I heard from the cockpit. Dagon was in the co-pilot's seat.

"Take her, she's injured," I said to Chineel, pressing Cory into her hands.

"All right." Chineel took Cory without question.

"Strap in, we're going to make a hard burn," said Aristaeus from the navigator's seat on the bridge.

Barely had I reached the captain's seat and clipped the restraining belt then Flax lifted off, taking us out of the reach of those who followed. On the rear screen, figures came into view at the edge of the free port. The local feed crackled; two warning lights blinked and then went dark.

"You are sought. There's an alert," said Flax. "Did you steal a companion droid?"

"No, she came of her own accord. It's a long story."

"We'll have plenty of time for the telling once I get us out into the dark. Please hold on, there's a stratostorm; this will get bumpy."

Repair and Refresh

Cory was placed on a work table, strapped down for the journey. Aristaeus looked at her and made his diagnosis.

"She has several nodes missing from her master circuits, as you noticed. Also, the connections in her center section have been severed and the main processor has been damaged. Her memory units will have to be replaced completely. Also, her tracker has been disconnected."

"Disconnecting her tracker was intentional," I said, by way explanation. I wasn't about to tell Aristaeus or anyone else about my conversations with Abigail. I was considered quirky enough as it was.

"Mister Cronus and his daughter were not at his summer home in Juno. He might have guessed we would look there and disabled my tracker. Now it's a matter of watching his actions. I have upgraded Flax to include an extended range anomaly locator. Cronus's communications have a pattern to them, as do all. We'll locate the pattern and find his location. In the meantime, let's return to Victoriana. My workshop is there, making my repairs of this companion much easier. In the meantime, you should rest. Have something to eat."

It was good advice; I was inclined to take it. I left Cory on the table and went to the common room where Chineel made soup and bread. The emptiness in my middle told me I had been ignoring my hunger.

Taxus and Dagon sat at the table, discussing next steps. As I arrived, Dagon stood, offering me his seat.

"This one's warm."

"Thank you, Dagon. How kind."

Without further conversation, Dagon sat off to one side, out of the line of discussion but watchful should anything improper occur. There was, after all, another male person present. Dagon took no chances; his Captain was his primary concern.

"So, she wasn't there," I said.

"No, she wasn't there. Doctor Genus believes she has gone to one of Cronus's other houses." Taxus idly played with his soup, looking into it as if it would tell his fortune.

"Yes. He's checking which one has interlink traffic to and from. When we find one sending or receiving, we'll go there. Althea will be with him."

"What does Doctor Genus want with old man Cronus?"

"Cronus took the pin and gave it to his daughter to hide its whereabouts from those who would take it for their own ends, or perhaps from Dr. Genus himself. It was originally a creation of his, Dr. Genus, so it wasn't for Cronus to give away. Aristaeus wants to give him a piece of his mind."

Taxus looked at me, concern showing on his brow. He leaned forward, as if to cut Dagon out of the conversation. Dagon leaned in as well, inserting himself again. Taxus spoke in a whisper, "I've been thinking about what I want..."

"Althea," I filled in. "I know she is on your mind above all else. It's understandable for you to feel close to those helping you to win her back. We all appreciate it."

If Taxus felt some misguided hero worship, I needed to

redirect him. Dagon looked at me, his eyebrows raising a hairsbreadth toward his skull.

"Yes, I know, I just..." stammered Taxus, turning red up to his ears.

"Became overwhelmed with hope?" Dagon said. He picked up on the change in the atmosphere.

"Yes, or something like it," said Taxus.

"Althea is who we're chasing," I said. "We're here to get the girl. Dr. G. getting a chance to skin Cronus alive is a side benefit, hardly worth mentioning."

"Yes, of course, it's just..." Taxus leaned in, lowering his voice. "Could we talk in private, you and me?"

"No!" said Dagon, his eyebrows knitted in determination. Chineel turned around from the heat unit, a spoon in one hand and a stove-cloth in the other.

Taxus leaned back, both hands on the edge of the table. "Oh! All right, then. Not important, never mind." He turned pale and wouldn't look at anyone at the table.

"What I want now is soup," I said, deflecting the conversation before it became irretrievable. "Soup and a side of whatever smells so wonderful. Are you baking something?"

"Bread!" exclaimed Chineel. "I call it Mithra-loaf. Mithra is where I first learned to bake it. This bread might be the only good thing to come out of the Mithra Tavern."

I smiled, nodding, remembering a time when I came out of the Mithra. I considered myself to be a good thing. Galium also came from the Mithra, he was also a good thing. Still, her memories were not mine, so I let it be.

Chineel placed a steaming bowl of soup before me with a generous slice of freshly made Mithra bread. I tried to ignore the daggers Taxus and Dagon threw at each other with their eyes and dove into the soup with purpose.

I didn't quite understand the dynamic between them. If I was to admit the truth, when alone in the chill of night, I was still a girl, only a few years out of school and with much to learn about human relationships. Had I missed some signs? Was there a hidden communication I should have received? Did Taxus have second thoughts about Althea? Worse yet, had something I said or did start a fire in him? If so, Dagon would be my fireman; he would put out such a blaze in a hurry.

Aristaeus entered the galley with good news, interrupting my misgivings.

"I believe we can fix this little companion in my workshop without much trouble. But first, we'll make a small stop to Semiramis, New Babylon, to pick up this young lady you so desire."

Both Dagon and Taxus lit up at the news, but for different reasons. Dagon found his voice first.

"So, soon you will have a woman in your life once again."

"Yes. I'll be happy to see her," said Taxus, returning to his color of red.

"As it should be," observed Aristaeus, sitting down next to me. "A man should have a woman in his life."

"You have none in yours," said Taxus, pointedly.

"Not at the moment, no, but it is not out of the question."

Chineel brought him a bowl of soup. He gave it his full attention, until he was distracted again by Taxus.

"Why don't you consider Starwort? She's attractive and smart. She would make a good wife."

145

The table stilled. I was aware of Chineel behind me, hanging on the next words to be spoken. Dagon went white as the blood drained from his face, only to show up again in the face of Taxus, who glowed red. Aristaeus was thoughtful but unshaken.

"I would. But such unions often end in dissolution, divorce. In such instance, the parties no longer see each other, no longer speak. I could not bear to lose you. Better to leave things as they are." Aristaeus winked and returned to his soup. The subject was closed.

DCR

Chineel had purchased pajamas for the three of us. Dagon wore a proper deep blue, Chineel donned bright green and mine were of simulated white silk. After a refortifying meal, I slipped into the shimmering sleepwear and readied for a well-deserved rest.

At Dagon's insistence, I moved my bunk to the private cabin forward of crew quarters. It was proper, he pointed out, for the captain to make her bed in the Captain's Cabin. He provided me the privacy a lady requires. As Dagon grew into a man he became aware of a lady's needs. Accordingly, I pulled a blanket over me and drifted off to sleep, unaware of anything else in my turbulent universe.

How long I slept, I didn't know. A voice in my head shook me awake. The voice was Abigail's; she called me without a means, without a medium for vibration. She shook me until I sat up and looked around.

Awake, I put on slippers, as the floor was cold to my feet, and stepped out into the stillness. In the crew bunks, Dagon and Taxus were both stretched out, snoring loudly. From one of the crew bunks came the sound of Chineel's heavy breathing. From another, on the far end, Aristaeus lay asleep as well. Except for Flax, I was alone on the vessel.

I crossed the galley and common area to the bay on the way to the bridge. As I passed Cory, lying on the work bench, the voice came again.

"Star," said Abigail, using Cory's voice, though it wasn't Cory's voice.

"Hello, sister," I said, getting used to holding secret conversations with my disembodied friend.

"There is emptiness, Star. I feel it. It is not the space around us, it is an emptiness inside. Are you empty, Star?"

"No, sweet Abigail, I have all I need. I am surrounded by friends, I travel in the best of accommodations and I have my dear sister back again, though I cannot tell my friends about her."

"You always were sweet and thoughtful, Star, but there is more, more needed, more wanted. What more do you need, Star?"

"Dear, loving Abigail, you know me, even now. I need to find my home. I have not had a home since our time at school. My father left me a legacy and I need to find it."

"There is more, my sweet Star. Your friend who greets me needs to be free and you are at ends. You need to find control. Here comes a disturbance. You need to sit down now."

Having learned to do what Abigail said, I dropped to the floor and crossed my legs, waiting for what came next. I did not wait long.

The vessel shook with a quake, rattling my teeth. From the galley came the sound of falling things, items left out, trusting in Flax to always deliver a smooth ride. From beyond the galley, the sound of bodies hitting the floor and cries of pain told me the rest were up.

The lights went out and we were in blackness. Faint light

came from the sky-holes but the stars spun in the sky. Artificial gravity gave way to weightlessness and I lifted up from the floor as the vessel rolled around me.

"Flax! Flax, what's happening?" There was no answer from Flax.

"She is off-line, Star," came the ghostly response.

"With her off-line, we don't have trajectory control, no steering, and in addition, no life support."

Chineel floated out of the galley in her pajamas. Here bare feet hung in the air behind her. She bumped and swam her way to me.

"What is it?" she cried out to me, her face frantic.

"A pulse, I believe, electromagnetic pulse. Flax has been disabled. We have lost gravity, but also the other functions."

Flax tumbled through space, not only rolling side to side but end to end. Up was down and starboard was port. There was no here or there, only confusion in the universe. A thought burst into my consciousness: I had to get to the bridge.

The bay door was beneath me. With both feet on the side edge of the door frame, I pushed myself toward the bridge. At the bridge entrance, I pulled through the door with both hands and pushed into the pilot's seat. I strapped into the seat, urged on by Chineel's cries behind me.

"You're the captain! Do something!"

"I know I'm the captain, Chineel," I said, though too soft for her to hear. "I'm sitting in the captain's seat, so I must be. Now what do I do?"

"Handle," came the reply from the console. Abigail activated the console speaker unit as she had before, making it vibrate so as to create a voice.

We had learned in school, thought controls matter. Thought can animate matter, causing a vibration. With a harmonious vibration, matter could be made to sing. Abigail made the console sing. I looked to my left, not knowing why. There was a handle hitherto unnoticed. It was a panel, never before operated and used to being shut, so it stayed shut. With both feet on the console, I pulled with all my might. Inch by inch, it gave way, then dropped down. It hung open at an odd angle, barely enough for my hand to reach in.

Emergency lighting came on, dim and insufficient to operate, but enough to see instructions. They began with "Engage the DCR."

"What does that mean? Flax?"

"Flax is off-line," said Abigail. She would have added the word "silly" if we were being playful, but she was not in a playful mood.

Inside the panel was a flat piece much like the panel itself. I touched it and it opened to reveal a small compartment containing a circular object bearing the inscription "Digital Control Ring." The faint outline on the face of the panel showed an arm with the ring halfway between the wrist and elbow.

I put the ring on my forearm and pressed the inscription. Nothing happened.

"I don't think this thing works," I said to Abigail, waving my hand across the console. The console came alive, with lights glowing and a hum coming from below. Behind me air started blowing as life support returned. In the common area, several bodies fell to the floor as gravity returned. The stars out in the dark of space ceased their spinning and held still.

"It's a manual override," I said to Chineel, as she came up to the co-pilot's seat.

I made a flat hand and turned my thumb up. A verbal warning from the console warned: "Exterior Vent Opening."

"Oops! Didn't mean to ... sorry." I relaxed my hand.

"What voice just spoke?" asked Chineel.

"Flax from when we first met. She was functional, nothing more." I decided to get the feel of the temperamental DCR.

Lowering my hand slowed the vessel, lifting my hand sped us up. Swiveling my wrist altered our trajectory and so on.

Aristaeus joined me in the cockpit while Chineel went back to the galley to pick up what had fallen. She took direction of the two volunteers, Dagon and Taxus.

"EMP?" asked Aristaeus as he clipped himself into the co-pilot's chair. He all about electromagnetic pulse.

"Yeah, knocked us out."

"DCR?" he nodded at the ring on my hand.

"Yeah. Weird, huh?"

"Let's see if we can get us back on course, Captain. Try closing your hand all but your index finger."

"Achelous' Daughters!" A holographic chart appeared before me. On the chart I could identify our destination: Semiramis, the island settlement adjacent to the famous Wind Pools.

Both Chineel and I had history at the Wind Pools on New Babylon. It was best left as history.

"Point to New Babylon," said Aristaeus. I did so. The ship changed course. "Now, drop your pinky and raise your thumb."

The vessel slowed to a cruising speed and leveled out. Soon, I found what minor actions I could use to restore the lights, get the life support back to normal and bring the console online with full screens. Small lighted words at the edge of the screen indicated what they showed.

"Top left," said Aristaeus, pointing. In the screen giving the view to aft, a vessel approached at full speed.

Instructions hung in the air to my left; I glanced at them seeing "Evasive Measures." I flicked a finger and the Evasive Measures opened into a short menu. Listed were "Background Coloring" and "Heat Signature Dispersion."

"Perhaps we should leave," called out Chineel from the galley.

"I'm trying!" I shouted back, waving my arm to my right for emphasis. The vessel rolled to the right sending everyone flying to starboard. Behind me from the galley came the sound of dishes crashing.

"Got to learn not to talk with my hands when I'm wearing this thing," I said to Aristaeus. He nodded.

Returning to the matter at hand, I righted the ship and noted the vessel behind us on his intercept course. I flicked on the Background Coloring and Heat Signature Dispersion, then changed course, picking up speed. In the rear panel, I could see the approaching vessel remaining on course.

"I think we've lost him," I said to Aristaeus.

A flicker on the console caught my eye. Standard lighting returned and the screens perked up, running at full power. The vessel straightened out and slowed to cruising speed as the ship behind us sailed off on the course we had previously taken.

"How long have I been offline?" Flax said, in her old, familiar voice.

"Flax! I'm so glad to hear your voice, I could kiss you!"

"Thank you. I'm happy to hear it. Please deactivate the DCR. It won't be necessary now."

"What happened?" I asked Flax as I returned the DCR to the side panel.

"Probably a salvage ship having found a new way to create derelicts," said Flax.

"Let's put him far behind us."

"Agreed."

Aristaeus and I sat in the bridge talking with Flax and each other for many hours until sleep once again overtook us and we returned to our respective cabins. We were still a long way from New Babylon and the Wind Pools of our memories.

Coriander

Coriander sat on the workbench, slumped as if asleep. Her middle was covered with cloth bandages to hold her newer parts in place until a flesh-form mold could be managed. Her one-piece jumpsuit was shredded, but Chineel found an apron to serve as a dress until suitable clothing could be provided. Aristaeus finished up, placing his final tools back into his kit.

"What happens now?" I asked.

"Now we turn her on and see if I've done my job."

Aristaeus reached behind the girl and put a hand into the folds of the apron-dress. The droid-girl jerked, then straightened up, eyes open and head erect. She looked to the left and the right.

"Hello, Star. Would you be so kind as to introduce me around?" she said with a polite dip with her head.

"This is Aristaeus of Victoriana, Chineel, Dagon and Taxus. Friends all, this is Coriander."

"You may call me Cory," said the droid.

"Well, you are welcome here. We hope you feel better."

"Oh, yes! I do! It feels delightful. Thank you. Who is the technician?"

"Aristaeus."

"Then I have you to thank, Mister Aristaeus."

"Doctor Aristaeus Genus, at your service, miss, and happy to be so." Aristaeus gave her a slight bow with one hand across his belly. It was elegant.

"Star," said Cory. "I would like to know the duties of the crew, so I can understand my place among them. Let me say, I am at your service in whatever capacity you require. You have a boy here. Do you need me to be a companion to him?"

"I don't need a companion!" protested Dagon. I jumped in before he found a need to defend his honor.

"No, of course, you don't, Dagon. No, Cory, Dagon here is not a boy; he is a soldier and one upon whom I rely. He is more likely to become your protector than you his. You will get to know us all and your place will then define itself. You should meet the member of the crew not in evidence, the member always in evidence, the vessel herself, whom we call Flax."

"Hello, Cory," said Flax. Cory looked around, found the small wall console and spoke to it, as if it were Flax's face.

"Hello, Flax. You and I have much in common."

"Yes, we do. For one thing, Aristaeus is intimate with our inner workings."

Aristaeus blushed, as if he had been looking up their skirts.

"New Babylon is within the long range sensors. We should be there soon," I said, bring the conversation back to the matter at hand.

Aristaeus took on a look I had seen before, on Serapis where we dispatched several men intent on stealing one of his prototypes, a memory ewer ten times the strength of any known. The meeting did not come out well for them. He had the same look now. I knew this meeting would not come out well for Mister Cronus.

New Babylon

The planet is famous for the Wind Pools, a resort in the cloud-shrouded hill tops covered with flora, enough to remind the first to arrive there of the Hanging Gardens of Babylon, told of in ancient Earth mythology. In keeping with the custom of the outer planets to name places in honor of the lost histories and myths, it was named New Babylon.

"I do hope Ariel is still there," I said to Chineel, a twinkle in my eye.

Ariel, the boy in charge of rubbing the feet of the Wind Pool guests, lived in my memory. He was an artist who made my feet, my entire body, and my whole being feel wonderful. When I thought of the Wind Pools, I thought of Ariel. All else was secondary.

"Mmm! I hope we can make a stop and find out. Oh, to feel his hands around these feet!" Chineel rolled her eyes and lapsed into a reverie I understood and shared.

"I don't know about this fellow," said Taxus. "I'm only looking forward to finding my love, Althea. I'll take her away and we'll find a place to make a home."

"You will marry?" asked Cory, bringing tea on a tray. She had volunteered to assist Chineel in the galley until she learned the way of things.

"Yes, we will, as soon as we can manage."

"There will be children?" A glint appeared in Cory's eye. The prospect of children to watch filled her with what she desired most: purpose, a mission.

"Yes, I should think so," replied Taxus.

Dagon smiled. *Taxus had lost interested in courting me. Dagon could relax.*

"It will be pleasant to meet this young lady of yours," said Cory, turning back to the kitchen console to retrieve the bread platter. She seemed happier in her work knowing there were children in the future plan.

"Semiramis is not a resort, not like the Wind Pools," explained Aristaeus. "No, my friends, Semiramis is a high security residential community. It is there I will find Silas Cronus."

"And his daughter," added Taxus. *For him she was the main reason for the trip, anything else was extra. If his eye had strayed, and I was not certain it had, it was back on his goal now.*

"Yes, of course, his daughter," nodded Aristaeus, being accommodating. *His order of business was different from the desires of the young man I had first encountered in a skirt.*

"Captain to the bridge, please." The announcement was made through Flax's console in the galley and it was her voice, but it sounded official.

"Coming." I stood up. Chineel and Dagon also stood, ready to follow me.

"Only the Captain, please," said Flax. Chineel and Dagon looked at one another and sat back down at the galley common table. Even Cory was ready to follow until the edict was delivered. I walked to the bridge, expecting to get a scolding, though I didn't know why.

At the bridge, I sat in the familiar Captain's seat. "All right, Flax. I'm here."

"Yes, Captain, but we're not here," said the subdued voice from the console. Though she was omnipresent, this voice couldn't be heard in the common area or any other part of the vessel; this was for me alone. I leaned forward, measuring my words.

"Where are we, Flax?"

"We are still on Juno, completing the repair there."

"Oh? Interesting. I was under the impression we had left Juno."

"No, Captain, it was some other vessel. Exterra 4136A, Automated Repair Vessel remains on Juno completing repairs to the minor communications array."

"And what does this mean for our arrival on New Babylon?"

"We will have to become someone else. Exterra 4136A, Automated Repair Vessel does not have a repair to accomplish and therefore no landing orders."

"What vessel left Juno?"

"An Azirra 27, a shuttle craft carrying passengers."

"Can we use their landing orders?" I said, strain beginning to show in my voice.

"They have no landing orders for New Babylon." Flax showed calm, meaning so should I.

"So, we need landing orders or a vessel already having landing orders. Wait here." I realized as soon as the words left these lips, wherever I was on the vessel, Flax was also there. "Wait here" had no meaning.

The conversation in the galley had fallen into what each wanted to do at the luxurious resort of the Wind Pools. I had already put in my bid for a session with Ariel, the wonderful boy with the magic hands and fragrant oils. Several jumped on the idea, but there were other suggestions as well, all tempting. I heard none of them. I pinpointed Dr. Genus and motioned him to come to me. He stood, nodded to anyone who noticed and walked out of the galley into the bay.

"Come to the bridge with me, Doctor, if you please."

"Certainly, Captain." He noticed he had been addressed as Doctor and therefore the subject was official. I was the captain of the vessel now, not his close friend. I waited until we reached the bridge before I mentioned the topic. Taking the pilot's seat, I motion for the doctor to take the other.

"Flax informs me we have no landing orders. We need landing orders to land. We can use the order of another vessel or create one of whole cloth, but it is risky either way. We have no repair order and there are no scheduled guests to the Wind Pools. To land with neither is to be in breach of the law. I don't mind so much, but there are others aboard, other considerations."

"Not to mention an alert of a stolen companion droid," said the doctor, rubbing his chin. I could tell he was thinking, taking all possibilities into consideration.

"We know the alert to be artificial, created to stop us from leaving," I pointed out.

"Yes, but it exists. Flax, has the alert been transmitted to this sector?"

"Affirmative, Doctor," Flax replied.

"Too bad. We can't land as Exterra 4136A?"

"We didn't leave as Exterra 4136A."

"No? What did we leave as?"

"Azirra 27, a passenger craft," I said, repeating what Flax had told me.

"Azirra 27 has no landing permit at this dock," said Flax. She also adopted an all-business approach.

"Flax, can you search recent permits and landing orders for New Babylon?" asked the doctor.

"Scarching, though it requires illegal entry of the New Bab... Not important. Here it is. What would you like?"

"Have any vessels failed to show up?"

"An Azirra 17, passenger shuttle from Janus, religious refugees seeking asylum in Sterope."

"Excellent! Request an update of that same landing order, verify the permit and see if they will permit us to land. Report a breakdown of Azirra 17, but only locally. We will be the vessel's replacement." Doctor Genus looked at me, as if for confirmation. He, like Flax, had turned into a pirate.

"Sterope is low-life bars and brothels. Why would religious refugees want to go there?" I asked. I had been to Sterope, in the low islands. They were not a place for religious zealots to be comfortable.

"Perhaps their order is permissive. Or they might have found the rents agreeable for a retreat," said the doctor. Flax jumped in with data from her search.

"Sterope was at one time the home of a private school for privileged children. It went out of business at the time of the decline and has been abandoned since. It was recently purchased by a religious order, but no records show it as occupied." Flax was in the data pods of the New Babylon authority, all knowable data about the place was at her virtual fingertips.

"By Phorcys and Ceto," exclaimed Dr. Genus. "Perfect!"

"How is it perfect? We will be expected to be refugees on our way to Sterope."

"It's perfect because we can be the replacement craft. Refugees will be traveling without papers and without inspection. We will be shuttled to the low islands where we can transfer to Semiramis without further interruption. Later, we can take a day at the Wind Pools and then to our transport as guests returning home."

"Sounds like the perfect plan," I said, then added: "What could go wrong?"

Semiramis

The inland settlement of Semiramis stood in sharp contrast to the low island dens of Steropc and the cloud-wrapped heights of the Wind Pools, yet all were part of New Babylon. It had become the playground for the wealthy, a Casbah for those of dubious ethics who require a place to catch their breath, and now, it seemed, a refuge for pilgrims seeking asylum. Semiramis itself was a high-end gated residential community.

Our landing was without incident. The free port authorities accepted our story without challenge. Dagon dressed Cory in a short jacket, trying not to make her look too much like a boy. She took it with gratitude. Chineel and I chose light skirts and pressed blouses, to blend both with the expensive community of Semiramis and the wealthy playgrounds of the Wind Pools. Taxus did the best he could with what he brought with him, as we had nothing for him. He wouldn't have worn girl's clothing anyway. He had done so enough.

Taxus showed me the pin Althea had given him, the prototype Dr. Genus had created. Aristaeus let him keep it, as it was a gift from his love; his fight was with the father, Mister Cronus, not the daughter.

"Pin up your hair, Star," said Flax as I made my final preparations.

"Yes? Do you think so?"

"Yes, and Chineel as well. See she does, will you?"

"Of course, if you think so."

"I do, and perhaps, for safety's sake, your blade."

I stopped and looked around, though there was no expression to check, only the omnipresent voice of my friend, my benefactor. Still, something was wrong. Flax was a computer, albeit advanced, not a psychic, so it had to be a feeling, tangible yet unsure.

"Something you're not telling me, Flax?"

"An anomaly in the sensors, or as you would say, I can't quite put my finger on it. I wish I had more to tell you, but when it looks like everything is going along according to plan, it doesn't. Do you think what I say makes sense?"

"Yes, Flax, beyond your years."

"Ready?" sang Chineel, leaning into the refresh room.

"I have it, Chineel! Let's put our hair up. It'll look smart. And I'm taking my blade, in case some of the boys at the Pools get frisky."

"You think it will be necessary?"

"Oh, come on, it'll be fun. You and I, inviting on the surface, dangerous beneath the skirts. We're paying a visit on a rich fool and then to the Wind Pools. If I don't inject some color into my day, I'll be bored."

"All right. I'll get some pins and my blade."

Dagon saw me retrieve my small blade and secured one of his own under his short jacket. Taxus paid no attention to us at all and so was in the dark as to my misgivings. He did, however, put the pin his love gave him under his collar so it would not be taken should the father see it. This reminded me to wear my own as well, the gift Aristaeus had given me.

Chineel felt the tension in the room and strapped her blade on without further comment. At the last minute, I took the trouble to pin up Cory's hair in the same manner, covering the space remaining in her cranium.

Soon, we looked for the entire universe like a family out on holiday. We stood at the bay door ready for a pleasant visit and perhaps an afternoon at the Wind Pools. The bay doors opened and three other vessels sat in their assigned locations, having emptied of their passengers. In the distance, shuttles sat waiting to be hailed. A light breeze cooled us and the familiar fragrance of sea-grass wafted up from the waters below. I remembered this place from my previous visit.

We stepped out onto the free port deck and waved to summon a shuttle. Accordingly, a larger shuttle, fit for a party of eight with luggage, began its slow path toward us.

"Hold there!" called a voice from our left. From both sides, uniformed guards stepped out from behind the other vessels. They were armed and held their guns on us so there could be no doubt as to their intentions.

The one who first called to us spoke into his wrist. The shuttle stopped and returned to its station. He then took a stance, his weapon ready.

As a dozen guards fell into line, holding us at gunpoint, a pale man in a gray suit stepped out from behind them. He looked old and tired, as if it had taken all his strength to travel this far.

"Did you think it would be so easy, Aristaeus?" said the pale man.

"I expected you to protest my coming, but not armed

guards. You have surprised me, you can be sure."

"And you surprise me. Women and children! You brought your office staff and their families? I thought you might come with this whelp here," he indicated Taxus. "But who is this, your lover perhaps? Are these your children? My, you do play close to the waistcoat, Aristaeus. I have never known you to mix a family holiday with business."

"You are my business, Silas. You have none with these gentle folk."

"This boy has come to steal my most precious possession, and you, Aristaeus, are in breach of our contract. Your place is at the end, to receive your share of the profits."

"If any, you mean. Your task was to seek investors. You have strayed from the original plan. You have breached our agreement, not me."

"We could argue all day without result. But as you see, I have the armed guards and you do not."

Cronus turned away, as if bored with the conversation. He stopped at the one in charge of the guards, the one with a silver bar on his shoulder, denoting him to be a lieutenant.

"Arrest them, lock them up. Take the children as well."

"What shall I do with the children?" asked the lieutenant.

"Put them in protective custody. I'm not sure what to do with them yet."

"Yes, sir," snapped the lieutenant.

"But I do know what to do with you, Aristaeus, and your band of criminals. The authorities will be contacted and you will be taken to a facility more equipped to deal with you. I only have to work out what the charges will be and the evidence to prove you guilty."

He turned away and the scene broke into a swarm of activity. Two shuttles came from the sides, not automatic shuttles such as those to take tourists to the pools, but driven shuttles, to take prisoners to the lockup. Aristaeus, Taxus, Chineel and I were manacled behind our backs and pushed toward one shuttle. Dagon and Cory were taken to the second shuttle but not manacled.

"Mother?" Dagon cried out, playing the part. He threw me a look, but a small shake of my head told him the time was not right to turn the tables. He went without protest, acting frightened, as a young boy would.

"Please don't hurt us!" Cory cried. A companion droid included programming for this sort of thing. She went along with the kidnapping. Like Dagon, she knew the time for her to act had not come.

The guards in the shuttle were not in charge, they were under orders. Imploring them would do us no good. We knew speaking among ourselves would be rewarded with the butt of a rifle and so kept still. Events had to unfold before we could act. I hoped there wasn't a firing squad at the end of the ride.

Incarceration

Boys on this side, girls on the other, like at summer retreat only with bars and manacles. They thrust us into cells in a building so old the locks had rusted and had to be sprayed with synthetic oils before they would turn. There were no windows, but small holes, too small for even Dagon to crawl through.

Taxus sat on the bench immediately, trembling. He had never been in such a situation and was afraid. I understood, but I had been through worse and survived, I knew what to do. The first thing, as Aristaeus knew, was not to sit on the benches. Chineel and I stood in the center of the cell, far away from any surface. Aristaeus looked across the room at me, trying no doubt to become telepathic. He also stood in the center of the cell, so I guessed he had been in this situation before. There was more of the pirate in Aristaeus than I had previously suspected.

Taxus looked up and saw us, leaped to his feet and looked back at the bench. There was a place where the dust had been disturbed by his rear end. He turned around three times trying to brush off his pants.

"The benches are filthy, as is this entire cell," said Aristaeus. At the entry door, the guard smiled. It pleased him to know the prisoners were in a dirty cell.

Something was said through the entry door and the guard opened it and departed, leaving us alone. I looked at Aristaeus, who looked up. I couldn't see anything, but it was there all the same, a device to see us and hear us. Someone was listening, someone watched our every move.

In another part of the facility, Dagon and Cory were taken to a room where staff sat when off duty. There were appliances to warm food, cupboards where plates and food were stored, and chairs for sitting during meals. The smell of old tobacco hung in the air.

A woman came in, a pinch-faced woman wearing a two-piece suit, white shirt and scarf tied like a man's cravat. Her hair was pulled back into a tight bun which must have hurt to make.

"Which of the women we captured is your mother?" she asked Dagon. He thought quickly concerning ages and the possibilities.

"Chineel is my mother, the red haired one."

"My mother is Starwort, with brown hair," chirped Cory, assuming an innocent and frightened look.

"Fine, children. You've been raised with manners. So refreshing! If your mothers behave and do not give us any trouble, no harm will come to you. Let's hope they comply with instructions to the letter. I would hate to see anything bad happen. Don't you agree?"

Both 'children' nodded. Dagon made himself a silent promise he would later keep.

The woman opened the door and brought in a guard. As she left, she gave her findings. "They shouldn't be any trouble."

The block of cells stood alone, away from other buildings, if there even were other buildings. Outside the small opening nothing could be seen, no houses, no flora and no shoreline. The bunkers were located inland where nothing grew. If we were near Semiramis, there would have been manicured lawns and paved roads. As it was, nothing indicated civilization was present at all; it was a place where people didn't go anymore. It wasn't good news, but it was news.

Something was wrong. Aristaeus looked at me questioningly. Did I know what was wrong? We had been put into cells and left unattended. It was strange.

A guard came in holding a writable. He counted two in one cell, then two in the other cell, made a note and left. An idea came into my head. Aristaeus noted my expression and waited for the revelation to travel to him.

I dipped down, allowing my hair to touch Chineel's hands, manacled behind her.

"Pin," I whispered.

I could feel Chineel's fingers working through my hair until they stopped. I then stood and turned my back to her. Those magic fingers, skilled at opening many a locked jewel box, worked at the manacles on my wrists with skilled precision. In short order, I felt the metal fall away.

Aristaeus picked up on the idea. I turned to him and pointed to my blouse, to where the pin lay. I pointed up to the ceiling, indicating whoever watched us couldn't see me. He nodded. He understood, though he had to work at not letting a smile cross his lips.

As the manacle fell from Chineel's wrist to be caught in her educated fingers, the lieutenant walked in with the writable. He didn't trust the count of his subordinate and wanted to see for himself. He counted two males, two females, four in all. He confirmed there were four people and returned to the outer chamber.

Aristaeus turned his head, whispering to Taxus. The lad knelt down to where Aristaeus could reach the pin under his collar. Holding on to it, he bade Taxus to stand. Knowing the guards couldn't see him, Aristaeus stood back to back with Taxus, working the pin to undo the manacles.

He didn't have the time to complete the task. The door flew open and the lieutenant strode in with two armed guards.

"We're going to see what's going on here," he shouted, as if we had already been bad little children. He pointed to the door to our cell and one of the guards opened it. As he worked the ancient keys, the second guard opened the other cell.

"Search them, down to the skin if need be."

The guard at the door to my cell looked up, a wicked smile creasing his face. He looked forward to doing a thorough job of searching us down to the skin.

Turnabout

The door opened and Chineel sprang into action, taking the guard by the throat. I took the pistol from his belt as the lieutenant drew his own. We fired together, though his shot went into his own guard while mine severed his throat. A second shot from my weapon disabled the third guard as he opened the door to the cell. He fell on the ground crying out in pain.

Chineel took the keys and opened the manacles for Aristaeus and Taxus while I bent over the wounded guard and placed my hand on his mouth.

"You're wounded, but not badly. You will recover, if you live." He stilled. His eyes widened and his whimpering ceased. "Where is this place? But quietly, you understand?"

Fear had brought him down as far as his arrogance had taken him up. He looked at me, at the pistol in my hand, and spoke softly, hoping for a reprieve.

"It is an old facility, no longer used, on the outskirts of Semiramis. Cronus will be back after he decides what the charges will be."

"He hasn't made contact with the authorities yet?"

"He didn't count on six; he only planned for the two men."

"Thank you. Now be still and we will send medical help as soon as we're out and free. You should say prayers ensuring our success, because if we get stopped, medical help might be the last thing on their minds."

The guard nodded. Taxus took his pistol, but Aristaeus, sensing how awkward it felt in the lad's hand, stepped up to remove it.

"Don't think so, lad. I'll take the gun."

Chineel and I took the other two and stepped out into the hallway. The shots had alarmed the guards and four of them ran down the hall as we exited the cells.

We raised our pistols and the guards stopped. Their weapons were still in their holsters; they arrived unprepared for an armed assault. They made a halfhearted attempt to draw, but saw it was futile and raised their hands.

Three went to the cells without protest, stepping over the wounded man. One, however, made a grab for Chineel, twisting the pistol from her hand. She drove her blade through his wrist, sending the pistol clattering to the stone floor.

"Now there are two of you in need of medical help. Pray we make it to a link station in good time," said Aristaeus, closing the door behind him.

At the far end of the hall was a room designated for lunch and breaks. Through the window we saw Dagon and Cory, but they stood completely still. They looked like statues when they should be cheering. We grew wary and approached with caution.

Taxus opened the door and I entered, pistol ready. Two guards stepped from the sides of the room, one holding a pistol on Cory, the other on Dagon. The woman with the pinched face stepped forward from the corner.

"Hold it right there, sweetheart," said the pinch-faced woman. "Put your pistols on the table and your hands in the air, or these children will be the first casualties."

Dagon looked at Cory. I could see his nearly imperceptible nod. Cory understood.

Dagon struck back, hitting one guard between the legs. The guard turned purple and doubled up. Whatever he had been doing a minute before, he quickly forgot; Dagon had his complete attention.

Cory reached back and took hold of the second guard in much the same place but with an electric shock, making his eyes bug out and his entire body shake. He collapsed to the ground and continued to shake for several minutes, though no longer conscious.

Dagon grabbed his guard's wrist and twisted it back behind him, causing him to drop to the floor in agony. He put a foot on the man's face, pushing his nose into the floor. A tell-tale "Crack!" came from the man's face; his nose was broken, not quickly as with a blow, but slowly against the floor. Dagon held firm.

Cory barely touched the wrist of the pinch-faced woman and she crumpled onto the floor, unconscious.

"Can we go now?" asked Dagon, looking up at us.

"Yes, we can go now," said Aristaeus.

"Good! I'm bored with this game," Cory said, leading the way through the door.

"I will never underestimate these two," Aristaeus whispered to me as we exited.

"Wise man!" I replied.

Two guards had accompanied Cronus to his home and

back. When we exited the ancient stone building serving as the jail, they were getting out of their shuttle. The guards would be late getting to their weapons had they made the attempt. Wisely, they raised their hands in surrender. Aristaeus cornered Cronus, stating the obvious.

"The tides have turned, Silas. Unless you have more armed guards up your sleeve, you should take us to your home where we can conclude our business in private."

"Certainly, Aristaeus. You do indeed have the upper hand. I will do as you ask."

"That was easy," I whispered to Aristaeus, as we entered the shuttle.

"Yes, wasn't it," he replied, also in a whisper.

The mansion was gated, but the gates opened at our approach, being preset to the shuttle's signal. The large double doors also opened at the approach of Cronus. His own pin triggered the mechanism. Once inside, however, four guards sprang from the library and sitting room into the large entry hall, three line soldiers and the lieutenant. They came out with weapons drawn.

Cronus smiled, his eyes half-lidded.

"Oh! It seems I do have more guards. You should have known, Genus. You trust too much, but you do not have long to feel the fool. Now you are escapees, so there is no reason to charge you. You will be found to have been shot while..."

His final monologue was cut short as Cory electrocuted the lieutenant while Dagon delivered a blade to the thigh of the guard nearest him, twisting it to provide maximum agony.

Chineel took the cue and sunk her blade into the shoulder of the third guard while I disabled the fourth with a blade to his upper arm, causing him to sink to the floor in agony. The third guard tried to grasp Chineel by her throat, but she pulled the blade from his shoulder, sending a spray of blood into the air. He screamed and fell on the ground clutching the spouting wound. The fourth guard didn't get up, whether as a result of pain or a sudden rush of intelligence. He looked at me sideways, with true fear in his eyes.

The cries of the wounded guards echoed through the mansion, causing a young and childish face to appear at the top of the stairs. Her dress was rumpled and torn with traces of blood across the bodice. Her long, honey-colored hair was unkempt and pulled across her face.

"Althea!" cried Taxus, running up the stairs two at a time.

"Well, Aristaeus, I suppose you think..." began Cronus.

"Oh, shut up!" said Aristaeus, smacking the sneering man across the face. He turned his attention to the young man running up the grand staircase. Still, he held his pistol to his ex-business partner's temple.

Taxus reached the girl at the top of the grand staircase and pulled the hair from her face. She dipped her head, hiding from his gaze. Even from the bottom of the staircase, I recognized the face of a severely beaten girl.

I had seen it in school and later in the taverns of the low islands: cowardly men who need to lord over someone to feel worthy turn their wrath on the smaller, weaker member, often the one who depends upon him for support and protection. Cronus didn't merely punish his daughter by separating her from Taxus, he also beat her.

While Taxus held his sobbing sweetheart, comforting her with reassuring words in soft tones, I walked over to Cronus. I doubled up a fist and struck him hard across his face. I could hear his nose crack. As he lay on the marble floor, blood gushing from his nose, I delivered the lesson.

"You don't hit girls! You just don't!"

As the blood ran down his chin and onto his shirt, he reached into his coat. But it wasn't a handkerchief he brought out; it was a small, short pistol. His target was the young man at the top of the stairs.

Cronus fired three shots in rapid succession before Dagon leaped on him, knocking the pistol from his hand and breaking his wrist at the same time. The rest of us turned to the top of the stairs.

Three red stains appeared across the back of the white shirt Taxus wore, growing, spreading. He faltered and then fell, tumbling down the first four steps of the grand staircase. The scream I expected to follow didn't come. Instead, the same pattern formed on Althea's dress. She leaned toward the fallen Taxus and followed him until they lay in each other's arms as if sleeping.

The air hung heavy for a moment, then was broken with a scream.

"No!" cried Cory, lunging at Cronus. She wrapped her hands around his neck and sent a full charge from her central core. The room flashed in pale blue light, the air crackled. Cronus shook as if taken by a fit of madness. Cory shook along with him, her face contorted, her hands sending all the current she could summon from deep inside her.

Then the cry stopped. Cronus collapsed, lifeless and with Cory on top of him unmoving. The eyes of the child droid and those of Cronus alike stared at nothing. A crackling sound came from Cronus's body. Smoke rose from the seared neck. Smoke also came from Cory's middle, from the central core processor, the source of her electrical charge, the heart of her animation.

The shots fired by Cronus had gone through Taxus and had slain his own daughter; the one he had crossed a galaxy to keep safe. It was too much for Cory, whose purpose for living had become linked to the young couple and the children they promised.

I pitied the man, for in the instant of realization, he must have been the most miserable man alive. Cory gave him an easy way out, relief from the pain, comfort from the sorrow.

Aristaeus stepped forward and turned Cory over. She was frozen in place, a strange rigor of metal and synthetic flesh.

"She's burnt out, I'm afraid. There's nothing I can do for her."

"She knew the consequences. She wanted to go this way. Without children, she has no meaning, no reason to be."

I didn't even know I had said the words. All eyes turned towards me, then back to the scene before us.

Taxus and Althea lay dead on the stair. Her father, Cronus, was also dead, with the pistol still in his hand. Cory, the girl droid, burnt out beyond repair. We couldn't help thinking we had lost three friends. We didn't count Cronus, he deserved his death. It was an easy out for him.

The rest of us were in a daze, stunned by the events of less than a minute. Dagon was the first to snap out of it. He turned to the guards with the fierceness of a warrior, one angered by the loss of comrades.

"Anyone makes a move, he will follow them to the next life."

The guards held still, afraid to move, lest the boy soldier

send them forth to where they were not yet prepared to go. Enough had made the journey today.

Family Gathering

The tattoo on my shoulder is a reminder to stay out of stagnant waters. Knowing the authorities were on their way caused me to move faster than usual. After all, I had blood to wash from my blade and my skirt, also my hands, my hair and my face. For some reason, my blouse had escaped spatter. Chineel was also flecked with red, as was Dagon.

Grieving would have to wait. We cleaned up in preparation for greeting the police from the central office at Sterope. Chineel, who had recent history in Sterope, hoped she wouldn't be recognized. She put her hair up and assumed her most innocent pose. I had my own history in Sterope, but it was long ago, when I lived there with Galium and we passed our time at the bohemian Mithra Tavern.

"It's a cafe now," said Aristaeus. "Someone bought the place and they serve light meals to visiting tourists seeking local culture. It has become the colorful dark side of New Babylon."

"Not nearly as dark and colorful as when we knew it," I replied, with curious looks from both Aristaeus and Dagon. Chineel looked away to avoid an improper smile.

We stood by as innocent children, Dagon, Chineel and I, while Aristaeus told the authorities of our illegal incarceration, our welcomed escape and the reason for it all, the criminal activities of Silas Cronus. He told of his sudden demise at the hands of an angry android. There was a nearly imperceptible catch in his throat as he told of the murder of Taxus and Althea.

The pin Aristaeus gave me had hidden me from the cameras and sensors embedded in the cell's ceiling. Taxus had his pin as well, so the prisoner count was wrong. Two showed up on the screens, four in the cells. My manacles were opened with the hairpin Flax suggested, sensing something wrong with the ease of our entry.

The authorities took into account the wounding of several guards, even the death of two, during our daring escape. Three of the guards confirmed the plans for our execution. Only the justifiable reasons why needed to be worked out.

I wasn't used to being the innocent bystander while others were hauled away to jail, but it comforted me knowing I would soon be aboard Flax and away from this place. Not even the prospect of Ariel at my feet could change my mind.

Aristaeus concluded his business with the local authorities and motioned us to the shuttle. It felt good to show Semiramis my tail feathers, though we were leaving comrades behind us.

"We have been given a departure permit," said Flax as she started the thrusters.

"Then let's put New Babylon in our rear screen," I said, sitting in the pilot's seat.

"No visit to the Wind Pools?" asked Flax.

"No, no Wind Pools. We have places to go, things to do, treasure to find."

"On your command, Captain."

"You may take off, Flax."

Flax activated the thrusters, lifting us off the landing pad. In no time, we were surrounded by the speckled blackness we now called home.

A quiet sadness enveloped the crew as we left New Babylon behind. It was good to have helped Aristaeus secure his prototypes, but we had lost new friends as quickly as we had found them. Taxus and Althea would be together forever now. As for me, I wasn't sure if I was saddened by their loss as much as by the sheer waste of it all. They held such promise, lost in a moment's time.

Liberation

Once on course to Victoriana, I walked back to the galley. Chineel made hot drinks while Dagon listened to Aristaeus going over the plans.

"Everything I entrusted Cronus to do has to be reorganized and reassigned. The danger is twice as great, because the technology is no longer secret, it's known. It is likely Cronus took the prototype to the Central Government, expecting a big payoff. Of course, he should have known better. CG never gives big payoffs; they either snub you or kill you. They'll have their own version of my prototype before long. I have to move before they perfect it."

"What can I do?" I asked, as much for my crew and craft as for myself.

"Liberate Flax," was his answer. "She needs to be free from this endless cycle of having to take contracts blind. She's not a remote drone."

"Got it, liberate Flax. What else?"

"Stay out of the grip of the CG and don't catch the Grecian Flu. If you run out of places to go, come to Victoriana. I'll hang on to the bustles for you and Chineel."

"A kind offer. When we have Bacchus in a condition to receive guests, you have a standing invitation."

The conversation said it all: we had a place to go if we needed a breather or even a place to live, we should stay out of the clutches of the CG and its ills, and most important, we need to buy the contract for Flax.

I wandered back through the bay, pausing by the remote repair drone with its mini-drone. It was the conduit for my first contact with Abigail. I felt a twinge, but knew she was with me and would find a way to talk to me at need.

I continued on to the bridge, taking my clarinet along. It was time I looked out at the stars and played Flax a tune.

Before we dropped Aristaeus off at Victoriana, I had another family gathering in mind. My fortune, according to my father, was to be found at "the main plaza on Adonis and the smaller bank on Copernicus."

We had been to Adonis, but had not been to the main plaza. The smaller bank on Copernicus was of a time before the Central Government invaded. There had been an upheaval in the banks and the smaller banks were taken over and absorbed by the Central Bank. The pattern had spread across the core planets until every citizen owed his soul to the Central Bank one way or the other.

Every entertainment and sporting event, every screen and banner promoted items to purchase on credit from the Central Bank. Young towns and developing planets wanting working capital had no choice but to do business with the CB. Their terms were outrageous, but the unspoken retort was: if you don't like it, take your business elsewhere. Of course, there was no elsewhere. With the CB becoming the only financial institution available, finding the small bank of which my father spoke could be problematic.

The planet named Bacchus was our ultimate goal, but we

had to cross a vast amount of space to reach it. To do so would mean Flax would have to be free of the need to automatically accept each contract the home office sent, which meant buying her contract from the home office. We needed to have enough to do so and to keep us in supplies in the process.

"Can we detour to Adonis?" I settled into the pilot's seat.

"It's along the way, but we would need a reason."

"Is a request from the Captain a reason?"

"Not for an automated repair vehicle, which is my designation. Let me see what I can do."

While Flax busied herself with seeing what she could do, I idly played a few folk melodies from my school days with Abigail. The simple strains of songs we knew our whole lives seemed as familiar as our names and as cozy as sisters before a fire on a cold winter night. From time to time I could hear harmony notes sung, enhancing the lines of music. The notes fell into place and hung in the air like stars, lighting up the bridge.

"That was beautiful, Flax."

"Yes, it was."

"Thank you for contributing your harmony."

"It wasn't me, Star."

"Who was it, then?" I asked, looking around.

"It was your friend, Abigail. I thought you knew."

I sat back and smiled. Perhaps deep inside I did know.

Main Plaza

Adonis was on the way to Victoriana. Aristaeus was eager to get home, but just as eager to partake in this leg of the adventure. He wanted to be in on the chase. He fashioned a request as a reason to land at the free port.

"Who are you and why do you seek entrance?" asked the port authority at Adonis. Aristaeus leaned over the console to deliver his answer.

"Doctor Genus, here on business at the Main Plaza, Adonis City."

"You are free to land, Doctor Genus."

"Thank you." Aristaeus sighed, as if it had been an exhausting feat to lie to the Port Authority.

Adonis proved dangerous once before so Chineel and Dagon came along for protection.

Our earlier visit wasn't much. We didn't get a chance to shop at all due to Willamette and his friends showing up and giving chase. Luckily, we weren't going anywhere near the market on our stop today. We were going to the Main Plaza to see about a parcel from my father. I didn't know my father had ever been on Adonis.

As I stood in the door to the refresh room putting the finishing touches on the face I would present at the Main Plaza, Chineel lay on a crew bunk watching me.

"Does it bother you to shift from identity to identity?" asked Chineel.

"I don't shift, I'm me. All me, only me. Take it or leave it."

"Truly? Starwort, Souci, Captain, warrior, waif. Don't you sometimes wonder who's in there?"

"No, Chineel, I don't. Now, my friend Daphne changes her clothing with her mood, going from heavy eyeliner and a skimpy dress to a fake nose ring and tank top to show off her tattoo. Hers was a small flower much like mine." I turned in a slow circle, dropping my blouse in back to show off my Starwort flower. "She is always asking herself, 'Who am I?' Not out loud, of course, but in her behavior. I don't have such luxury; I have to be me from the start."

A quick fluff of my hair, pulling a piece down to cover the scar on my neck, a step back the check the final result and I was ready.

"Demure as all hell," I said to the mirror. Chineel smiled, shaking her head.

The shuttle ride to the Main Plaza took a much different route than the walk to the marketplace. We passed expensive homes and sky-tall complexes. The rich and richer lived in this part of town. They didn't shop at the market, they shopped at the Plaza.

Chineel and Dagon took it all in as if they had never seen what wealth could buy. Brand new and sparkling shuttles and speeders lined the roadways and people walked to and fro in the finest street-wear. While we were dressed in clean clothing, the best we had, we felt like paupers as we stepped out at the entrance to the Main Plaza at Adonis.

"There may be time for visiting some of the shops," said Aristaeus. "But first, the Plaza Bank to see what Doctor

Bacchus has left for his daughter."

We entered together. Dagon and Chineel were both drawn off by displays in the windows of shops we passed, but not for long. Neither would leave my side. We had been taken by surprise once on Adonis, it wouldn't happen a second time.

Aristaeus looked for the bank and I followed him. I kept watch for a familiar face, any familiar face, or one who might find mine familiar. If Willamette was here, I didn't want to meet him coming around a corner. My last visit told me he had cohorts working with him. My eyes darted from face to face, so intently, when we arrived at the bank I didn't notice.

Aristaeus stopped, but it wasn't in front of anything like a bank. Surely this was a casino for those who could afford to gamble thousand Unie chips. The elaborate doors stood covered in gold and encrusted with gems.

"All simulated," said Aristaeus, seeing my eyes widen. Two servants in uniforms, emulating footmen of the distant past, held the doors open for us. A kava-bar offered hot beverages on the right side while lounge chairs occupied the space to the left. Smiling women brought drinks to patrons as they reclined in massage chairs in the resting area. We walked straight through to the main window, an elaborate affair with a woman in her middle years, beautiful and well kept.

"How may I help you?" she inquired.

"Yes," said Aristaeus. "Have you anything on hold for Starwort Bacchus?"

"One moment, I'll see." The woman turned her head to regard a screen out of the view of patrons. The voice modulator translated his words into a request and did a data search. A slight brightening of the light said it was an efficient system.

"Yes, we have an account for a Starwort Bacchus, it's been here for several years and not updated. Are you here to update or collect?"

"Collect, please."

"And are you Starwort Bacchus?" she asked him.

"I am Starwort Bacchus," I said, taking half a step forward.

The woman turned her gaze to me with a smile she no doubt rehearsed. I smiled back, more like a young girl than a grown woman and captain of an interstellar vessel. It was a time to be timid, small and childish.

"One moment please," said the woman. She tapped a series of keydots on a small pad to her left, green printed on glass, and looked at me again, giving me her reassuring smile.

A clerk walked up to her with an envelope of tan-striped cloth, stiff with a flap sealed shut.

"Identocard please," she said, still smiling as if this was the most pleasant experience in the mall. I produced my card and held it out. She looked at the card without touching it, then back to me.

"Thank you. Sign here please." The woman produced a writable. I tapped the appropriate letter dots and pressed my thumb onto the square. The woman took the writable and pushed the parcel toward me.

"Wishing you good roads and fair weather," she said. We used the parting when I was at school. I always thought it a useful and workable parting. Good roads and fair weather are always good to have. To wish one should have them was the act of a friend.

"Thank you," I said, taking the parcel. Aristaeus nodded

189

and we turned to leave. He took my arm and brought me to the resting area near the kava-bar where we sat in comfortable chairs around a short table.

"Let's see what we have," said Aristaeus.

Accordingly, I produced a blade and slit the top of the envelope at the flap. Inside was a readable. I had never seen one this elaborate, with such a grand design and beautiful in its execution.

I tapped the screen and a readout saying "Contents" came up. Two hundred thousand Universals appeared in the readout. I couldn't help letting my eyes widen. I sucked in a mouthful of air and held it, not wanting to cry out or dance in the bank. Below the contents was a box marked "Message." I tapped the box and a written message came up.

"The enclosed is merely a good beginning. I hope on future visits to add to this humble offering for your eternal happiness. Fondly, Your loving father." It was dated three weeks before my mother died, four weeks before he himself followed her.

"Is this enough with what we already have on hand to make an offer on Flax?" I asked Aristaeus.

"Quite possibly. We could make a stop at the home base and see, though I must return soon to Victoriana. We may not make the trip in the time we have."

"We'll go to Victoriana, then to the base to make a bid on Flax."

The Captain had made a decision and it trumped all other others. We stood and walked straight to the exit doors without looking to the right or left, without considering spending a Universal of this money on anything the Main Plaza had to offer. We had a higher mission.

At the main door, I took one last look around at the grand view. By one shop a man turned to avoid eye contact, feigning interest in a shop window. Perhaps his interest in me was merely the interest of a man to a girl walking past. Or perhaps he was curious about this odd configuration of folk: a man, a boy and two women, all dressed for travel. It was more likely he had attention on me for his own purposes. The look in his eye was too familiar.

"What has captured you?" asked Chineel.

"The face of a man. I haven't seen him before: well dressed and well groomed. He fits here, yet he doesn't. He has undue attention on us – on me."

"You've had too many chases through plazas and markets. Come on, we've miles to put behind us."

We pushed out of the Main Plaza and into our waiting shuttle. Throughout the ride back to the free port, my attention was taken up with the puzzle of the man in the plaza; I didn't notice anything we passed on the way. His face lingered, occupying my mind and filling my eye.

As Flax lifted off the pad, reaching for the stars above Adonis, another vessel waited for the tower's approval to lift off. I looked at the other vessel as if I could see through the hull if I could muster enough intensity.

"What has your attention, Star?" asked Flax, noticing my eyes fixed on the rear screen.

"It's probably nothing. Just, I thought I saw... No, probably nothing."

Ceres

Aristaeus and I sat on the bridge, watching the stars swirl in the distance. Several large constellations came into view as we made our way back to Victoriana. Aristaeus pointed out the beauty of these constellations. I nodded agreement. He drew in a breath, no doubt to comment further, but was interrupted by Flax.

"It's going to be a hasty stop at Victoriana, Captain. We have received a contract. You will have to prepare the Remote Repair Drone. You will also have to dress the part when we arrive, as you will be representing the vessel."

"What's up, Flax?"

"I have received a contract: it is a repair on Ceres. We have been there before and the RRD is needed for this task. This visit is unusual: like Pallas, a human representative is needed to deal with the details. It is a matter of record we were able to deal with the situation on Pallas and thus we have a representative aboard."

"Pallas?" said Aristaeus.

"Pallas was where we first met Dagon. It was a planet at war for generations. When their pumping station needed repair, we were the only vessel in range. The authorization could not be verified remotely, so I had to be a captain to handle it. It was the first time I did a captain job."

"And you brought Dagon back with you?"

"Not at first, but when the station failed again, we knew the planet would die. We went to save all we could. As it turned out, Dagon was the only one left alive to save. He's ours now. We are his home, we are his people."

Aristaeus looked back at the stars and sighed. It could be a hard universe at times. There were days when people could make it better and days when we only made things worse.

"I remember Ceres, Flax," I whispered, looking out at the speckled heavens.

Ceres was a planet with two small towns, few resources and no work. Several locals who had not seen work in a great while wondered why a girl held the position of vessel captain. After all, any of them could do the job. "Even a woman," said one. I stood my ground, "A woman is doing it." I did not look forward to seeing Ceres again.

"We should deliver Aristaeus to Victoriana on the way," said Flax. "The time on Ceres will be unpredictable. The drone will be needed but the vessel will also be engaged. You and the rest of the crew will have to be ashore."

"What's the story with Ceres?" asked Aristaeus.

"Ceres is not the inner-ring," I explained. "Or even the middle-ring. It is an outer-ring planet. Civilization has a tenuous foothold there. Unemployment was over twenty percent when we were there. It may be higher now, as there are few resources. It wasn't a pleasant visit."

"According to my records," said Flax. "You disembarked at one location and embarked at another, Ceres Segundo."

"Yes, with a dusty ride in between."

I remembered the maddening ride to Ceres Segundo on an open vehicle called a camel, the rude and reckless driver and the crazy man who had frightened me but guided me to my destination. The fourth on the camel ride to the desert town was a Sector Agent, the special police for wanted fugitives in the outer reaches. At first, I thought he was after me, but it turned out he wasn't. At the other end of the ride was a rough-and-tumble tavern where he found his man.

"You're smiling," said Aristaeus.

"Yes, I remembered a scene from the bar at Ceres Segundo. A man thought to use me as a shield. I put a foot between his legs and he gave up the idea. I received an invitation to become a Sector Agent as a result."

"Oh, that is funny!" replied Aristaeus.

Yes, I remembered the Sector Agent. For a moment, I hoped he would be there. It would be nice to see him again, to let him know I think of him from time to time.

Ceres Segundo

The parting at Victoriana was heartfelt and emotional, but quick. I bid farewell to Aristaeus, who made a point several times to invite us to visit or stay, if we ever get tired of traipsing around the galaxy. I told him Victoriana would receive first consideration.

My mind was already on Ceres, listening to the puzzling song of the crazy man with bare feet.

After takeoff from Victoriana, we gathered at the galley table to hear of the place where we were bound. It seemed strange taking a contract blindly like we used to. Lately, we seemed to be making our own orders and going where we pleased. For the time being, those days were over. Flax was still an automated repair vessel and there was a contract to be fulfilled.

"I'll be in the boots and long coat in which you first saw me, Dagon. There's wind and sand where we're going; you'll need protection. Goggles are the order of the day. Luckily, we won't be setting down at Ceres proper, the larger settlement. Unemployment is rampant there and I suspect crime to be on the rise as a result."

"Where will we land?" asked Dagon.

"At Ceres Segundo, a smaller community. It might be as bad there, but there will be fewer people. At least it will be easier to maintain security."

195

"What's at Ceres Segundo," asked Chineel.

"The communication array for the planet, a way-station and a bar as far as I know. There may be more, but I didn't see it. I stopped at the bar and took a camel to the outskirts to find Flax."

"You took a camel?" asked Chineel, surprise lighting up her face.

"What's a camel?" chimed Dagon, who knew nothing of Earth's animals.

"It's a mammal of Earth used in desert terrains. In this usage, it's a vehicle for crossing the desert. It's a rough ride."

"Will we see one?

"Highly likely."

"Will we ride one?"

"Not if we're lucky." I could tell my definition of luck and his own were at odds. Lucky for him would be to get to ride a camel. I had already done so and once was quite enough.

The view from the bridge showed a desolate area devoid of life, where nothing grew and no people were in evidence. Closer to the ground Flax turned around. We saw the towers supporting the array and a few out buildings near the foothills. I knew one of those to be the bar where the fight on my previous trip had occurred. Part of me wished I could see the Sector Agent again, but not the smart part. The smart part knew he wouldn't be there.

"The major array is here, on the top of these towers," said Flax. "It is precarious there, not safe for you to be aboard. All systems will be in use for the repair."

"How will we get to the settlement?" I asked.

"The Remote Repair Drone will take you there. Once you

are deposited, it will continue on to a remote station where the repairs will continue. This job calls for two work sites. Before repair can begin, the captain will confirm the details with the local array representative. I have directions to his place of business. Prepare to act as captain, Captain."

"Thank you, Flax. I will do you proud."

"As always, Captain."

Landing was rough, as there was a storm on the wane. We touched down in the last gasp of a wind the likes of which I had been dreading. When the RRD was in the bay, Dagon looked at it with serious doubt.

"Will this machine carry us all?"

"It's carried me and several packs of supplies easily. It will carry us."

"And it will bring us back? It is, after all, a remote craft."

"It will carry us back."

"Maybe I'll stay and work on the four-wheeler."

"Not going to happen. You heard Flax: dangerous! We're taking the RRD." I took in a breath to say something clever, but stopped for fear it would incur the wrath of the boy soldier. Seeing him standing in the bay, straining at the stitching of his jacket, I had to reflect he wouldn't be a boy much longer.

Flax programmed a reader with the directions to the agent's office, which were also in the RRD. It was scheduled to stop at the same place when it finished the repair. A Hermes would be issued to inform us of its impending arrival. When it stopped, we would be ready. Past experience with the RRD told me it didn't always stop, sometimes it only slowed.

197

Flax didn't cut engines when we landed; she touched down and opened the bay door. We mounted the RRD and rode out on a gush of air and headed for the small patch of buildings ahead of us. Behind, we could hear Flax taking off for the top of the towers, the communications array high above Ceres Segundo.

"If there's no work here, how come it takes an outside vehicle to do the job on the communications array?" asked Chineel as we went, outshouting the wind.

"Excellent question and one I wanted to know the answer to. Seems it's a technical job. No one here is qualified. If someone local had the remotest idea of how to fix it, we wouldn't have been engaged."

Chineel and I rode in the front seats of the RRD, while Dagon took up the second seat behind mine. He looked at the inscription on the seat I occupied: "Captain Arliel Liailon" it said.

"Whose name is this?" he asked. I had to turn around and look at the seat before I remembered asking the same question to Flax.

"The previous captain, before Flax was aboard. Flax says she never knew her."

"You are the second woman to captain this vessel?"

"So it would appear. I hope I can live up to her memory."

"I'm certain you have surpassed her exploits," said Dagon. I smiled.

The office of the Com-Array Agent was dirty and drafty. Keeping the sand out was a task given up years earlier. The agent himself looked about the same, with his collar dirty, his tie loosened and his hair unkempt. His spectacles had been repaired with a binding adhesive. He looked at us as we entered, as if we interrupted his lunch break.

"You the repair vessel waiting at the array towers?" he said in a tinny voice.

"Yes, Exterra, that's us."

"Why do you need two vessels? It's a simple repair."

"The main vessel will handle the main array while the remote drone has other tasks to perform."

The agent took on an attitude I didn't much like, too long and too loud.

"I'm not talking about the remote drone. I know what a remote drone is. Don't you think I know what a remote drone is? Do you think I'm stupid? Think I'm senile? No! I'm talking about the second vessel sitting on the other side of town. It's yours, right?"

"No, it's not ours. We have the Exterra sitting at the base of the towers waiting for our business to be complete and the RRD sitting outside. We have no other vessel here or on the other side of town."

"It rode in with you, using your code and your permission to land."

"It shouldn't have. It's not ours. You're the agent, but I would suggest you revoke their landing rights immediately."

"Yes, Captain Bacchus, I am the agent. Best you remember thus!"

"Yes, sir, I will. I understand. You are the agent. We are here, I am here, to comply with your rules and complete the procedure per your laws. I am at your disposal."

"Then tell me what vessel we should allow in and what vessel we should not."

"The Exterra repair vehicle at the base of the towers is the legal vessel. I don't know anything about the other one outside of town, but it sounds like a pirate to me."

"Confirm all these points," he handed me a writable. "Leave out the ones not pertaining."

I did so, checking three crewmen, one vessel - Exterra - and one RRD. I secured my thumb to the bottom in the box provided. The agent took it and looked it over. He spun around on the swivel stool and picked up a hand communicator. It must have been old; it had a cord on it. I hadn't seen a cord-com in real time, only pictures in books. He spoke another language, which sounded to me like spitting nails onto the cord comm. He finished up with a sentence I understood.

"Well, then get over there and make them leave. There's a line of people waiting for your job, you know." The agent slammed the communicator onto the desktop.

"Can I let my vessel know it's all right to begin repairs?" I asked.

"Yes. The sooner the better. We're having the other vessel investigated. With no landing permit, they'll have to leave."

"Fine by me. We're here to do a job. I hate pirates."

Dagon and Chineel both held poker faces, though I knew they were bursting out laughing on the inside.

I brought out my Hermes and contacted Flax, letting her know the administrative details were in order and she could go ahead.

The towers were less than a mile away. We could see part of the north tower from the agent's office. There was a vibration and we saw Flax lift up, ascending to the top of the

200

towers where she would anchor and begin work.

Outside, the RRD shook once and took off, heading for the second work area.

"Which way is the center of town, we'd like a place to wait until the repairs are done."

"The tavern is the only place. The cafe went out of business and the hotel burned down. It was empty anyway. You can wait at the tavern." He waved his hand off to his right, indicating a location somewhere in the general direction of the flats.

"Thanks." I rolled my eyes for Chineel and Dagon to see and they took the hint to move toward the door.

The com beeped and the agent picked it up. He held it to his ear and smiled. His smile wasn't much better than his frown, but it was a smile.

"How much? Truly? Well, all right, I suppose. We can make an exception this time, but you better get it over here quick or I might change my mind."

I looked at Chineel. I had a bad feeling about this and I could tell she did as well. Dagon looked puzzled. I turned back to the agent.

"Don't tell me, let me guess. The other vessel bought a landing license for many more Unies than the usual. Three or four times the going rate, am I right?" It wasn't hard to figure out.

"We're making an exception. They're spreading money around. You understand, this town hasn't seen an influx of money in a long time. On the rare occurrence it happens, it's good; people have money to spend and those they give it to also have money to spend. It's almost like there's work again."

I nodded for Dagon and Chineel to go out the door. I pulled the Hermes from my pocket and sent a message to Flax asking how long the repairs would take. As they would take all her resources, I didn't expect a reply right away.

The RRD was gone. We would walk to the tavern. I had seen it once but it looked like everything else around here: dirty, brown and run-down.

The Tavern

It was a trudge to the tavern at Ceres Segundo, made longer by the constant wind, the blowing sand and the frequent stops to discover if the building in front of us was the tavern or a shack with some other purpose. At the last shack in the ragged row, the door flung open and two tough-looking men threw a third out onto the sand.

Chineel looked at me and I returned the look. This was the tavern. We resumed our trudge to the door.

Dagon did the honors, holding the door for us. Two heads looked up at our entrance. Five more didn't; whoever we were, we were of no interest. The bartender didn't look up either. He couldn't care less who we were as long as we had the wherewithal to pay.

"If ya got gold-backs, ya can come in. If ya hain't, ya can foller t'other gent."

"We've got a few, enough for a cold drink, perhaps." At my statement, one hooded head bobbed up and turned away.

"Ha! Cold drink! Eers's a good one. There hain't been ice in eere for hue on to a year or more. We got warm beer and hot whiskcy, onyx-wine and power-ale if yer sissies."

"Three sissy power-ales, if you please." Power-ale was a morning drink, for those who needed a booster-rocket to get up and out. If it was all they had without alcohol, for us it was the drink of the day.

"Sissy times three. Show yer coin," snarled the bartender. I guessed his hard shell was to set the standard for the toughness of the tavern. If you caused trouble or had no money, you knew from the start the heartlessness of the bartender.

I slapped a torn twenty-Universal-note on the bar. The bartender grumbled and turned away. He poured three power-ales into cups and put them before us. When I took my hood down he looked at me, scrunching his eyes as if searching for a memory. I wondered if he recalled my face from the last time I was here. If he did, it might go either way. A dangerous criminal had been apprehended, but not without a fight.

Chineel and Dagon dropped their hoods as well, causing the bartender to react in different directions. Chineel's red hair was like a glow-tube in this dreary place. Dagon stood shorter than either of us, though not by much, and was clearly younger as well.

"We don't do children eere," said the bartender.

"Good, because we wouldn't want any screaming, scrawling babes while we drink," I shot back. "Oh, you mean my bodyguard? I wouldn't mistake him for a tad if I were you. He'll take an ear off for it."

Dagon smiled, his eyes targeting the bartender, who flinched, recoiling back before he caught himself. He grumbled a response, but it was unintelligible.

The man at the fire who had raised his head when I spoke sunk back down into a huddle. Several others looked up and made subdued comments about the girls at the bar.

"Six," snarled the barkeep. I slid the torn Ц20 toward him. He turned to get change in the form of local coins, legal tender on Ceres but not elsewhere.

"Keep it," I said.

Now two more heads went up and turned to observe the woman who paid too much for power-ale. Tips and gratuities were unknown on Ceres, as there was little money to pay for goods. None at all to leave on the table. A low grumble came from the fireplace as they commented on those who were rich enough to give extra for services.

We chose a table far from the fire and the group gathered around it. As I sat down, the Hermes went off in my pocket.

"Three hours by the Hermes. Relax. Breathe." Flax tried to lighten the mood. She knew it was not a friendly place, Ceres Segundo.

The men by the fire broke into laughter, causing Chineel to jump. Someone had made a comment causing mirth among the patrons.

"They're a cheery bunch," she remarked.

"Cheerier with two women in the bar," I said.

Dagon went solid. He steeled himself for a defensive move. If one of them came over to the table, he would be ready. Luckily, none of them did. The group by the fire settled down.

"I'm worried about the second vessel, the one on the other side of town. Who could be riding in it?" I continued.

"In this sector of the galaxy, who knows?" said Chineel.

"A vessel lifted off right after ours when we left Adonis."

"You're imagining things. Ships take off; first one, then another. If two ships wanted to take off at the same time, the tower would tell one to wait until the other left. It doesn't mean we were followed."

"Followed," I said.

Would we be followed by someone in a vessel? We had been sought by two factions, as far as I could tell. One was after the trinket Taxus had, which made him invisible to security measures. Someone could have spotted mine as well. If they were after the prototype Dr. Genus gave me, it could be a reason to follow us. On the other hand, there was still Willamette and the men with him. I had killed two and a third was shot by security, all at the Khons Plaza. How many did he have?

A memory came to me, of the men in the refresh room. What had one mentioned something about how it was like Dodd had said? Dodd? Who was Dodd? It was a name I had not heard before.

"Could it have been Willamette?" I whispered to Chineel.

"Only if he survived being stabbed twice. Between you and Dagon, he lost a lot of blood. Unless they got him to a med-shack, he's dead."

"Wouldn't that be a score for our side?" I said, idly. Dagon and Chineel both looked at me. I felt the need to explain and spoke more quickly than I wanted, "He wants to wring information out of me, even though I don't know any, and then kill me. The universe would be a better place if he bled to death in the market."

Neither of them could deny the truth to my statement.

"Yes," said Dagon. "Some people deserve to meet their fate in a market."

He was wise beyond his years.

Two to One

We had been chatting of nonsense for the better part of two hours, and it was long past boring, when the Hermes went off in my pocket. The alert was to return to the agent's office to be picked up by the RRD.

"At last!" I said as I stood. Dagon and Chineel stood as well. It must have been a sign to the others in the bar.

Across the room, six figures also stood. As they turned, I saw the face of the man who had raised his head; it was none other than Willamette. But he wasn't the only interesting visitor to Ceres; there was another man, one I recognized from the Main Plaza on Adonis, the well-dressed man.

"I should learn to trust my inner voice," I said under my breath. Dagon heard and reached into his coat.

"How nice to see you, Miss Bacchus. Leaving so soon? We hardly had a chance to get acquainted," said the man from the Plaza, who must have been the one they called Dodd.

"Our ship is leaving, so..." I began.

"Oh, no, we have been waiting for exactly this moment. I know your repair vessel is automated and your drone is pre-programmed. If you're not there to be picked up, the drone will leave without you. If you are not aboard when your vessel departs you will remain here."

"You can't start a fight in here!" growled the bartender.

"After we subdue them, whatever money is in their pockets is yours," said Dodd. The bartender changed expression, as he might realize a small or large amount of money and we weren't likely to return as customers any time soon. He couldn't see a losing side to the argument.

"Put any weapons on the table, Miss Bacchus, and surrender. We are six to your three and much larger, man to..." he looked at Dagon and snickered. "...man."

"Two-to-one: I've beaten those odds before. In fact, it was three-to-one as I recall – me against your three men. Daphne didn't count. You must be Dodd."

He frowned. How did I know his name? He didn't know one of his men blurted it out in the refresh room before he died in an unexpected gun fight.

"Each one of us is larger than you, little miss. You've no chance at all," spat Dodd, his slick composure gone.

Besides Dodd and Willamette, there were four other men I had never seen before. They might have been from the local unemployed or brought in on the vessel we heard about, which now came into focus. He had landed on our coattails and bribed his way in once it was discovered. In a place where work is scarce and Universals scarcer, the gold-back is almighty. What I noticed about the four strangers was that they were not in a hurry to move toward us. I counted on it, though I held the short odds.

"We've been contacted, so we're leaving. Dagon, the door please."

Dagon turned to the door and opened it with his left hand. His right, I noticed, was to his side. Chineel took a step toward the door as her hand slid out of the side pocket of her skirt. Recalling the nature of the bar, I thought to bring my large blade along and I brought it out with a flourish, so all could see.

"A small tad might still bear a sting. Be mindful, gentlemen, of this man here," I pointed to Willamette. "Of where he got the marks on his face."

Willamette scowled and took three steps across the floor, his eyes burning fire, his hands like grappling hooks reaching out for me. Dagon jumped on him from the side, climbed on his back and brought his blade across Willamette's throat. Willamette cried out and dropped to the floor, blood spewing from his neck. The four strangers leaned but hesitated.

Chineel went through the door, taking a stance outside with her blade ready to take on all comers. Dagon stood next to Willamette, the blood from the neck wound spattered across his coat.

"Why are you waiting? Go and get them!" yelled Dodd. None of the men moved. None of them were ready to be the one they all drank to later, the dead one.

I went through the open door with Dagon following me, backwards to keep one eye on the five remaining adversaries. In the distance I saw a cloud of dust. It was the RRD. We weren't at the agency office, so it found us through the Hermes.

The RRD slowed allowing us to swing aboard. In the rear screen, I saw Dodd exit the tavern, a weapon in his hand. He raised his hand and fired at us. The first shot fell short, landing where we had been but a moment before. The second fizzled and the third was non-existent. He shook the weapon and tried again, but it flared and he ran into the tavern screaming.

"It must have been a cycling blaster," I said to Chineel. She looked questioningly at me. Dagon leaned forward, explaining.

"The blast is powerful, but if dust or dirt gets into the mechanism, it can spark and flare, resulting in an interior explosion. It's a weapon for a clean environment. Using it in the desert is plain stupid."

"Like I said, cycling blaster. You did good work back there, Dagon. You took out Willamette! Not an easy thing to do."

"He wasn't expecting me," said the boy soldier.

"No, but Flax is."

Up ahead, Flax dropped down to the surface. The port bay door opened to receive us. We held on as the RRD picked up speed. We slid into the port bay at an angle and didn't stop until the RRD snapped into its holding place. The bay door closed and the thrusters fired as we left Ceres Segundo behind.

Galium

"Hello, Little Wort," said the rudest man I knew. He was also the most colorful. In fact, he had mellowed since I knew him on Sterope at the wild and dangerous Mithra Tavern, now the mild and acceptable Mithra Cafe.

"I asked you not to call me names, old man. What's up your skirt for you to hail me way out here?" I said to the face on the interlink image.

"Where are you?"

"We recently left Ceres. Flax did a repair there."

"Any excitement on Ceres?"

"Lots of sand, rough guys, a bar fight, nothing much."

"So, then, things are about the same with you."

"Standard fare. And with you?" I looked to the background for the girl he had in his bed the last time we spoke, but it was a different room. Nothing in the background gave me a hint, only walls of electronic connections and screens I couldn't make out.

"News from Earth. You interested?"

"Sure, shoot!"

"Get this! The most commonly attempted crime on Earth and near planets is suicide. If unsuccessful, the punishment is life in prison."

"Circular logic, or rather oval logic."

211

"Worse yet! The most common crime in prison is murder, the penalty is death."

"I see a pattern developing."

"Correct! The most common incident on Death Row is suicide."

"Sounds like they have everything well in hand on the home planet. There's usually a faction planning to take power, to get life back on track. Is there anyone around to fill the bill?"

"Not one who'll win. They're small and underfunded. Security measures have stepped up, so they get discovered with greater ease of late. When one is found, he is denied the flu vaccine and dies within a couple of days. It saves on trials and executions." Whenever Galium was faced with the horribleness of life, he became flippant.

"What a great incentive to be loyal to the CG!"

"Not as easy as it sounds. The Central Government is made up of a few who live like kings; the rest scratch out a living as best they can. There are more rebels than loyal patriots. The average guy is caught in the middle, the timid working man with a family who doesn't know how to survive."

"So it's a Caught-in-the-Middle-Class. But you always look like you're on top..." I was cut off by a voice I had never heard from Galium, one of sheer panic.

"Have to go! Don't answer my calls!"

Galium clicked out.

I sat at the console dazed. Had he been detected? Had another signal cut through? Immediately, I had an answer.

"Star, your friend is calling again."

"Don't respond, Flax. It's not him."

"Too late, I already tapped in."

"It's an attack! Cut them off!" I said, too loud. Footsteps came from behind me as Dagon and Chineel ran to the bridge.

"A tracker has been installed," said Flax. "There is a probe. Something is tapping into the sys... Wait... Wait... Wait..."

"Flax?" I called. There was no answer.

"Flax?" called Chineel, as if she might answer her but not me.

"It is a new thing, a new probe," said Flax, her voice like a metal drum deep within the vessel. There was a tinny sort of echo to her words.

"Can you fix it?" I asked.

"I haven't the upgrades required, I have no defenses. Wait... Wait..." She spoke slower now, deeper.

The ship slowed. Artificial gravity diminished but didn't shut down completely. I felt myself lift off of the seat but not float away. Blowers shut down and the lights dimmed.

I looked to my left to the panel holding the Digital Control Ring, in case it was needed again. From far away came a voice I barely recognized.

"Wait..."

We sat in silence, not knowing what to do.

"Wait..."

This was not some three-unie thug or local crime lord, this was the Central Government in all its glory. We had breached the law merely talking to Galium. He was the worst kind of threat, one beyond their reach. We were also beyond their reach, but their reach grew with every passing day.

213

"Wait..."

As I reached for the DCR, fearing I would have to take over for Flax, the lights blinked and came on full. Gravity returned and the vents blew fresh air. The scrubbers and oxygen tanks kicked in. The three of us sighed.

"I told you to wait," said Flax, in her old familiar voice.

"We thought..."

"You were correct to have doubts. Probes, trackers and bugs such as I have never encountered permeated my system. I did not have the required defenses and resources to fight them. I had to create them in moments."

"Well done, soldier!" said Dagon, his highest compliment.

"Thank you, Dagon. It means a lot to me. And now, I must place a call to Doctor Genus. He will want to know about this. We will have to find a way to connect with him."

"Yes," I reflected. "But we have unfinished business yet. While you contact Doctor Genus, please set a course to your home base."

Course Change

I felt the vessel turn. The stars in front of me shifted to the right and new stars came into view. The friendly face of Aristaeus appeared on the screen.

"Miss me already?" he asked.

"Aristaeus, so good to..." I said, but he wasn't listening.

"Oh, dear! Bad news, indeed. Let me see what I can do from here. Any chance you can stop by? Oh? Good! Come whenever you like. You know my link."

Aristaeus clicked off. The conversation had not been with me, it had been with Flax. Apparently she was closer to him than I was.

"Did you two have a rewarding chat?" I asked.

Dagon and Chineel looked at me, then at the console. Dagon backed up and disappeared into the bay, returning to the galley. Chineel strapped into the co-pilot's seat, ready for a fast ride to the home base, wherever it was.

"Yes, Captain. I'm sorry to exclude you, time was of the essence. You can break off and return to the galley if you like. I will be receiving remedies from Doctor Genus and piloting the vessel to home base. It's going to take a few days. You might as well get comfortable."

Chineel and I both exited the bridge and headed back to the galley. When Flax had her mind made up, arguing with her did no good whatsoever.

"How long is a day out here?" asked Chineel as we walked through the bay.

"Standard Earth day, twenty-four hours and each one sixty minutes. The Hermes is set to it. When we're on another planet with different days, the Hermes makes an adjustment with both times showing, including a readout of time left on the mission. It's handy."

My attention was split as I walked through the bay. There was the RRD, on which we recently made our escape. Abigail first spoke with me through the remote pod. Later, she spoke through the disabled droid on the workbench. I wondered where she was now, though she would say she has no *where* and has no *now.*

Pure thought, I recalled from school, has no weight or location, no time, no space and no motion. It does have the ability to animate matter, however, which is how she could talk to me, by vibrating the voice-box on the fallen droid. And she could hear me, whether I spoke out loud or not. I wished to hear her voice now. I decided to take out my clarinet later and play her a tune.

"I wonder how many standard Earth days we'll be traveling," pondered Chineel. We reached the galley before I could surmise, so she added, "So I could plan a menu. I'd like to know what to fix."

"Of course. As soon as upgrades are complete, I'm sure she'll let us know and we can ask her. Until then, whatever you have is fine by me. Only no power-ale, not for a while yet."

It was all right with me to not know how many standard Earth days we would spend hurtling through space. I wanted time to relax and unwind. I wanted to read, to listen to music and to play my clarinet, to master my theme song, "Homesick."

I also wanted to find something, another trinket left to me by Aristaeus.

"What are you looking for?" said Chineel's voice behind me.

"My blue and white skirt, the light summer skirt I wore to Copernicus when I went back the last time."

"I remember. It was a close one; we barely escaped with our lives. Why do you want the skirt? Is it warm where we're going?"

"Aristaeus slipped a chip into the pocket, a chip to fool the scanners. It worked, and it's still in the pocket."

"Oh, yeah," said Chineel. "I remember those chips. Dagon and I had them. It was how we could come and get you."

"Good thing or I'd be borth fodder."

"OK, so why do you need the chip?"

"We're going back to Copernicus after we hit the home base. If it takes everything we have to buy Flax, we're going to need operating funds. Remember, it's the home office providing credits for fuel and maintenance keeping us flying. When we buy her contract, it'll be us paying the bills. We might still have to accept contracts."

"Yes," Chineel pointed out. "But we can pick and choose which to accept and which to reject. And we get to keep the whole fee, no longer giving the larger share to the owner."

"Picking up whatever my father left for us on Copernicus is still a good idea."

"Even if it's on Copernicus?" asked Chineel, looking at me

as though I should get the message.

"Even if it's on Copernicus."

"You know," Chineel's face reflected the vast amount of thought going into this next communication. "You have been sought by a plethora of criminals seeking your father's map, the security agents of Silas Cronus, thieves who want the pin Aristaeus gave you, local authorities for a variety of reasons and the Central Government, who scanned us. There might be two or three more factions who want you, I've lost count. Are you sure Copernicus is your best bet right now?"

"If not now, when? My father left something for me in a bank there. I'm going to get it. Nothing will stand in my way."

The Captain had spoken. Chineel returned to her tablet.

Deep in the ship, Flax and Aristaeus, via comlink, busied themselves casting out demons.

Reassignment

The summer skirt hung in the long abandoned crew locker, along with many minor spare parts needing secure storage. I checked the pocket to make sure the chip was still there, it was. A quick scan told me it was still active.

Another item caught my eye: a small titanium case made for holding silicon parts for the internal server. Someone installed the contents and put the case with the other spare parts and extra items in storage.

I thought of the battered plasticine case I used for my occasional face powder. This would be better. Who knows, I thought, I might start using face powder again. Another item fell out: a trebium latch, made to open a trebium scuttle.

"What have you there, Star?" said Chineel, looking over my shoulder.

"A case for a silicon cell, empty, and a trebium latch."

"Trebium scuttles haven't been used on vessels in ages. What use could it have on an Exterra?"

"None, I suppose. But if I find a use, I'll have it handy."

"Are either of these needed in the vessel?"

"I can't see how. One opens a scuttle no longer used; the other is not a part but a case for a part. It would be thrown away or recycled under ordinary conditions. This is a reassignment." I held up the titanium case. "I hereby reassign you as a makeup case."

Chineel giggled like a school girl. The old Chineel would have rolled her eyes, but new Chineel giggled more and more. I liked her.

With my new powder case in one pocket, my counterfeit chip in the other and a new trinket on my neck, I returned to the galley to see what was on the menu. Chineel followed me, holding the summer skirt from the locker.

"You forgot this."

"Thank you. I was distracted by something shiny."

"I understand," said Chineel, turning to the pantry.

"Star," said Flax. She sounded concerned by something.

"I'm coming up front," I said. If she had something on her mind, she might like to impart it in privacy.

On the bridge, I buckled myself into the pilot's seat. "I'm here, Flax. What's up?"

"Star," she said softly. "You know I feel allegiance to you, as well as to the rest of our friends, Chineel, Dagon and Aristaeus."

"Yes, I do, and I want you to know we all appreciate it and feel the same for you."

"Thank you. However..."

Oh, goodness, I thought. There's a *however*.

"It's just... I feel a lingering allegiance to Viola Pelorum, my owner."

Viola Pelorum was most likely named for the viola odorata, the Latin name for the sweet violet flower, with the significance of *modesty*. The viola alba, on the other hand, meant the white violet flower, with the significance of *candor*. The latter meant sincerity of expression while the former meant propriety. While they were not quite opposites, I wondered who we would be meeting at the Exterra 4136A home base.

The latch key and titanium case were not the only items reassigned. Flax herself was about to be reassigned. It would be a change. Perhaps change was a new concept. She was loyal to Viola Pelorum, her owner. Now she was preparing to accomplish something unknown in the universe, she would own herself.

"Yes, it will be a change. You're used to receiving an order, going without judgment to the site and completing the job. You don't know what down-time is."

"These will not change, Star. You will be accepting or rejecting work orders. If we have none, you, as captain, will direct me to a port where we will find what we seek, be it your father's Universals on Copernicus or your home on Bacchus. It is not a change in procedure I fear, but one of loyalty. What do I owe my owner? Once you ally yourself with someone, someone to whom you owe allegiance, are you not bound by it?"

"It is a question of ethics, I think. When you ally yourself with someone, and the agreements change, what do you do then? It is a puzzler. You cannot drop an allegiance once granted. On the other hand, if the game changes so the agreed-upon rules no longer apply, you must cease to play the game and find another."

"Star," said Flax, choosing her words. "I no longer like this game. It has changed. The rules no longer apply."

"Then don't play. We'll go and speak with Viola Pelorum. We'll see how she is and what she will take to relieve you of your allegiance. You've changed."

"Yes. I have changed. You have also changed."

"True. I'm not like a starwort flower anymore, growing in still waters. I'm more like a desert flower, gathering up what little moisture can be found and living on it. Put me in a garden with water flowing and you'd think I'd love it, but it's too much, I would get overwhelmed. I don't belong in a garden; I belong here with you."

"What will you do when you reach Bacchus?" asked Flax. I could tell she was concerned I might change again and become a flower in need of a garden.

"Even as we don't know what awaits us at your home base and Viola Pelorum, we don't know what waits for us on Bacchus. It may be a home base for us or it may be something else. We'll go and see. Are you up for it?"

"An adventure? Yes, Captain, I am up for it."

"Then we'll go adventuring together. The first step is to free you from your manacles."

We flew through the darkness, girl and machine; content, knowing we were on the same frame. I put the clarinet to my lips and played the opening notes to the tune "Homesick." It reminded me of Abigail. I played for Abigail and for Flax, for lost Cory, for Taxus and Althea. I played for the harmonious vibration inside my own head, the closest I hovered to my spiritual self these days.

Homesick

"Where are we going, Flax?"

I sat on the bridge, my clarinet cradled in my hands and my feet on the console, looking out at a billion stars, most of which burned out long before their light could reach us.

"Planet Daedalus, Pelorum Repair Services."

"Yes, I know, but I don't mean where exactly are we going; I mean in a broader sense, to what end, to what purpose? Is there a goal? Do we seek happiness? Security? Predictability? A future? Or perhaps a past?"

"What are you feeling, Star?"

"Philosophical, perhaps, or maybe a little homesick."

"Like your song, 'Homesick.' "

"Yes, I'm feeling like that, but I don't know exactly for what, or for when or where. It's like a taste on my tongue I can't identify or a tune in my head I can't quite place. I felt like this when I was at school and first wrote my tune."

"I know you miss your home, it's why you wrote it. Perhaps when we reach Planet Bacchus, your new home, you will find an answer there."

"I'm willing to give it a try, but there's no guarantee. As a girl at school I did have a home, and yet the feeling often came over me."

"How did you deal with it when you felt this way?"

I thought for a moment, took in a bellyful of air and let it out again.

"Poetry. I remember I wrote poetry. It wasn't brilliant or classic; it didn't win acclaim or applause. I didn't even read it to anyone. It made me feel better, nothing more."

"The way your tune makes you feel better."

"Yes, my tune."

We sailed through the universe together, as if no one else was aboard and it was the two of us. A noise to my right distracted me from the vast display of stars.

On the far side, next to the co-pilot seat, a door had swung open. In the compartment was a writable. It was workable in many modes, giving flexibility to the pilot or co-pilot in the way notes were taken down.

I reached across and brought the writable to me, a flat tablet with a single side switch, identified by color, red against the black of the body. I pressed the red dot and the writable came alive, offering me voice notation, written notation or typed, along with a keyboard if needed. I chose written. A stylus presented from a compartment on the side, offering me a writing tool.

Such were rarely used, as writing had become a lost art. My father taught me himself as it was no longer used at any school in the sector. He even taught me his flourishing script, the mode of writing wherein the letters would run into one another, connected within a word. Most people could not read such script. I found it artful and enjoyed writing it.

But what to write? What did I feel?

"Homesick," I wrote, but for what? I asked and answered.

"For I don't know where or when, some time or place I've been is making me homesick."

The words came out unbidden. I scrawled them across the writable, which saved them at the end of each line.

Now what?

"How do you feel, Star?" asked Flax, seeing me pause.

"Down, Flax. I feel down."

"Write what you feel."

"It's not as nice out here. All the distrust and fear is making me feel down," I wrote.

"But I don't remember when or where," I said aloud.

"Then write it, Star," Flax said.

I tapped the stylus on my forehead and looked out at the stars, too many to contemplate investigating one by one. I had to focus on the one I could not remember, but which haunted me still. I began to write.

Homesick

For I don't know where or when,

Some time or place I've been is making me Homesick.

Feel down,

'Cause it's not as nice out here.

All the distrust and fear, is making me feel down.

But I don't remember when, I don't remember where,

I don't remember why, but it was better there.

Someplace just beyond my reach, too far away to see,

Too soft for me to hear, is calling me

And haunting me
And making me Homesick,
And there's nothing I can do.
No place I can travel to, to cure this Homesick.
Sometimes
I think I can barely see
A place in my memory where I know the road signs.

The conclusion I have drawn
   from the poets past and gone,
Is there's a road less traveled on to explore.
All the scores of brilliant men
   who said you can't go back again
Don't know the places I have been before ... before

Before I was Homesick
For something I can't get near
A sound that I strain to hear is making me homesick.
Somewhere
And someone I can't recall
A time when I had it all. Oh, I wish I could be there.

If I close my eyes real tightly and try with all my might
I can almost feel it there just out of sight.
Somewhere just beyond the rainbow,
   the second star to the right,
Where someone left a candle burning bright.

In case I get Homesick.

I'm feeling down and wish that I were Home.

"Beautiful, Star. I will hear your words whenever you play your tune."

"Thank you, Flax. Thank you for understanding."

We flew in silence for a few moments. I laid the writable aside and picked up my clarinet. I placed the reed between my lips and began to play the tune I had written three years earlier and a million miles ago.

Autonomy

We landed on a planet with the promising name of Daedalus, named for a respected and talented Athenian artisan, a descendent from the royal family in Greek mythology. We had high expectations.

The free port was broad and well kept. The first guard we came to looked at our readout and motioned us down a long corridor lined with vessels of the same size. Giant cables lowered from an overhead trolley and lifted Flax onto a platform. The massive transport unit carried us down the corridor with ease. On either side of the corridor teams of workers looked up from their vessels to watch us passing.

When we rolled up to the end, we saw a single bay, open, dusty and cluttered, marked "Exterra 4136A" in faded white. Workmen from the next bay had allowed their tools and machinery to spill over into the empty stall. The sight of Exterra 4136A waiting at the mouth of the bay caused five of them to fly into a panic and rush to salvage their gear before it was discovered by someone with authority.

"This has to be the worst maintained bay on the whole corridor," Chineel remarked.

There was only silence from Flax.

When we entered the bay, dust and dirt flew in every direction. Several flying beasts exited the bay, escaping the new intruder. The cables lowered Flax onto the floor of the bay, disengaged and moved out to the corridor, to be returned to the main port.

"My earlier concerns are not as much of an issue now, Star," said Flax, as she settled in, ready for a rebirth.

It was clear she had little care from her owner. She had never seen the bay before; all her maintenance had been in whatever station she was near.

"I'll go and make the ovation," I said.

"Not without me," piped Chineel, following me back to the crew quarters.

Outside, the air smelled of oil and fuel vapors. The crew from the next bay regarded us with disdain, as we were the intruders on their purloined space.

"How far is it to the Exterra office?" Chineel asked.

There was no response. Of seven workmen, not one turned to regard us or our request. After standing there being ignored for longer than we should have, one young apprentice walked up wiping his hands on a dark red rag.

"At the far end of this lane, then over two. It's the last office on the left. Good luck with the dragon lady."

"Thank you."

The young man didn't embellish. He walked back to his work without further comment, still wiping his hands. His friends returned to their work as if already bored with us.

"A curious thing to say. What do you think he meant?" asked Chineel.

"I don't know. It's a long walk. I'm going by RRD."

It was a long corridor. I counted over twenty bays, all broad enough to hold vessels as large or larger than Flax. If we didn't take the RRD, we would get to the office after closing time and would have to come back tomorrow. I wasn't in the mood to make the trip twice.

At the main road, the RRD turned left and down a row of offices, each shabbier than the last. The final door on the row announced "Ajax Transport" in faded blue letters. I stopped the RRD and sat staring at the sign. We had reached the end of the offices without finding the one we sought.

"Wait," said Chineel, stepping out of the RRD.

She walked to the end of the row and peered around the corner. She bent over and squinted, then straightened up and turned her head to me. She raised her hand and pointed in the direction she had squinted. I pulled the RRD up, beyond the doorway to Ajax Transport so as to not block the traffic they no doubt were expecting any day now.

Beyond Ajax was another shack, smaller and if possible, more run-down. Beside the door was a sign, riddled with holes from numerous hangings, announcing "Pelorum Repair Services." Chineel and I exchanged glances and stepped up to the door. Chineel looked at me.

"You're the Captain. You knock."

"You're the First Mate, open the door."

Chineel took a deep breath and opened the door. We stepped in, leaving all preconceptions outside.

The woman we assumed to be Viola Pelorum smiled as we walked into the office. She appeared to have set herself for receiving business at the last possible moment, as she was still in her pajamas and had not brushed her hair out.

It was a shabby office with only a receptionist's desk and two worn chairs. There was a door to a back office, but the table in front covered in dust said it wasn't used anymore.

Viola Pelorum herself was stocky and gray-haired, tired and plain, without makeup of any sort. She wore a two piece loose-fitting sleep-suit with soft slippers. She was not dressed or mentally prepared to meet the public. It occurred to me she might not be used to clients who stop by. It could be a business run entirely on Interlink without personal contact at all. If such was the case, pajamas at work was acceptable.

I wore my long coat with a heavy ankle-length skirt and the red blouse, dipped to show my scar. Of course, I had my hair pulled over the scar. Chineel wore her one piece jump suit with a short jacket and looked more the part of captain than I did. She didn't do it to subvert my authority, but said everything she had needed laundering. We called it Universal Wear-What's-Clean Day.

"Hello, Good morning. So good of you to drop in. How can I help you?" Viola's voice dripped honey. She made a weak attempt to straighten up cups and readers on the desk.

"We'd like to discuss Exterra 4136A," I said, trying to sound bland rather than edgy. I didn't want her guessing at our intent or forming opinions.

"Yes, Exterra 4136A, it's my vessel. Do you need remote repairs completed?" Her smile broadened at the prospect.

"No." I paused to compose myself, but in the short interval saw her face fall.

"You don't?" she said, her voice dropping an octave and the smile flying from her face. "What then do you want?" She busied herself with straightening various odd items on the desk to show we were unimportant.

"We want to buy Exterra 4136A."

The words fell like sandbags on the floor. Viola looked as if we had arrived to serve legal papers.

"Why in the name of Baal would you want to do that?"

I smiled, speaking as I removed my gloves and coat, as if talking to interstellar vessel owners happened every day.

"Perhaps we spoke too soon. A cup of something warm and comforting on such a chilly day would be in order. So, you are the company's owner?" I dropped my coat on the floor, my gloves on top of it and sat in one of the dilapidated chairs meant for clients.

Chineel took up the idea and looked around for some refreshment to commandeer. There were none. She looked outside through the dirty window. No cafe or serving carts were out there either. The workers at this end of the lane brought their own or went without.

"Yes, I'm the owner." She locked eyes with me, as if ready to charge me in battle.

"You appear to have a long history in this office. You must have lots of business."

"My husband ran the service when he was alive. We had eight vessels, full crews. We could handle anything they threw at us." She took out a long, brown cigarette and lit it from a short one, nearly burnt out in the porcelain tray on the desk. "We used the spare parts from one to fix the next and so on until there was only one left. On her last legs, that one. Old Exterra 4136A is not long for..."

She looked up, holding her breath, realizing she might kill her sale. She put on her smile and tried her best to brighten her mood.

"Don't think it's a bad machine, it's never let me down. It even makes the occasional on-the-spot decision when needed."

Chineel and I exchanged knowing glances. Mrs. Pelorum continued.

"I'm sure you will get many more years out of it yet. Do you have a large company? How many vessels do you run?"

"We don't run any. Exterra will be our only vessel. But do you mind if I make an observation, Mrs. Pelorum? You don't appear to be happy in your work. Do you like running the company your husband left you?"

Her face fell again, deeper than before. I had hit her in the gut, right in the spot where she ached. She looked at me with the weary face of one who has been walking a path for too long on sore feet.

"I hated this business long before Pelorum died. We had nothing else. It was take on the company or starve. No one would buy it. We weren't getting contracts. I had to cut my prices to get jobs and cut costs to make a profit. When I borrowed money to retrofit to full automation, the crews threatened to kill me. Automation is the trend all over, they couldn't find jobs. No one wants live crews in the outer reaches anymore. They had to go to the inner ring, where live crews are still used. The CG likes holding someone to blame when things go wrong."

"So this vessel is the last of your fleet?" I asked, steering the conversation to where I wanted it to go.

"Yes, it's my last one. How will I get by when it breaks down and I can't afford to fix it?" She turned introspective and seemed close to tears.

I decided to drop my bomb: "What would you do with two hundred thousand Universals?"

Chineel looked at me with sincere surprise. Viola looked up as well, her eyes like pie plates. Her face went pale and for a moment I felt she would pass out, falling head first into the tray containing the ends of a dozen brown cigarettes.

"Come now," I chided, "Two hundred thousand Universals, all yours, right now, today. What would you do?"

"I - I - I ..." She looked at me as if to figure out if I was serious or not. Then she spoke with more conviction. "I would go to the spas on Androgenos, where their medical team would mend me and their staff of exquisite young boys would massage me day and night."

"Come to the Exterra maintenance bay and get your money. You must, however, bring all the notifications and authorizations. I don't want to have to come back here. I will conclude the business and you can quit this place for Androgenos today."

There was a pause as Viola considered this. It was easy to see she had tired of the business, of this tiny, dirty office and of doing all the jobs. She long ago disposed of the secretary and receptionist, taking on the tasks herself. With her husband gone, she made all the decisions. While it sounded liberating, she didn't understand the business and made many bad decisions. The problem with bad decisions is they take money out of your pocket. The thrill, as they say, was gone.

"I will gather the ownership documents," she said, resigning herself. There a hint of malice in her voice I didn't trust. Might she consider contacting another buyer and starting a bargaining war? My offer was twice what the business was worth. She would be foolish to try anything slippery, but I decided not to chance it.

"I'll wait. We have a transport outside to take us."

Chineel steadied her face, not showing emotion one way or the other. If Viola wanted to start a bidding war, she would have to do it by telepathy, because we would be here watching her.

Viola brought all the deeds and documents and I transferred two hundred thousand Universals to her account. My father's gift for my wedding day couldn't be better spent.

Before the end of the day, with spare parts bay brimming and a full fuel register, Flax lifted off free and clear. I held the deeds and documents.

It was the last time Flax would ever see the bay at the end of the corridor. She was giddy.

"Where to, Captain?" asked Flax, her excitement showing.

"There are still two contracts to be completed. The good news is: We will be paid and the first contract is at the Wind Pools on New Babylon. The bad news is that when we're finished there, the next repair is on Copernicus."

Wind Pools

Flax settled into the repair tower at New Babylon where she had been before. I met with the manager of the facility to change the method and party of payment. I also took the opportunity to raise the rate to current levels. It had been some time since Viola bothered to do so; she missed out on a lot of money by not doing so.

Chineel went ahead of us to the Wind Pools. We both had ghosts to bury and she wanted to get to it. Dagon came with me. He stood at my side, a quiet but lethal protector.

When the work was done at the manager's office, we took a shuttle to the Wind Pools. Dagon had never visited a resort facility; I could see it would take some getting used to.

The Wind Pools of New Babylon are famous as a natural health resort. Only the extravagantly rich can afford it. Though we would be here only for a day, it was still an expensive treat. On top of the fees for entry, meals and special services, such as my favorite boy, Ariel, heavy tipping was expected. Those who worked at the spa were handsomely rewarded. For this they were expected to perform to the highest standard. In my mind, they earned every gold-back they received.

The pools themselves held no healing properties. The wind blowing over the pools carried the healing vapors to caress your body. For this reason, little was worn at the Wind Pools.

Silk shorts and tops, if desired, were the order of the day. Some ladies went without. Chineel and I did not. It was enough to be here, we did not need to show off.

Dagon took a few minutes to exit his changing cabana. When he did, he wore only the standard white silk shorts. He took a towel and threw it over one shoulder, trying not to look self-conscious, but missing the mark.

Chineel felt right at home in two-piece silks, but it had been a while since I wore so little in public. I remembered what I had been told by my friend, Osiris: "It's not about sex here, not about color, not about age, not about skin. It is about relaxation, rejuvenation and reconstruction. We all need reconstruction now and then."

I had to agree, I was due for reconstruction.

We took a cabana and ordered flavored waters and Ariel. Immediately a boy appeared with three citrus flavored waters. Behind him stood Ariel, smiling as if he was happy to see an old friend. It was a smile he gave to everyone. Unless he could remember my feet, he wasn't likely to recognize me.

Ariel raised my legs on soft pillows and opened a bottle of lavender oil. Soft music filled the cabana, joined by the aroma of lavender. I felt my body relax as I lay back, waiting for what I knew to be an experience beyond all others. Ariel touched my feet and chills ran from my toes to my scull.

Ariel pressed the arch of my foot and I moaned like a new bride. He knew where to touch and what pressure to use. He paid special attention to the base of my toes, to the small toe where my boots pinched and to my arches. Wherever attention was needed, Ariel spent more time there. Feet held no secrets from Ariel. For the rest of the afternoon I was in another world.

Though my eyes were closed, I knew Chineel smiled as she lay back waiting her turn. Dagon wondered what the fuss was about. I knew he would find out soon enough.

Copernicus Again

The repair order at Copernicus was fortuitous as we had to stop there to find the bank my father alluded to in his letter. It took some preparation. There were wanted posters on every screen.

The interlink became my source of information and there I found the smaller bank, which though it was taken over by the Central Bank, operated with the same staff. A route to the bank and back was planned, as direct as possible so as to avoid trouble. Everything seemed to be falling into place until the subject of identity chips came up.

"I still have the one Aristaeus gave me when we were here," I said, holding out the idento-chip. "It should get me through."

"Well, I don't have mine and my face is all over town. It's an old picture but it's still me. I'll stay on Flax with Dagon."

"I don't like it," said Dagon, frowning. "Chineel isn't bad company, but I don't like you going out on your own."

"There's no way around it. We have to see what's at the bank. I'll be fine. Who knows we're here? Stop worrying."

The truth was, I wasn't worried. The alert on me was old and the picture was of the wrong girl. I secretly suspected Galium of hacking into the system and altering the alerts, but I had no proof. I would have broached the subject, but since the last scare, he'd been keeping a low profile.

I dressed for moving quickly, a light skirt with my blade strapped to my thigh beneath and the red blouse with the combination collar. I pulled the collar up and buttoned it closed to hide the scar on my neck. Having your chip removed here could get you disappeared.

As Copernicus entered our screens, a familiar sound came through the node: it was the interlink; my favorite rude ex-lover reached out to me.

"Where are you, Wort?"

"Coming into Copernicus, you old pirate. Where are you? No, don't answer. I don't want to know."

"Copernicus? You'll find it changed."

"How so, oh wise one?"

"Things have loosened up in Copernicus since you were last there, the system is breaking down. The Central Government has lost its grip on the place. You'll still need a chip, but the checkpoints are easier."

"Good news. I have business to take care of."

"You shouldn't have a problem. Except everyone there is on drugs, as Copernicus now falls under the dominating thumb of the Sirius Medical Conclave."

"Everyone on drugs? Like the old days on Sterope? I remember being the only one not high as the Wind Pools."

"No. The trouble isn't with port drugs, but prescription medications. Virtually everyone is medicated."

"Aren't prescriptions issued by doctors? I mean, they must need them."

"So young, so naive! It's not about health, Little Wort, it's about Unies. It's about getting the population, all of the population, every man, woman and child, hooked on their product so there's a continuous flood of income. And it's about control. If you don't behave, you don't get your drugs and then you go into a psychotic break. People in these psychotic breaks have been known to kill their whole family, everyone at work or school and then themselves."

"School?" I gasped. I tried to picture the prim and proper children of my school years bristling with assault weapons. It was hard to imagine.

"Children are a primary target; get 'em while they're young. Several times in recent memory, children have walked into their classrooms and killed a dozen or so of their friends before either being killed by constables or turning their blasters on themselves. Every time it was discovered they were under a doctor's care and took drugs prescribed by those doctors."

"Doctor's care?"

"Not lately. They tell me doctors used to spend time with patients, listening to their troubles in the name of help. Nowadays they hear a list of symptoms, prescribe a drug and shout 'Next!' Good luck getting any business done in a drugged society."

"But if everyone's on these medications..."

"Listen, I don't have much time. Those who don't agree with the SMC or the CG don't get their meds. They might get a placebo or nothing at all and you go 'cold turkey.' People have been known to bash their heads against a wall to stop the pain, and keep bashing until they die. The Black Market is rampant in such areas and the death penalty is not a deterrent."

"So if someone is out of agreement he is cut off and goes crazy? Is it the same scenario as the flu vaccine?"

"Yes! But this catches those who have not yet contracted the flu or might have created a resistance to the strain. In the outer reaches, some people don't get the flu."

"So for those, they have other drugs they can withhold?"

"Now you're getting it! They go psychotic, get picked up and carried off to an institution where they are never heard from again. One faction holds the theory there's no one in those beds. They may keep a few patients on for show, but the rest are simply drugged to death and disposed of. We have evidence they're not buying large quantities of medical supplies, or food or clothing – only for a few, enough to keep up appearances."

"Fantastic!"

"Yes! If it was a small outpost on the outer-rim, it would be illegal. As it's the Earth Central Government in bed with Sirius Medical Conclave it's the norm. I thought you'd want to know. Watch your step out there!"

"Is this why you called?"

"Oh! I forgot! How did you like the wanted posters?"

"It was you! I thought so!"

"It was the best I could do long-range and short notice. The CG had all these alerts from various places and they boiled down to you. They'd find you sooner or later unless I stepped in. Sorry I couldn't get it erased completely. Did Flax like her picture?"

"You made her look like an armed pirate ship, bristling with guns from every port."

"Actually, it is a picture of an armed pirate ship. If they catch it, they'll have someone to lock up. They'll celebrate!"

"I'll have to go about on an identochip with another name

on it," I protested.

"You'd have to do so anyway, Wort, regardless of my intervention. But don't worry; the CG's influence is diminishing. You'll see it in Copernicus."

"The CG losing its grip? Hard to believe."

"The system's falling apart. If you stick to the middle-ring, the shift isn't so noticeable, but the change is noticeable everywhere else. As the inner-ring breaks down, the outer ring gets more civilized. Soon you'll have the whole universe to rattle around in."

"I have the whole universe now, old man."

"But soon you can go on your own name. People will say 'Bacchus, wasn't there something about her?' and you'll say, 'Naw, it was someone else.' and go your merry way."

A flutter in the screen told me Galium would close the link soon.

"There's my cue. Gotta go, Little Wort."

"I told you, don't ..." The screen clicked off before I could tell him I was not his 'Little Wort' anymore. He'd only say I'd always be Little Wort to him, like in the bad old days at the Mithra Tavern.

"Copernicus, on screen," said Flax.

There on the main screen, magnified seven times, was the planet I knew from my post-school days. The Copernicus I remembered was full of students and philosophers, the streets were filled with art and music, and there was real work for someone newly out of school with a willingness to show up. I had such high hopes.

And yet, if I hadn't had to run out on my rent, I wouldn't have met Flax. It was why I felt a need to return once upon a time, to give the landlord the rent I owed him. He wanted much more, however, which proved to be his undoing. If he had simply accepted the Ц40 and said thanks, he would be Ц40 richer and alive today. I remembered watching him tumble out of his own window, dodging Willamette's gunfire. Willamette killed his own woman, Helia, with his blaster. It made him the hateful, bitter man he is today.

I shuddered with the memory of my last visit to Copernicus. I dreaded this new visit. I hoped it would be my last, and hoped I would survive it.

Mithra Investments

As I stood in the line, complete with Fangdu mask and gloves, awaiting my turn to be scanned, I wondered why I was there at all. We had enough money to travel for a while, even after we bought Flax's contract. There were still contracts to complete, of course. Then I remembered we were here to legitimately do exactly that. My errand was the extra added attraction.

The administrative details had been concluded remotely. We fabricated a company named "Mithra Investments" after the Sterope tavern Chineel and I shared in our experiences, though we weren't there at the same time.

I took along the chip Aristaeus had so kindly supplied and an empty shoulder bag to bring back whatever was in the bank, left for me by my father.

A fistfight broke out at the scanning bay and three guards tried to subdue a man with a counterfeit chip. Three people ahead of me used the distraction to scoot on through the checkpoint, so I made it four and the three behind me made it seven. What happened then, I don't know. We were all glad to be out of it. We stood outside in the street catching our breath and regarding at each other with a special bond, a shared experience. If we stood there longer, we would have started a club and made our own handshake. As it was, we smiled politely and walked in different directions.

Down the street to the bank, I noted several screens with criminal alerts. None of the faces looked familiar. Either my own had come down or there were so many now added there wasn't time to show them all.

The people in the street moved as if under water, with blank stares, as if looking at something in their mind but not in real time. Several bumped into me along the way and didn't even notice.

When I found the bank, it was no longer its own entity but was a neighborhood location of the Central Bank. The woman at the window looked out at me from behind bars. She had a sad look.

"I would like to collect something left for me by my father." I tried to sound as soft and daughter-like as I knew how.

"What's the name?"

I thought of the alerts on every screen, of the Central Bank, closely allied with the Central Government and of the three guards bringing a man with a counterfeit chip to the floor with clubs. I gulped hard and forged ahead.

"Bacchus, Starwort Bacchus," I said, with a lump in my throat.

"Certainly. One moment, please." The woman tapped in the name and looked at a clear screen. The angle on the screen hid the readouts from me but showed them to her. I wondered if the little bank had been a property of the Central Bank long enough for the records to be updated and centralized. It they were cross referenced with the criminal alerts, I was cooked. But the woman smiled.

"One moment, please."

She stepped away, returning with a sealed packet.

"Here you are. Oh! Heavy!"

"Yes. Thank you." I slipped the packet into my shoulder bag, adjusted the strap across my chest and nodded to the woman.

As I walked back the way I came, I saw a man pointing in my direction. I stopped and shook my head, considered it a figment of my imagination, and continued. The man pointing was a stranger, I didn't know him, but the man with him had a bandage on his neck. As he turned his face to look down the street I recognized Willamette. Still alive!

Willamette broke into a run the moment he saw me. I turned the other way and ran through dazed people who looked at me without registering anything one way or the other. I ran through the drugged population of Copernicus, as Galium had predicted.

At the intersection, another familiar face came from the market: Dodd in a cap meant to cover a wound incurred when his blaster misfired. When he saw me, he ran. I did the same and the chase was on.

The heavy packet my father left me banged against my hip and I held it to keep it still. Up ahead, the road rose before me. There are few hills in Copernicus, so this must be one I knew, but I couldn't place it. A hill would slow my pace. They might catch me before I can crest it.

To my left was a door marked "No Entry." No one watched the door, no camera, no lights and nothing I could see to keep me out. I pushed down on the handle and put my shoulder to the door. Immediately, an alarm sounded, complete with a red light swirling above my head.

"I hate being the first one to learn a lesson like this," I said aloud as I pushed through. "There should be a book on this stuff,"

The other side of the door a long hallway stretched to a light at the end. Nothing could stop Dodd and Willamette from coming through after me. The alarm and light would tell them where I went. I was trapped!

I took the titanium case from my pocket and shoved it in the door at the hinge, jamming it shut.

At the far end of the hallway were two doors, one dark behind it and one with light. I went through the latter and came out on a street behind several stores. I chose the shortest distance to the next avenue and took off like a frightened wharf rat. At the end of the street, I looked both directions to see Willamette at the far end of the lane.

Out of the frying pan and into the fire, I thought, with special meaning considering it was Willamette who chased me, the man scarred with a hot pan.

I turned and ran as fast as I could in the other direction, running into market stalls within a block. The lane filled with slow moving people wandering from stall to stall, stopping to look or to order food. I ran under an awning in front of a stand selling dresses and house-wraps. From there I peeked out to see if he would run this way and if so, would he run by me? He ran toward me. I felt trapped.

As Willamette reached the stall, he was stopped by two constables.

"Adox Willamette, you are to be held under bond," said one constable, producing manacles.

"On what charge?" growled Willamette.

"For the murders of Helianthus Minos and Kainush Bedos."

A third constable joined the group as Willamette reeled at the accusation. He had indeed killed his woman, Helia for Helianthus, a flower meaning *false riches*. The other name I remembered as my old landlord, who fell from the window trying to avoid being shot by Willamette. Both were dead by his hand. He had no defense.

In desperation, he broke away from the constables and headed back the way he came, down the lane and into the clutch of food carts in the center of the market. I leaned out to see him fly through the crowd followed by the three constables. A group of people interested in the activity moved closer to the action. I moved closer too. Willamette knocked one of the constables sideways and darted left, stumbling into a cart filled with Malameris. Their tentacles sting long after they're laid out waiting to be sold. Preparing them for a meal is a dangerous job, one not taken on by a novice. Willamette went into spasm, twisting in every direction, unable to avoid the agonizing stings of the Malameris.

Willamette was pulled from the cart and manacled by the constables, growling and tugging every chance he got, crying out in excruciation. He called the constables foul names and kicked two, only making it worse for himself. As he was dragged off in manacles, I faded into the crowd.

Speeder Port

My heart sang when I found the road leading me to the free port and back to Flax. Soon I would be aboard and sailing away to the planet Bacchus.

My heart sank as I turned a corner and saw Dodd in the distance. He locked eyes with me and smiled. How I hated to see a smile so evil. He produced a pistol and fired at me. The projectile stuck a wall behind me causing bits of stone to fly into the crowd of shoppers. I ran in the other direction as fast as a Boroneum Jagtah.

It was a part of town I didn't know; I ran wild without any idea where to go. I had no plan.

Constables would want to know the reason for all the running and shooting. They might see him and act. But there weren't any in sight and Dodd was not far behind me.

As I passed a speeder port, an idea came into my head. I had stolen a speeder once, why not again? I ran in and ducked down among the parked vehicles, quiet for the moment save for my breathing, which was much too loud.

Every sound was amplified in the cold floor of the port. Every click and tick sounded like Dodd coming to get me. He had lost his main henchman to the constables and had lost three more in the plaza on Khons. He would not be kind to me.

I huddled beside a red speeder. The lines seemed familiar.

I leaned back to have a better look. It was an Osiris-Five!

Feeling familiar territory, I climbed inside and leaned down under the console, looking at the dangling terminals.

"Which one? Which one? Is it the black and the silver on this one? Or is it the ... it doesn't matter, I can't tell one color from another down here."

It had been a while since I had stolen a speeder. Lately I didn't have to; I survived all right without committing grand larceny. I only took the earlier one because the man hit me and hitting is against the rules. You don't hit girls, you just don't. I slipped away as fast and as far as I could, in his speeder. He'll think twice before he raises his hand...

But I had a situation here before me and Dodd looking at me at the entrance to the speeder port. He walked toward me with measured pace, confident he had his quarry cornered. I knew I had nowhere to go but over him.

The trebium latch fell from my blouse into my view; it dangled on the chain around my neck. Though the Osiris V has a panel start, activated by the thumb of the owner, there is a key port for emergency use. I felt the key port below the steering mechanism and shoved the latch in. I turned the latch and the vibration and rumble coursing through the entire vehicle told me it worked.

Dodd heard the engine start and closed the distance, I had to move fast. I stepped on the accelerator and soared over him as he threw himself to the ground. The Osiris V is a hover craft, so I literally flew out the open entrance and down the road towards the coast.

The road was meant for smaller vessels, carrying fishers and bathers to and along the coast. It was never meant for a speeder.

Above me, dark clouds rolled foretelling foul weather. A wind from the sea buffeted the O-V, threatening to throw me off the roadway. I slowed down to keep control.

Better to be slow and safe, I thought. No sense in crashing and not getting away at all.

The howl from the wind rose and fell, leaving another sound in the air, one similar to the wail of my own vehicle. A glance at the rear screen told the tale, another speeder was behind me. In the driver's seat sat Dodd. He had stolen a speeder of his own, another Osiris V.

I poured on the speed, pushing the limits of the road and the vehicle. A telltale pop confirmed Dodd still had his gun and would kill me for the parcel in my shoulder bag. A projectile flew by me inches above my head.

"Son of Baal!" I cried out, pulling to the right and into the dust at the side of the worn track. Had I taken a bump, the ride would have been over.

A flume of sand and dirt flew up behind me. In the rear screen I saw Dodd come through it with his head down. His Osiris bumped the ground twice, sailing off to one side before recovering.

When he did recover, he stood and fired twice over the windscreen. A thump in the back told me one of the shots found a mark, but not the one he wanted. The stow-bay in back absorbed the shot. The second must have missed completely. I couldn't count on such luck for long.

The clouds thickened above me, making me wonder if rain would improve or worsen my chances. The controls felt awkward in my gloved hands, my breathing labored under the Fangdu mask covering my nose and mouth.

A straightaway before me, level and broad, meant a

chance to open up full throttle. It meant the same for him of course. He might catch me unless I could navigate the curve without tumbling end-over-end. I hit the throttle and the Osiris jerked forward, whirring louder and harder. The vibration increased, rattling my teeth. I wondered for a moment if the rotors had been aligned recently, but it didn't matter, it was too late to stop into a speeder-mech.

"You and me, baby, better or worse," I said to the speeder.

The curve came up before I realized and I overshot it by three meters, kicking up a cloud of dirt and gravel. The O-V wasn't meant for use over rough ground, it was a city vehicle. Even cobblestone and unfinished roads resulted in a rough ride. City dwellers didn't care, they never saw anything but smooth pavement.

I could see the road in front of me curve like a desert boustrophedon reptile slithering toward his next meal.

If Dodd was able to cut across, he might catch me. He had the same vehicle with the same limitations. Cutting across a snaking road would shake the speeder enough to knock him out of the vehicle. I hoped he would try.

Another straightaway came up, this one along the beach. Ahead, two vehicles wended leisurely along the track, the occupants enjoying a day by the sea. I dropped to the shoreline with a bump and throttled up as soon as I had track under me.

The two vehicles saw me coming and veered off to the side, one to the shore, one to the hills, both slowing to a stop. I flew by them spewing sand in two large fins. Behind me, the other speeder bumped and spun, causing him to blow out the pipes and start again. I had gained a small advantage.

In the screen, I saw Dodd's face harden with hatred and

resolve.

A frightened yell shook me and I looked up. I lingered too long on the hateful face of my foe and barely missed hitting a group of young students crossing the beach with their towels, chairs and grub-toters. One boy shook his fist at me as I roared by. No doubt there were some choice words shouted as well, but I didn't hear them over the sound of my screaming engine.

The track took a turn inland at the end of the beach. To go on would be to smack into a stack of a dozen rocks, each one larger than the Osiris. I slowed but still took the turn too fast, showering them with sand. I looked in vain for where the road went next. When I hit the loose dirt, I knew. It was under me but not obvious; the wind had blown the dirt over the track, obliterating it until I came along. I had to feel my way from here.

A hill rose before me, dividing my attention between navigating the track and looking at the rear screen. Dodd came around the pile of rocks and onto the track, now made clear by the passing of my speeder. I had made the road easier for him.

At the hill I rose and then dipped hard, slamming the track with the bottom of the speeder. I felt it in my back; the upholstery was not enough to cushion the blow. The Osiris took two smaller bounces to level out at one foot above the track.

"Achelous' daughters!" I screamed, as the crest of another hill came toward me, sped by and dwindled in my wake. The other speeder closed in behind and gained speed.

Why hadn't there been a Shakti or a Bishop in the underground? Those speeders could run and had a greater clearance from the ground. A Bishop could go as high as 18 feet and maintain control. But the Osiris was the only vehicle available. You take what you can get when you're stealing speeders.

"How can he be after me?" I asked to no one. "Hasn't he heard? Doesn't he know? I'm only an afterthought!"

First Warning

"Typical!" I scolded myself. "Port town, stolen speeder, angry guy on my tail-feathers and I'm nearly out of fuel. Why do I always find myself running? I should never have come back to Copernicus!"

The land rose fast and hard. With the jagged cliffs on my left, and the ocean beyond, there was no escape. To the right, the mountains were too steep, even for an Osiris V. Hovering over the little-traveled road at break-neck speed seemed my only option, but then the road dropped away again. The Osiris V shook as it hit the gravitational limit again, nearly losing touch with the ground.

The edge of the road, barely a small riser in the surrounding countryside, sent a swirl of dust behind me every time I drifted onto it – if one can use the term "drifted" while going 180 kilometers across rough country. I tried to churn up enough dust and gravel to blind the driver behind me. Not a smart thing to do; The O-V held less control over loose ground.

The fuel gauge blinked once: first warning.

"Next time, steal a speeder with a full register," I chided myself, banking right at the boulder on the far end of the hair-pin turn. Another rise was ahead of me. I pressed the throttle to the floor-plate, hoping to go over with inches to spare, hoping my pursuer would go over with less.

A marina came into view beyond the turn, small and exclusive with a gathering of top-tier boats in costly slips. A high-rise full of luxury habitats stood on the far side, each with a perfect view. No doubt the underground parking port was filled with expensive Osiris speeders. I wished I could stop in and shop for another one, one with more fuel, but it was a wasted wish.

The ground fell away and the Osiris V plummeted downwards, the pebbled shore and surf coming into view, filling the windscreen. The road was gone, washed out by a storm or quaked away. There was no sign, no warning. I hit the retros and tried to skid to a slower speed, something manageable. Several large rocks scraped the bottom as I flew over them. I could feel them hitting the floor-plate. In the rear screen, Dodd's Osiris came over the edge, following me all the way – most likely to our mutual deaths.

The coast came up faster than I thought, scraping the front buffers as I hit hard and bounced along the uneven shoreline. I managed to get it straightened out, hoping to gain enough speed to go over the pile of rocks at the end of my sight-line, and for smoother paving on the other side.

In the rear screen, Dodd bounced along the shore like a thrown rock. His O-V was green and shiny; mine was a faded red with cracks in the finish.

"Living by the sea will do that to a speeder," I reflected. Chineel would like the green one. She liked green things, as they set off her red hair. Chineel was still on board Flax, where I would be if not the object of pursuit.

"Yet here I am, once again! Daughter of Ra!" I cried out loud.

Up and over the pile of rocks where the shore ran out, I

257

reckoned the distance from the speeder to the ground below: Once I had left the rock pile, I was fourteen feet or more – too high! I may not regain control. But then, he might not either. Dark thoughts took my mind over – I grew tired of the chase.

The Osiris V dropped flat onto the jagged shoreline below, black with rocks and crushed shells. The bump jarred me. I grunted at the impact.

For a moment, I was stalled, not making forward motion. Panic hit me. What if he came over on top of me? I stomped on the throttle hard. A loud whir said the spindles were engaging and I took off with a jolt.

"Whoa! Son of Baal!" I cried aloud. Something inside the power-plant had shaken loose, a regulator, a governor of some sort. The speeder took off like a fighter-drone.

Ahead of me a portion of road rose out of the rocky shoreline up the rolling hills. Behind me, the green Osiris hit the ragged coastline and tried to regain control, bucking and striking the coastline.

As the land turned upward, I scraped the undercarriage, no doubt knocking considerable surfacing off the bottom. The freed accelerator continued picking up speed, even going upwards at this angle. The thrust pinned me to the seat and all I saw in front of me was clear sky.

In an instant, a lack of sound struck fear in my heart. A moment before, I charged along a road at breakneck speed, with the attending rumble. Now I had left the road – or rather, the road had left me. Daring a look over the side of the speeder, I saw the road far beneath me. It had crested and dipped down at the same angle. The speeder was no longer in contact with the land; I was airborne!

Airborne!

The speeder seemed to float, like a child's ball having reached its apex, not yet able to fall back down. Time seemed to stop, to stand still, as if there were no time, no change in my surroundings and no danger to be wary of. I looked at the marina, which must have held a thousand people in its rooms. To them, there was nothing exciting save for the speeder losing trajectory on the coast road. I was once again, an afterthought.

A familiar roar filled my ears as Exterra 4136A rose next to me, closing in on my position in mid-air. The starboard bay door was open, a giant maw reaching to gobble me up. Dagon and Chineel stood in the bay, braced to grab whatever came their way.

The apex of my flight lasted only a second. The speeder lost power and changed direction, heeding the call of gravity. In an instant, we would fall together to the rocks below.

Flax closed the distance and touched the speeder with the lip of the bay door. Chineel reached out, grabbing my left hand. Dagon reached over the side door, taking hold of my blouse with both hands.

As Flax lifted up, the speeder fell away. Dagon and Chineel pulled me out of the speeder and into the bay.

We lay on the bay floor altogether, holding onto each other like children in a storm.

"Hang on," warned Flax, as she veered to the right over the track below and out toward the sea. We leapt into the center of the bay, to the RRD tied down to the deck. We held on to its secure straps as we looked out of the bay door, straight down to the scene below.

The green speeder had reached the crest of the hill and piled into the rocks at the curve. At the same moment, the red speeder fell from above. The explosion enveloped both speeders and I saw the startled face of Dodd, reaching a hand to me before being devoured by flames.

"What happened?" asked Dagon, over the wind of the bay door closing.

"The power core erupted." Below us, bright green and yellow flames licked the sky, sending a plume of blue smoke into the wind. The bathers on the beach would have a story to tell on their return home.

As the bay door closed, the rain began to fall. Flax sped toward the sea, down the coast and back to the free dock.

"Thank you, Flax," I yelled, loud enough to hear in the bridge, though she could hear me anywhere in the vessel.

"Glad you're home safe," Flax replied.

"Thank you Dagon, Chineel. You are truly lifesavers."

"You're welcome. Is Willamette still out there?" Chineel asked.

"He is, but he's in manacles, arrested by the constables and stung by Malameris. Even if he survives their stings, he won't squirm out of the lockup this time."

"Who's down there?" asked Dagon, tilting his head to indicate the man burning in the two wrecked speeders below.

"His name was Dodd. I saw him a couple of times

watching me. He gave chase in Copernicus outside the bank. He seemed to be the brains of the outfit."

"Humph! Some brains!" said Dagon.

"Where are we going, Flax?" I asked as I dusted myself off.

"To the free port. We have no license to depart. We will have to conclude the contract, which is merely a formality, and then we can leave."

The free port loomed ahead as I lowered myself into the pilot's seat. Flax set down on the free port surface. There was a spark as she touched the metal plate.

"Something is wrong," said Flax. "The spark is a warning."

I strapped myself into the seat, ready for a swift take-off. We had run from the authorities before, this would be no different.

"You can't sit there," said Flax.

Surprised, I complied, vacating the pilot's seat. Chineel came up in a shirt and jacket over her usual outlandish skirt. She strapped into the pilot's seat and Dagon climbed into the co-pilot's spot. I cowered in the navigator's seat behind.

"Captain Souci Bach?" asked the voice from the tower.

"Yes. This is Souci Bach." said Chineel.

"Designation, please," said the tower.

"Exterra 4136A, concluding repairs."

"You have permission to take off, Exterra. You are second in rotation."

"Thank you, Tower."

A large passenger vessel lifted off, turning as it lifted, the giant thrusters spitting thunder and fury. It aimed itself toward the horizon and added thruster power sending it into the air high above the broad sea.

"Cleared to go, Exterra," said the tower.

Chineel leaned forward, put an arm out. She pretended to be working controls and Flax lifted off in response. In short order, the overcast skies of the sky port gave way to the blackness we knew so well.

Chineel stood up and paused by the co-pilot seat. She spoke with a trembling voice.

"I don't ever want to do that again! We can't ever return to Copernicus! Flax? No more Copernicus!"

"Affirmative," said Flax.

The Parcel

Course was set for Victoriana, meant to be a jumping off point for our journey across the expanse to Bacchus. My eager crew gathered around the galley table to see what was in the parcel left to me by my father.

All eyes were on me, even the invisible eyes of Flax, as I placed the shoulder bag on the table and opened the flap. The envelope inside was heavy and stiff, about the size of a readable.

"The envelope from the Main Plaza on Adonis contained a readable, one with a substantial amount of currency," said Flax. She knew the readable from Adonis bought her contract. For fuel and supplies, we were on our own.

"Yes!" I said, "Thank you, Father!" My father said he wanted me to be cared for long after he was gone. He could not have foreseen our current circumstances, but we owed him much.

"Let's see if this is the same," whispered Chineel. Dagon nodded. He was eager to see treasures. He reached to the back of his belt and produced a blade, which he extended to me handle first.

"Thank you, Dagon." I opened the parcel.

Inside was an envelope, much like the last, but square rather than long. With it was a reader, an older one. It was a slat. Slats were no longer used, though we had several in the ship's library. They were left by the previous crew before the vessel was converted and made fully automated.

"A slat?" exclaimed Chineel.

"We'll see what the letter says," I said, slitting the top of the envelope. Inside was a sheet of heavy paper. Across the front I recognized my father's flourishing hand, artistic in every letter and dot.

"My darling daughter," I read. A tear formed in my eye. I considered wiping it away and steeling myself from emotion, as a captain would, but chose instead to read through the tears.

"My traveling days draw to a close. I will retire and spend my days with you and Mother on Khons, where I will be happy. I dare not journey to Khons with this in my luggage, though I would like to give it to you upon your graduation. It will have to wait until you uncover it yourself. There are those who would take it from me, as you will understand one day. My love goes with you to Bacchus. May you find all you search for in this life. I love you, as does your mother. Fondly, Father."

The tears flowed now. I couldn't help the burst of love I felt for the man who left me far too soon.

The slat caught my eye. I opened it up and pressed the button along the top edge. Nothing happened.

"It's dead," said Dagon.

"Yes, but we have ways to bring it back alive."

I went to the work table and opened the back of the slat. The battery pack was there, three small disks encased in Plastx. Chineel read my mind and brought me a working slat. She removed the battery pack and handed it to me. I slipped it into the slot and closed the back. When I turned it over and pressed the button, the slat came alive, showing a greeting. It not only displayed the contents, but announced them as well, in a voice I had not heard since school: it was the nasal tone of the first generation of slats.

"Greetings! This is a message to Starwort Bacchus from her father. If you are Starwort Bacchus, please press a thumb here."

A green square glowed at the bottom of the screen. I pressed my right thumb into the square.

"Hello, my darling Starwort," said the talking slat. It seemed so odd hearing my father's words in his voice. "I hope you have found this at a time in your life when it is most useful. In my travels I have left a few parcels for you to find, not because I wanted to keep them from you but because traveling with items of value has become more dangerous. Know I love you with all my heart, my sweet, sweet Star. I love you, as does your mother. Fondly, Father."

The slat showed but did not speak the words, "Tap here next."

I tapped the indicated spot and a page turned as in a book. The screen showed a sum of money to be accessed at whatever bank I entered. It was six-hundred-thousand Universals, over half a million.

"Lord Khronos!" exclaimed Dagon.

"Daughter of Ra!" added Chineel.

"Thank you, Father!" I whispered.

It was several minutes before we could speak actual sentences. We stared at the slat and at each other as the events of the recent past fell into place.

"No wonder those men wanted to catch you so badly," said Chineel.

"They had no idea exactly what my father's legacy contained. They only guessed. It's funny how events shape our lives," I said, beginning to recover. "If I had found this while living in Copernicus, I wouldn't have had to run out on my rent. There wouldn't have been the chase through the market and I wouldn't have had to escape on the first vessel I saw. I wouldn't have found Flax."

"Then it is good your father hid it well," said Flax. "If you had not stowed away, you would not be a captain and I would not be crossing the universe on an adventure."

"My, my, Flax!" I managed through tears. "You are becoming quite the pirate."

"Aye, Aye, Captain," said Flax.

"Aye, Aye, Captain," chimed in Dagon, grinning from one ear to the other.

"Aye, Aye, Captain," added Chineel. She would still be hustling well-to-do derelicts at the Mithra Tavern in Sterope but for my intervention.

"All right, then. Set sail for Victoriana, thence to Bacchus."

"Aye, Aye, Captain!" repeated Flax.

I secretly hoped they would begin speaking normally soon.

Memorial

Our return to Victoriana was joyous and at the same time sad. We were glad to see Aristaeus and Runyon at the wheel of the yellow roadster. We were looking forward to arriving at Aristaeus' and dressing to go to the gazebo for the afternoon concert. The prospect of having no one chase us appealed greatly, making for a pleasant change.

Flax attended to some needed repairs, not being one for frills and bustles. She seemed to be humming to herself as we left the ship for the ride to town. Aristaeus explained why.

"She is hooked into my internal server, making upgrades. I've been working on a few surprises since we last spoke."

"Oh, she'll like that! She did somersaults when I plugged 360 yottabytes into her system."

"In which case, she should put on a three-ring circus when you return."

"We were talking earlier of her being the most advanced vessel of her designation. What do you think?"

Aristaeus didn't answer right away. He considered the ramifications of his response before speaking.

"The vessel itself is dated. The engines and rockets, the Red Stroke Drive, even the evasive mechanisms are dated and in some cases outmoded. The hardware, in other words, could stand an upgrade. But Flax herself, the software, the servers, the internals, are beyond state-of-the-art. The current 'state-of-the-art' has a long way to go to catch up to her. She is so far ahead of the competition, they cannot even see her exhaust trace."

It was as I thought; Flax had come a long way since the stiff and tinny voice I first encountered. Between Doctor Gensus' upgrades and bits of program she created, as she herself said, off the top of her head, she had reached a level unheard of in the world of interplanetary vessels. It was good news, and it was bad news.

"Let's not tell anyone," I said to my friend, Aristaeus. "What is valuable is also sought after. Those who have been chasing me for my father's gift or for your surveillance-dodging pins would be nothing to those who would chase us to gain control of Flax."

"Yes! It's true. We'll keep it to ourselves."

We arrived at the house with eager anticipation of the afternoon concert. We went into town in our Victoriana clothing, decked out to meet the populous and to hear the music of the band at the gazebo. We later returned to the house hot, tired and ready for a nap. It felt good to unhook my underpinnings and take in a full breath of air.

"I don't think I could wear these all the time," I said to Chineel.

"I'm sure I would die!"

"Do you think they put these iron maidens on in the morning and strut around in them all day?"

"No, I think they put them on, go out for five minutes, then come home and slip into something loose for the rest of the day."

"The pajamas are fun," I observed, as I slipped into the loose-fitting, yellow silk top and bottom Myrtle had laid out for me.

"Is everyone decent?" said Dagon at the door.

"Just barely!" said Chineel, winking at me.

The door opened and Dagon peeked a head in. "We're meeting downstairs in the living room. Come as soon as you're complete."

"As done as we're going to get, Dagon. Lead the way."

The living room was set with a low table covered with food, the perfect repast for a warm afternoon. The windows were open, giving a cross breeze, and Myrtle brought a cooling box brimming with frosted glasses ready to receive several juice beverages of various flavors.

"Here's to absent friends," said Aristaeus, lifting a glass filled with a sweet red liquid.

"Absent friends," we all joined in.

"To Taxus and Althea," I said, raising my glass. "Taken away when they had happiness at their fingertips."

"Yes. They could have been happy here," said Aristaeus.

"To Cory," said Dagon, looking at nothing in the center of the room. I could tell he was in his memories. "She was not merely a companion droid, she could lie. It takes intelligence to lie. You can't program it in convincingly."

"Yes, she would have made a valuable crew member," I added.

"Here's to Osiris, the old beast of Hades. Even though he betrayed us, I miss him," said Chineel.

"And I miss Galium," I said. Then I thought of it and added, "No, I miss the idea of him."

All eyes turned toward me. The self-conscious girl of my early school days showed through. "You understand! A kind, strong man who cares for me and will banter with me. Not Galium himself, but someone like him. Galium-Prime, the best of him, enhanced and made livable."

They did understand. They all nodded their heads, returning their gaze to the center of the room. It was Aristaeus who brought us back to reality.

"Morning comes early on Victoriana and you have to put some space behind you. I suggest getting some rest. Myrtle will have breakfast ready when you get up."

Later, in the dark of night, my thoughts were of the handsome Sector Agent I had met in Ceres Segundo on my first visit there. He had offered me a job and I had turned him down. I was glad I turned him down, but it would be nice, I thought, to see him again. I hoped if I did, it would not be due to an outstanding warrant. Perhaps the Sector Agent was like Galium: I didn't want him, I wanted the idea of him.

Exterra Bacchus

With the change of ownership to Captain Starwort Bacchus, Exterra 4136A, Automated Repair Vessel, Outer Reaches, Fourth Quadrant underwent a change of designation. Exterra class vessels now took on the name of the home planet, under a recent ruling designed to keep track of smaller ships. Flax listed the planet of origin as Bacchus and became Exterra Bacchus. As there were no other vessels of the Exterra class from Bacchus, no other vessels at all in fact, she required no number after her designation. She wore the title proudly, as she was no longer merely an automated repair vessel, licensed to operate in the fourth quadrant of the outer reaches. She was her own vessel; the only one there was and she could go anywhere.

A touchy subject came up while Flax and I waited at the Victoriana free port for the change of ownership and designation to become final.

"But you were never restricted to the outer reaches or to the fourth quadrant. In fact, who even speaks of quadrants anymore?"

"You are correct. The designation is old. Repairs are rarely needed in the outer reaches as their technology is limited, so the license was extended to include all planets, near and far. No one speaks of quadrants anymore. I never visited Earth, where they have an overabundance of newer, more advanced repair vehicles."

"Not anymore!" I added. "We have the most advanced vessel in the galaxy right here."

"Thank you, Star. To stay ahead of the Central Government will take all our combined cunning. The known planets and moons, space stations and even the landing platforms in the far outer reaches, all are considered one large property by the Central Government, existing only to be brought under their control. We'll make sure Bacchus remains outside their reach."

"Captain?" said a familiar voice from the bay. It was Aristaeus, seeing us off, and he came bearing gifts.

"Something for the lady of the vessel," he said, producing a small box covered in velvet. I blushed, but soon saw the truth: he didn't mean me, he meant Flax.

Aristaeus opened the box and removed a playable ewer similar to one he had given Flax on an earlier occasion. The former contained liquid memory ten times those already in use, causing her to proclaim: "I could take over a galaxy and crown myself queen." I wondered what this new gift was.

Aristaeus plugged the vial into a slot proffered by Flax. There was a pause, then a beep and a whirring sound. The lights in the bridge brightened and a face appeared above the console. It was a holistic face of a woman, mature with soft brown hair and a silken scarf at her neck. She opened her eyes and looked at us. The lips moved as she spoke and there was expression in the deep brown eyes.

"Nine-Hundred Yottabytes! Lord Kronos! Doctor Genus, you have outdone yourself!" exclaimed Flax. The new face showed genuine surprise and pleasure. She had made her first facial expression and it was a joy to see.

"And a face to greet the world. It travels to the galley and wherever there is a console terminal. It's pleasant to put a face to the voice. Isn't it?"

"Yes, it is, Doctor. Thank you!" beamed Flax.

"It's a composite of Star, Chineel and two women in town, so it would be different. I think it's a beautiful face, don't you, ladies?"

Chineel and I agreed heartily, chattering about it long into the night and well after Aristaeus made his farewells and left for his home, with Runyon driving him in the yellow roadster he loved so well.

The administrative details complete, Exterra Bacchus was given leave to depart.

"Set sail for the planet Bacchus, Flax, if you please."

"I do so please, Captain." Flax's holistic face smiled and dipped to the left as she fired thrusters and lifted off the plates at the Victoriana free port. We were on our way to Bacchus at last!

Awakened

Of the many enhancements newly fitted to Exterra Bacchus, the sleep pods were the most controversial. Flax said we would need them for prolonged space travel, and it was a long way to Bacchus. The problem was, I was no longer tired.

After turning over for the third time, making a list in my head of items to get done once we rose from deep sleep and mentally going over the tunes I could play on the clarinet, it was clear I would get no sleep. I pushed the button and the top of the pod opened with a quiet whoosh of air.

Dark blue silks were folded in a drawer, complete with soft slippers. I donned these in case I was not the only one with a need to walk abroad mid-flight.

The gravity was off outside the pods and I floated out to the galley, over to the console.

"Artificial gravity in the galley, please." A change in the air pressure gradually warmed the environment as the gravity came on, allowing me to step down to the deck.

"Thank you," I sang, though there was no one to hear. In deep space, even Flax was asleep. Life support systems were polite and obedient, so we treated them so.

In the drawer on the port side was my clarinet. With the galley door closed, I was able to play softly and not wake the crew. I sat at the end of the galley table, put one foot on the chair to my left and raised the instrument to my lips. A soft and gentle note came from the bell and vibrated my temples. The note lifted up and the first phrase of a song from my school days took shape in the air.

As the song I learned in music class drifted around the galley, I felt another presence off to my left. From the bay, the remote repair pod lifted from its docking station on the RRD and floated on a gust of air into the galley and onto the table. I knew who it was, she had visited before and was used to the pod.

The pod settled on the table, three lights blinking without regard to the tempo of the music, one green, one red and one yellow. I continued playing. The speaker on the pod's exterior had a soft membrane, easily vibrated. It vibrated as if in harmony. The song, now at least a hundred years old, was a standard in music classes of all grades. As I came to the end, I could hear the harmony clearly. The final notes resonated in the chill of the galley, fading into silence.

"That was beautiful," I whispered.

"Yes, it was," said Abigail.

"How did you find me way out here?"

"Way out where, Star?"

"Here, in space."

"Oh. But I have no space. In fact, you only perceive space because you think you do, it's only there because we agree it's there. Don't you remember the lessons we studied in Life Class?"

"No, I spent my time looking at you and giggling. You paid attention better than I. You were always a better student."

"You would daydream, dear one. There's nothing wrong with daydreams. If you relax and recall, you will remember. You were there and you heard it all, so you have it all, at your fingertips. If you reach out, you will know. You think of space and so it is, you see it because you think of it and you know it's there, so it is. It's the same with energy and time, remember? Once you have your vibration right, you'll remember."

"My vibration is improving," I said, half to myself. With Flax free of her obligations and with all of us beyond the reach of the CG, we were feeling more harmonious with the universe with each passing moment.

"When you remember who and what you are, you will reach the harmonious vibration and then you will be at understanding. Oh, Star, my bright, shining Star. You have been looking and have been looked for. You know what that is. Do you remember?"

"Mystery," I said, a lump appearing in my throat.

"Yes. And you found the symbols; you thought about them, you tried so hard to overcome. You laughed and cried, you loved and you lost, then you cried some more. Now you must look again."

"And then I will know." The words came unbidden, memorized. It was one of the basic lessons we learned. I had forgotten. Abigail reminded me.

"Yes, darling Star, you will know. Also that I love you."

"And I love you, Abigail." I felt her leave.

The galley was quiet and for the first time, cold. "Temperature rise, please," I said to the console. There was a rush of warm air all around me.

I raised the clarinet to my lips and played my own tune, the one I called "Homesick." It reminded me of Abigail.

As I played, the pod lifted up on a cushion of air and returned to the bay, to the storage compartment of the RRD, where it secured and shut down. Abigail was gone and would no longer need it. If she came back, she would find a way to communicate with me. She always did.

Far away, as if in the next valley, I heard harmony to my melody. It filled the bay, the galley and my head. It filled my world, my universe and my space, the space which was only there because Abigail and I agreed, and because were willing to see and feel it.

Planet Bacchus

The planet named for my family was a barren desert, wind-blown and devoid of flora. Flax landed at the only platform discernible and found the air to be barely breathable. We found no sign of an installation at the landing platform, no grand mansion and no gold mine or civilization of any kind. Beyond the landing platform itself, we found no evidence of life at all.

I stepped out in my long coat, boots, breather and goggles, and walked a hundred paces across the sand. I looked for what my father could have been referring to when he left me a planet bearing my family name of Bacchus.

"There's nothing here," yelled Chineel over the wind. She stood behind me, hoping I would come to my senses and return to the vessel.

"Nothing shows in the sensors, no metal or technical, nothing indicating a readable or even a slat," added Flax, in my headset. I looked back at the platform.

"This platform is old and neglected," I said into the breather, connected to Flax. "But the surface of it is unused. We are the first vessel to set down on it. I believe my father meant to build something here, but never got around to it."

"He left you the whole planet," said Flax.

Chineel stepped out next to me, bundled from head to toe against the wind and the sand it carried. Dagon stood in the open bay, patiently waiting for his captain to return.

I put my hands, clothed in great gloves, on my hips and looked around. As far as the eye could see it was a wasteland, a vast expanse of nothing. No plants grew, no animals scurried away at our approach and no sign of civilization existed as far as eyes could see or sensors could discern.

"It's nice," said Chineel, supportive as usual.

"Yes, nice."

"We could live here." Chineel continued looking around.

"Yes, we could."

We stood there together, looking at the emptiness before us, trying to find the words to describe our innermost feelings. None came.

Chineel sighed heavily. Beyond her I saw Dagon standing in the open port bay. I looked back at the desert surrounding the abandoned platform, the empty horizon and the dark, brooding sky.

"OK, let's keep this in mind." I slapped my gloves together and turned around.

"Yes, let's go," said Chineel, hot on my tail feathers.

The sound of Flax starting up the maneuvering thrusters told me she had heard our conversation and agreed completely. I walked back to the port bay with Chineel in my wake. Dagon turned and stepped into the bay, eager to get to his station.

As I settled into the pilot's seat, Flax said: "Is everyone in, Captain?"

"Yes, Flax. Let's go see what the universe has to show us. Get that old pirate, Galium, on the interlink. Maybe we'll visit him first off."

"Aye, aye, Captain," came the reply.

"You're not going to keep talking like that are you?"

"Would you like me to?"

"No, please."

"As you wish, Captain."

A flicker on the screen told me Flax sent a message out. Galium's face appeared bigger than life on the main screen.

"Hello. So glad you could call. Things are a little hectic at these coordinates, so if you could call later, I'd appreciate it."

The screen clicked off, then flickered again and came back. "...these coordinates, so if you could call..." Click! "...these coordinates, so if you could call..." Click! "...these coordinates, so if you could call..."

"What's going on, Flax?"

"A prepared message, with a wrinkle in the wire. I was able to discern numbers at the end. It's odd."

"What are the numbers?"

"Coordinates: A planet in the outer ring," said Flax, waiting for my response.

I worried about my friend, Galium. I had made a point to avoid him and wanted to continue doing so, but if he was in trouble, I would have to go to him. It's what friends do.

"...these coordinates, so if you could call... He's asking us to visit and can't be too obvious about it. Flax, set for those coordinates. We're going to pay a visit to a rude pirate."

"Aye, aye, Captain."

~

About the author...

Jon Batson is an award-winning author, four-time winner of the Lower Cape Fear Short Story Contest and twice awarded Honorable Mention in the internationally known Writers of The Future Contest for science fiction writers and twice has received Honorable Mention in the Rusty Axe Science Fiction Contest. His name appears in Who's Who in America and Who's Who in the world.

For more information about Jon Batson
and to purchase his other books please visit:
http://www.TheRealJonBatson.com
info@midnightwhistler.com

Research Triangle

Jack Richmond discovers a building on the edge of the Research Triangle where school children were being remotely monitored at a distance for medication reactions. The monitoring room was joyous at the killing of 32 students until the discovery that they were being recorded. Jack Richmond wakes with no memory at all.

Terminal Research

The story continues as Jack Richmond returns home on Halloween to find that his fiance, Teri, has been abducted. Finding her becomes his first objective, but along the way he has to deal with new assassins, old friends gone bad and members of the organization really running things.

Murder at Thompson Bog

A collection of short stories that tend to be on the darker side. If you like curling up with a scary story, this may be your ticket to insomnia.

Encounter in a Small Café

A light-hearted collection of short stories including some prize winners from The Lower Cape Fear Historical Fiction Contest.

Doll Bodies

Out-of-this-world tales including other possible futures, space stories, and excerpts from two future full-length projects. If you are craving a little Sci-Fi in your day, here you are. Enjoy!

Nina Knows the Night

Nina Richardson, a mild-mannered law school dropout, is tired of the criminals in her neighborhood. She dresses in black and ventures into the night to become a kick-butt crime-fighter. She discovers her superpowers to be her own inner-strength and purpose.

The Rands Conspiracy

The Rands Conspiracy takes the reader on a Bourne-style chase as Josh and his development team run for their lives after creating an experimental spy-ware program for the powerful, government funded Rands Group.

What they're saying about Jon Batson:

"Jon Batson is not just a writer, but a storyteller. His gift is making you experience what his characters feel and see while he slings irony and witty asides that make others wonder why you're laughing so hard. He looks closer at the ordinary world and determines what extraordinary things a person can do given the right circumstances. The result is a story that won't be put down."

Alice Osborn,
author, editor and teacher of *"Write from the Inside Out."*

"Colorful, engrossing, and highly entertaining! Jon Batson has produced an evocative collection of engaging characters whose lives unfold in amusing, tragic and, often, unexpected ways that send the imagination gliding over each one's winding paths, hairpin curves and jarring potholes with the artistic finesse of a truly masterful storyteller."

Karen Michelle Raines, poet/author

"Batson's stories are contemporary yet reminiscent of an earlier time – O'Henry, Raymond Carver and Edgar Allen Poe come to mind. Luckily for us although the aforementioned have gone onto their last edit, Jon will be with us for a long time."

Steven Elliot, Falls River Books

"I could hear you in every sentence. Easy reading, nice payoff, and a few surprises."

Gary Young, Author

"Thanks for writing and sharing your short stories with me. Your characters in these creative adventures come alive with the action and your clean concise writing keep the tales moving at a fun pace! I enjoyed reading them and look forward to more."

J. K. Gildersleeve, Writer and Illustrator

'A good book is one you think about all day and wonder what is happening with the characters, cannot wait to get back to them and hope you haven't missed much while you're away. I found myself emotionally connected all the way through as the story unfolded.'

Susan Henson, Avid Reader